Irres

"It is true. I ____
ever dazzled me as you have, Miss O'Connell."

Once again, Megan felt her heart thumping. There was a sheer magnetism about Prince Mikhail Kirov that was very hard to resist.

"So you say, Your Highness. But you make love so charmingly to everyone. Is it possible for a woman to trust your words? Or should I listen even more closely to the warning given me by your reputation?"

Prince Kirov closed the distance between them. "Believe this, mademoiselle." He caught up her hand and placed it firmly against his breast. She could feel the strength of his heartbeat beneath her palm. Her fingers trembled. He looked deeply into her startled eyes. "And believe this." He gathered her very gently into his arms.

Megan lifted her head to meet his kiss. She had been kissed many times since she had come to St. Petersburg. But she had never been kissed by a man whom she found so compellingly attractive. . . .

A Magnificent Match

Gayle Buck

A SIGNET BOOK

SIGNET
Published by the Penguin Group
Penguin Putnam Inc., 375 Hudson Street,
New York, New York 10014, U.S.A.
Penguin Books Ltd, 27 Wrights Lane,
London W8 5TZ, England
Penguin Books Australia Ltd, Ringwood,
Victoria, Australia
Penguin Books Canada Ltd, 10 Alcorn Avenue,
Toronto, Ontario, Canada M4V 3B2
Penguin Books (N.Z.) Ltd, 182-190 Wairau Road,
Auckland 10, New Zealand

Penguin Books Ltd, Registered Offices:
Harmondsworth, Middlesex, England

First published by Signet, an imprint of Dutton Signet,
a member of Penguin Putnam Inc.

First Printing, December, 1997
10 9 8 7 6 5 4 3 2 1

Chapter One

Miss Megan O'Connell set spur to her mount. The gelding's powerful hindquarters bunched. Horse and rider soared over the tall wooden gate and landed with catlike grace.

"Bravo, Megan!" The young ruddy-faced gentleman applauded. "You've got the brute well in hand."

Megan brought her horse alongside her brother's mount. "I cannot take all the credit. It is as much Father's hand as mine," she said, patting the gelding's warm muscular neck.

Captain Colin O'Connell shrugged his wide shoulders. "Oh well, of course. Father bred him and brought him up. But even Father recognizes the talent you have for training the horses and bringing out the best in them."

They started walking their horses across the muddy field. It was a cool fall day. The air felt damp against Megan's face. The soft Irish morning was quiet. Megan responded to her brother's comment with wry humor.

"Yes, I am every bit as valuable as a good undergroom," she said dryly.

"Here, now!" protested Captain O'Connell. "You know that isn't quite true."

Megan glanced at her brother curiously. "How odd. You have been in the military scarcely two years now, Colin, yet you have managed to forget so much. I find it wonderful."

Captain O'Connell frowned, disliking his sister's statement but too honest to deny its veracity. He had deliberately set himself to forge a new life in the Lifeguards and in the process forget his former one. It had been an uneasy childhood for them all. They had all been left to scramble for themselves. The one common thread that bound the O'Connells was the land and the horses that were bred on it.

Brother and sister rode in companionable but pensive silence for a few moments. "I wish it was different for you," said Captain O'Connell abruptly.

"I do not complain, Colin." Megan glanced at his frowning face with dawning surprise. "Why, do you pity me? You should not, you know. I have had a number of advantages that the rest of you did not."

Captain O'Connell snorted. "Yes, farmed out to this place or that so that you would not be underfoot. That was certainly an advantageous upbringing."

Megan chose to ignore her brother's derisive statement. Firmly, she said, "And I now have dear Mrs. Tyler for company. So do not repine on my behalf. Rather pity Celeste, who is anticipating her fourth lying-in."

Captain O'Connell stared. "No! Megan, you must be jesting."

"I would not say it if it were not true," said Megan with a smile. She was glad to have successfully sidetracked her brother's attention from herself. She disliked brooding upon what one might perceive as injustices. Nothing ever came of it except dissatisfaction and bitterness and that robbed one of what joy one did have.

"Why, Celeste was delivered of a brat not eighteen months ago. You wrote me yourself of the happy event. She cannot possibly be expecting again," said Captain O'Connell, still disbelieving.

Megan laughed. Her eyes lit up with amusement at his expression. "But I promise you that she is. Have you not wondered why she does not come downstairs until luncheon? Celeste is horridly ill every morning, poor thing."

Captain O'Connell grimaced. "It never occurred to me, no. Poor Celeste, indeed. I thought only that she had chosen to conform to our mother's indolent habits."

"Did you? More shame to you, then, Colin, when Celeste is your own twin. She was always one to be up with the dawn on horseback just as you were," said Megan.

"We may be twins, but we are poles apart in our likes and dislikes," retorted Captain O'Connell.

Megan understood him perfectly. "You must try to like

Patrick, Colin. He is extremely good to Celeste and the children. She is happier than she ever was before."

"I allow there to be truth in that. However, I find our estimable brother-in-law to be something of a bore," said Captain O'Connell frankly.

"He is rather difficult to abide on occasion," admitted Megan.

Captain O'Connell gave a crack of laughter. "That is an understatement, dear sister. I am only glad that I am not forced to sit at the table with him except when I am on leave."

"Well, I am not either, except when you are on leave," retorted Megan. "Patrick and Celeste prefer to stay at home, content in their domestic bliss. They bestow upon us an extended visit only when it becomes known that you are returned. So you see, Colin, you are paid a fine compliment. Patrick is partial to your graceless company."

"Heaven help me!" said Captain O'Connell, appalled.

Megan chuckled. She glanced at him sideways. Hesitantly, she said, "Can you not delay for a bit longer before you must return to duty? I would suffer even Patrick's most longwinded report of his crops for the continued pleasure of your company, my best of brothers."

Captain O'Connell reached out to squeeze her elbow in a sympathetic gesture. "Not even for you would I extend my leave. I promised to remain only through our mother's dress ball. Otherwise the lack of family feeling in our parents' house would have long since driven me back to England."

Megan smiled. She had not really thought that he would change his mind. Her brother was fond of her, but his attachment was not of a sort that he would put himself out for her. "I do understand. How I wish that I could go with you just once. I would so like to see something of the world."

There was an unconscious yearning in her voice that pulled at Captain O'Connell's self-interested heart. With suppressed violence, he said, "It is barbaric the way you have been used! You should be gracing the *ton,* established in your own household and holding fashionable rout parties. Instead of which, you are buried here with not a hope of anything else. If I had a wife, I'd see to it that you were properly brought out."

"If you had a wife, you would be as busy as Patrick and Celeste in setting up your nursery," retorted Megan. "There would not be time to spare for a spinster sister."

She was touched by the unexpected depth of her brother's concern, but also too wise to show how deeply she was affected. Colin must not end his leave feeling troubled and bothered on her behalf. That would be an unnatural state of mind for him and it would undoubtedly result in him becoming annoyed with her for being the cause of it.

Captain O'Connell reddened and mustered a protest. "Now see here, Megan! You shouldn't speak such warm thoughts. No, nor think them either!"

"Come, Colin, I am not a complete ninny. I have grown up with horse breeding all of my life. No one ever thought to send me out of the room when proper breeding points and lines were discussed," said Megan.

"Yes, well, but that is an entirely different matter," said Captain O'Connell, looking ill at ease.

Megan eyed his discomfited expression and her eyes gleamed. She then proceeded to tease him until they rode into the stableyard.

There the riders were met by a stocky gentleman dressed in well-cut tweeds. His heavy locks were cut in a tumbled fashion, setting off his broad forehead and handsome face. The Honorable Lionel O'Connell, the eldest of the siblings, was the very picture of a prosperous country squire. "Well, you have certainly been gone long enough," he grumbled, pointedly flicking open a gold pocketwatch.

"Yes, it has been an enjoyable ride. We came back across the fields," said Megan, accepting a groom's help in dismounting. She shook out her riding skirts, her crop in hand.

Mr. O'Connell looked sharply from one to the other. His blue eyes hard, he snapped shut the watch. "Not the Patterson gates, I hope?"

Captain O'Connell had also dismounted. He was considerably taller than his brother, a fact that Lionel O'Connell disliked intensely and which Captain O'Connell well knew. Captain O'Connell leaned his tall frame against the horse for a moment, regarding his elder brother from under half-lowered lids. There was a gleam of dislike in his eyes. "The gelding jumped beautifully. A pity that you did not see it, Lionel."

Mr. O'Connell did not rise to this provoking gambit. Instead he rounded on his sister, his expression flushed with anger. "I told you that the gelding was not ready."

"What nonsense, Lionel. Of course he is. I have told you so all week," said Megan calmly. "There was not the least quiver of reluctance in him. He performed handsomely."

The horses had been led off and Mr. O'Connell followed after them, fuming. "I shall see if they have taken any hurt from your reckless impudence!" he flung over his shoulder.

Captain O'Connell grimaced and fell into step with Megan as they crossed the yard to the manor house. "Our Lionel is scarcely a conciliatory sort. I do not understand how you bear him. I cannot!"

"He is as single-minded as Father ever was," said Megan with a slight shrug, entering the hall with Captain O'Connell close behind her. Once again, she turned the conversation away from herself. "Sophronia has quite given up on him, I suspect. She has turned to her own interests these days. She breeds pugs and when she goes to Bath, she orders out a special carriage for them."

"Bath! Pugs!" exclaimed Captain O'Connell. "Whatever does she do it for?"

"Why, Colin, isn't it obvious? Sophronia has decided to be a hypochondriac, which gains her the notice in Bath that she cannot arouse in Lionel's breast, and she breeds pugs because they annoy him so," said Megan, laughing.

"Lionel and Sophronia—that is an ill-managed pair! Then Celeste, who eloped out of the schoolroom with stiff-rumped Patrick, while I demanded a commission from my father so that I could escape into the army," said Captain O'Connell, shaking his head. "What a family we are!"

"Yes, are we not? Every one of us is selfish to the bone and unwilling to give up our own desires for any of the others," said Megan, suddenly sobering.

Captain O'Connell unexpectedly snatched up her hand and kissed it. "Except for you, Megan. You are the best of us all."

Megan looked up at him, raising her brows slightly. "You

are quite out, Colin. I am as selfish as the rest of you. Do not deceive yourself on that count, I pray you!"

She left him then, walking gracefully up the staircase, the hem of her riding habit draped over one arm and her whip clenched tight in her hand. Captain O'Connell watched her ascend, a somewhat startled expression in his eyes.

At the first landing, Megan was intercepted by one of the domestic maids. "Oh, miss, there ye be! 'er lidyship 'as been asking for ye this quarter hour past."

Megan glanced down at herself. There were splatters of mud on her habit and her half-boots were also soiled. She would have liked to have put off the riding habit before attending her mother, but she knew Lady O'Connell's impatient nature. "Thank you. I shall go at once."

Chapter Two

Megan traversed the long winding hallways to her ladyship's apartments. She was expected. The maid immediately ushered her inside. In a hushed voice, the maid said, " 'er lidyship is trying her jewels, miss."

Megan smiled and nodded her understanding. She walked into the dressing room and paused, not wanting to interrupt at an inopportune moment.

Lady O'Connell was seated at her dressing table. Her dresser, a woman of superior attitude, respectfully stood by. Her ladyship picked up a glittering diamond and sapphire necklace out of one of the three jewelry boxes opened on the dressing table. Lady O'Connell held the necklace up to her throat, glanced at herself in the glass, then dropped the necklace carelessly onto a tangled mound of earlier rejections. "No, it simply won't do. Too insipid by half," uttered her ladyship discontentedly.

"Perhaps the garnets, my lady," suggested the dresser.

"You wished to see me, Mother," said Megan, advancing into view.

Lady O'Connell did not turn around but instead met her daughter's eyes in the mirror. The faintest flicker of annoyance touched her features. "Oh, yes! I had almost forgotten. Simpkins, find me the garnets. I shall try them." The dresser acknowledged her ladyship's order with a nod and began to look through one of the jewelry boxes.

Lady O'Connell turned at last to face her daughter. With a sigh and a weary smile, she held out her hand. When her daughter came forward and lightly clasped her fingers for a moment, she said, "It is so fatiguing at times to make the proper decision. One must be so very careful to create just the right nuance, you know."

"Indeed," agreed Megan, knowing that it was expected of her to enter into her mother's preoccupation with self-adornment.

There was a striking difference between mother and daughter. Megan was dressed in a green drab riding habit that had seen better days. The cuffs and hem had been mended and the stock at her neck was yellowed with innumerable washings. Lady O'Connell was attired in a frothy dressing gown of pale sea-green gauze and lace. Bracelets circled her wrists and rings sparkled on her fingers. On the bed was laid a day dress of exquisite watered silk awaiting the moment when her ladyship decided that she wished to be dressed.

Lady O'Connell had once been a beautiful woman. Her gold hair had paled slightly and her figure was not what it had once been. But time had not altered her fine facial bones, nor the graceful line of her neck. As a consequence, her ladyship was thoroughly obsessed with necklaces and acquired costly new ones whenever the whim struck her.

After a glance at the dresser, who was still rummaging through the jewelry boxes for the garnets, Megan asked, "What is it that you wished of me, Mother?"

"What did I wish you— Oh, yes! Dear Megan, I have had the most delightful communication. Let me see where I have put it. Ah! Here it is, stuck in the side of my mirror so that I should not forget it." Lady O'Connell plucked the folded sheet from her mirror and waved the white paper languidly. "My dear friend Princess Elizaveta Kirov has written to me. You do remember her royal highness, do you not? She stayed with me briefly two years ago in London when you came for your first visit to a decent modiste."

"Yes, I do recall the princess," said Megan, nodding. She had a vague recollection of a strikingly handsome, very autocratic woman to whom she had been briefly introduced before being dismissed again into the hands of her companion. "Princess Kirov impressed me as a very grand lady."

Lady O'Connell was pleased and her expression showed it. "Oh, I am glad that you took a liking to the princess, for it makes things all the more delightful. Megan, Princess Kirov has extended a gracious invitation to you to come to her in St.

Petersburg. She assures me that she will see to it that you will be introduced to simply everyone and that you will have a wonderful time."

"That is gracious of her highness, indeed. However, you had told me that this year I could make my London debut," said Megan calmly. "I should like to do that, I think."

Lady O'Connell frowned. She tapped the invitation on her chair arm. "I scarcely recall. But it makes little difference, after all. The London Season does not begin for months and months yet. You may very well fit in a trip to St. Petersburg before we must think about the Season."

Megan knew that once again, as had happened for the past two years, her mother had sidestepped a commitment to bring her out in London. Lady O'Connell enjoyed a very active social life. She was extremely reluctant to interrupt her own pursuit of pleasure in order to take on the task of bringing out and shepherding a daughter through her first Season.

This invitation from Princess Kirov had come at a convenient time for Lady O'Connell. Her ladyship had developed a habit over the years of giving over the responsibility of her youngest daughter to others. Once Lady O'Connell had found a way to dispense with her maternal duties, she would conveniently forget Megan's existence.

Megan knew the futility of argument. Lady O'Connell was not moved by anything but her own desires. The hope of a come-out in London receded farther and farther out of reach.

Megan was nineteen. Soon she would be considered to be on the shelf without ever having had the opportunity to see anything of the world except their own estate in Ireland and that little bit of England where her maternal relations resided. It was a pity, as Lady O'Connell had once remarked, that her aunt Leonora was bedridden or otherwise she could have enjoyed her aunt and uncle's chaperonage for a Season by now.

Megan had once cherished hopes that her elder sister, Celeste, upon her marriage might sponsor her, but Celeste had never shown the least desire for anything other than acquiring a large family. As for her sister-in-law, Sophronia, Megan had quite decidedly turned down that lady's once-issued lukewarm invitation to join her in a pilgrimage to Bath. Taking the waters and walking wheezy pugs was not Megan's notion of enlarging her scope of experience.

On the spot, Megan decided to make the most of this particular opportunity. Half a loaf was better than none. If she was going to be shuffled off to Russia, she wanted to at least make something useful come of it. She had told her brother Colin that she was as ruthlessly selfish as any of the rest of the O'Connells and she felt that it was quite true. "I suppose that Princess Kirov has offered to bring me out into society?"

Lady O'Connell brightened considerably. "What a wonderful idea! Of course she shall, for Elizaveta is my dearest of friends and will do anything for me. I shall write a letter at once that she must do so and you may carry it to her. My dear Megan, nothing could be more fortuitous! St. Petersburg is famous for its cosmopolitan atmosphere. I have heard that the capital positively teems with bluebloods and well-connected diplomats. You will make your debut there and try your wings a little. And naturally you must make the most of your opportunities." She smiled archly. "I would not be at all displeased if you were to form a suitable connection, Megan."

"Nor I," said Megan with a smile. She longed to be given the opportunity to see a little more of the world and to form friendships with others who might have interests that had nothing to do with horses and horse breeding. As for acquiring a husband, that was farther afield in her thoughts just now but certainly she was not completely adverse to the notion.

Lady O'Connell's expression was softened by a degree of warmth. "I have always liked you, Megan, for you have never been a bit of trouble to me. So biddable, so even-tempered! I am fortunate that you are not a selfish, forward minx like so many of the daughters of my London friends."

"Thank you, Mama," said Megan, a little taken aback.

"I shall do my very best on your behalf, my dear Megan," said Lady O'Connell, feeling expansive. "I shall particularly make known to Princess Kirov that she must act as my deputy on your behalf. Then you may be quite comfortable in consulting Princess Kirov regarding the eligibility of any offers that you might receive. There! Is that not handsome of me?"

"Indeed, ma'am. I do not know what to say. However, I am certain that Princess Kirov shall regard your confidence just as she ought," said Megan dryly. "Pray convey my regards to Princess Kirov and my acceptance of her gracious invitation. I shall be most happy to join her in St. Petersburg once I have acquired a suitable wardrobe."

Lady O'Connell looked taken aback. "A wardrobe?" she faltered. "But I do not think—"

"I could not possibly go to Princess Kirov otherwise, ma'am. Why, I have not been to a modiste in two years," said Megan.

"But a new wardrobe," said Lady O'Connell. She shook her head. "It is out of the question, Megan."

"You would not wish the sophisticated gentlemen of St. Petersburg to stigmatize me as a dowd, Mother," said Megan, gesturing down at her drab mud-splattered riding habit. "None of them would look at me twice unless I was tricked out in the very latest styles."

Lady O'Connell looked unhappy. "No, of course not. Very well, then, I suppose that I must accompany you to a modiste. It is very inconvenient. I have several friends coming to stay in a few days."

"I cannot conceive any reason why you should disrupt your own schedule for me, ma'am. Why do I not have Mrs. Tyler accompany me? She has quite good taste. You have said so yourself," said Megan. "And since Colin is shortly to return to England, he may very well accompany me there."

Lady O'Connell brightened. "The very thing! Of course! Colin can have no objection. And dear Mrs. Tyler, what a dear she is. She will know just what will be best. Yes, that is the very thing."

"I will convey your wishes to Mrs. Tyler on the instant, as well as your insistence that she procure a few items for herself. I know that you will wish her to be well-provided for on the journey to Russia, as well," said Megan. Her mind was working quickly as she tried to catalog everything that would be needed to accomplish such a long journey.

"Do I?" Lady O'Connell looked startled.

"I assumed, of course, that Mrs. Tyler would be accompanying me as a trusted chaperone on the journey. It would not be at all the thing for me to travel alone," said Megan. "You have told me many times that I could not go up to London without someone trustworthy to keep me in hand. And Russia is a good deal farther away than London. Besides, I do not know what Mrs. Tyler would do with herself while I was gone. Perhaps she might make one of your retinue. But I do not think that is a happy solution."

"No, nor do I," said Lady O'Connell, with perfect truth. Her widowed cousin was completely suitable to be her daughter's companion, but she was scarcely a valuable addition to one's own entourage. "You are entirely correct, Megan. I entrust you completely to Mrs. Tyler's capable hands. She will know just how to look after you on the journey to Russia and will be your guide in all things proper." She beamed at her daughter. "I am glad that it is all perfectly settled. Now you must be off to tell Mrs. Tyler the good news."

Lady O'Connell's interest in the conversation was already waning, but Megan was not yet ready to be dismissed. She held her ground, determined to have all pertinent points settled. "Shall I have the modiste's bills sent to you or to your man of business?"

Lady O'Connell had already turned away. Her dresser had located the heavy garnet necklace for her inspection and the subject was already exhausted as far as she was concerned. Without glancing around, Lady O'Connell waved her hand in a dismissing gesture. "Send them to Henry, of course. I do not care to have anything to do with them. He shall take care of whatever transactions you may have."

"Very well, Mother."

Megan curtseyed and left the bedroom. A smile curved her mouth. She was slightly ashamed of herself for pushing forward her own interests so blatantly. However, Megan soothed the twinge of her conscience with the reflection that once she had made the decision to make the most of Princess Kirov's invitation, it was imperative that she gain all that she wanted at this single interview. Once the question of Megan's going to Russia had been settled, Lady O'Connell would not give the matter another moment's consideration.

Megan knew her mother well. Lady O'Connell concerned herself in her daughter's affairs only when Megan became something of a distraction to her ladyship's own pursuit of pleasure. Her ladyship would have sent Megan off to Russia willy-nilly, without giving a thought to wardrobe or funds or protection.

It was not that Lady O'Connell was particularly a cruel, cold woman. She was simply too vain and self-centered to want to be bothered with anything that did not have to do with herself. So Megan had herself put forward those things that she deemed important to her own well-being. If she did not, who would? And now she was going to tell her favorite person in the world of the treat in store for them.

With a growing sense of adventure and lively excitement, Megan went downstairs to find her mentor and friend, Mrs. Tyler. She found the trim widow in the parlor, engaged on a new embroidery design.

Mrs. Tyler was two-and-thirty. When she had been left a widow by an unfortunate road accident, she had discovered herself to be in uncomfortably straitened circumstances. It had been an unlooked-for blessing to have been accepted as Miss O'Connell's companion and she was highly appreciative of her good fortune. Though her cousin, Lady O'Connell, preferred not to acknowledge her, the daughter had proven to be an easy and surprisingly amicable charge.

Shutting the door, Megan smiled across the room at her companion. "Gwyneth, I have just been told the most extraordinary thing by her ladyship. I am being sent to Russia to stay with my mother's friend, Princess Kirov, in the capital of St. Petersburg. And you are to go with me."

"Russia?" Mrs. Tyler dropped her embroidery to her lap. She looked at her charge in mingled amusement and dismay. "But isn't that a very long way from Ireland?"

"Yes, indeed. Thousands upon thousands of miles," said Megan cheerfully. "Only think of it, Gwyneth. The whole Russian empire at our feet. We'll be the toasts of St. Petersburg. It will be a positively grand adventure."

"I don't know that I am the stuff of which an adventuress is made," said Mrs. Tyler.

"Oh, Gwyneth, how can you say so?" asked Megan quizzingly. "You are forever reading the latest romances and you followed every word that was printed about the war and the diplomatic intricacies and you have wanted to travel for ages and ages."

"Yes, that is as may be," agreed Mrs. Tyler with a show of spirit. "But it scarcely follows that I wish to be whisked off to the ends of the earth."

"Not to the ends of the earth, just to St. Petersburg," said Megan, sitting down on the silk striped sofa next to the older woman. "Only think, Gwyneth! I shall be brought out into society in St. Petersburg by Princess Kirov and meet all sorts of exotic princes and fascinating people."

"That is something, indeed," said Mrs. Tyler, much struck. Better than anyone, she knew and understood Megan's frustration at not being allowed the come-out that was a young miss's introduction into polite society. "St. Petersburg is not London, of course. But I have heard very good things said about the Russian capital. Personages from all over the world visit St. Petersburg at one time or another."

"You do see how good it will be for me," said Megan. "I shall simply waste away another year unless I make the most of this opportunity."

"Oh, yes, there is no denying that! It is past time that you were exposed to more society than is to be had here," agreed Mrs. Tyler. She sighed. "I have always wished that you could have the opportunity to spread your wings. Indeed, I have spoken to her ladyship on more than one occasion on this very subject, but without success. I suspect that her ladyship hopes that you will be as accommodating as Celeste and bestow your hand on one of the local gentry before she is absolutely forced to do something for you."

"I have no intention of running off with anyone," said Megan. She was not at all shocked by her companion's frank assessment of her situation. She and Mrs. Tyler were scarcely a dozen years apart in age and had formed a friendship that went far beyond that of mistress and companion. Mrs. Tyler had never pretended ignorance of the cold atmosphere in the O'Connell house, nor tacitly condoned it by downplaying a young girl's hurt. In addition, Megan and Mrs. Tyler were much alike in temperament and spirit, so that sharing of interests and confidences came easily.

"I should hope not, indeed! I trust that you will show a bit more sense," said Mrs. Tyler. She took up her embroidery again and set a stitch. "I must be fair to Celeste, however. She had little hope of contracting a marriage in the usual way and she knew it. It is something to be thankful for that Patrick Kennehessey turned out to be such a doting husband and father. Most such marriages are generally unhappy affairs."

"My father's extreme disapprobation could not have been anything but a blight against their happiness," said Megan. "He refused to acknowledge them for months. Yet I do not think that either Celeste or Patrick have ever held it against him."

"Indeed, their forebearance has been remarkable. However, it would have been so much easier on everyone if Celeste had had the advantage of a London Season and had been courted in the usual way," said Mrs. Tyler, shaking her head as she recalled those turbulent times. Her thoughts naturally turned into common channels. "What a pity that you have not yet had a Season, Megan, for I believe that you would go off very well."

"Dear Gwyneth! I think that you harbor greater hopes for my future than I do," said Megan, smiling at her companion.

"Nonsense! Only see how excited you are at the prospect of a come-out in St. Petersburg," said Mrs. Tyler, glancing up with a smile. "I do hope that Princess Kirov does well by you. Indeed, I pray that she does. It would be the height of anything were you to meet some eligible gentleman."

"I had supposed that you might wish to accompany me, Gwyneth. I own, I would feel more comfortable with a friend beside me. But if you prefer to remain here in Ireland with my mother until she returns to London, I shall not be inconsolable," said Megan.

There was a moment of silence. Then Mrs. Tyler said feelingly, "You are an awful girl."

"Then you'll go?" asked Megan.

"Of course I shall, as you well knew," said Mrs. Tyler tartly.

A smile hovered about her mouth. "Perhaps I shall meet a few princes myself."

Megan hugged the shorter woman. "I knew that you would prefer to go with me! And so I have already persuaded my mother to allow me to outfit us both with proper wardrobes. I envision a perfect orgy of shopping, Gwyneth! You cannot be a respectable chaperone and accompany me to balls and other functions without looking the part."

Mrs. Tyler chuckled. "I own, it does sound to be rather fun."

"Good! I intend to leave for England directly after the dress ball. Colin is to escort us over. We shall stay at the town house while we are in London, of course," said Megan. "I shall write a note to that effect and put it into the post today. I do not know how long we shall be there before we depart for Russia. Indeed, it depends entirely upon the extent of our wardrobe requirements."

"But do you know of a decent modiste?" asked Mrs. Tyler.

"Indeed I do." A hint of mischief entered Megan's smoke-gray eyes. "We are going to visit my mother's very own modiste," she said, rising to her feet and going to the door again.

"Isn't Mademoiselle Rochet rather expensive?" asked Mrs. Tyler hesitantly.

"Shockingly so," said Megan cheerfully. "And we are to send all of the bills to Mr. Henry for whatever we need. My mother explicitly said so." Her eyes twinkled. "I anticipate needing a terribly lot, Gwyneth."

"Oh, my," said Mrs. Tyler with perfect and dismayed understanding.

Megan laughed and whisked herself out of the parlor.

Chapter Three

Once each year during her annual sojourn in Ireland, Lady O'Connell held a dinner and grand dress ball. It was not that she particularly wished to do so or even enjoyed it. In her opinion, nothing which was not done in London was of any interest. However, the dress ball was extremely important to Lord O'Connell and she perforce bowed to his wishes.

Lord O'Connell was one of the few Irish landowners who still had hereditary lands. Once impoverished, he had managed to keep hearth and home together by consistently winning races with his own well-bred stock. Then he had had the good fortune to marry an English heiress and he was able to enlarge his stables. He began to sell racers, hunters, and jumpers.

The annual grand dress ball was not so much an entertainment as it was an opportunity to extoll the good points of Lord O'Connell's stock. Personages from all over Europe regularly journeyed to Ireland for a long house visit at the O'Connell estate. The grand dress ball was the opening gambit of the gathering and was followed by shooting forays, steeplechases, and foxhunting. Through it all, business was conducted. The negotiations were heavy and long, but several lucrative transactions were always completed. Thus was the wealth of the O'Connells generated over and above what the estate might ordinarily bring in.

Lady O'Connell was bored by the incessant talk of horses that pervaded the entertainments under Lord O'Connell's aegis. She much preferred visiting with her own set in London and Paris, but she knew what her lord demanded of her. Lady O'Connell had always collected acquaintances with ease and frequently these same individuals descended upon the Irish countryside in the dreary winter months. It was the only entertainment that Lady O'Connell could look forward to during her exile from the cosmopolitan world.

Lord O'Connell had no objection to his wife's friends. They were potential buyers, after all. Nor had he any objection to the wife of his bosom fleeing to London as soon as spring announced its coming. He was content as long as he had an efficient hostess for the fall and winter months when he entertained the world and sold his horses.

His lordship's heir, the Honorable Lionel O'Connell, had embraced the horse-based economy of the estate with a passion that was nearly equal that of his parent. He pursued a possible transaction with the tenacity usually reserved for a lover in pursuit of the object of his affection. His wife, Sophronia, had good reason to know that she was not particularly important to her husband's comfort. Thus she rather monotonously complained about the advent of the guests and gleaned all that she could about each personage's personal limitations in finances in order to prick her husband's hopes of making a good deal.

Each year Captain Colin O'Connell made his annual pilgrimage to his parents' home. His presence was acknowledged not with fondness but with satisfaction. He was wanted solely for window dressing. There were not many who could equal him as a rider. He made the horses look and perform at their best. If it were not for his sisters, Celeste and Megan, he would have stopped coming back to Ireland altogether.

Megan was regarded in much the same light as her brother, Colin. She had light hands and an unexceptional seat on any mount. Her erect, graceful carriage on a horse enhanced its good points. During company, she was always tricked out in the finest of riding habits. Indeed, she practically lived in that attire year-round, preserving her best habits for the annual houseparty and wearing her old ones for everyday use.

There was little place in Megan's life for an extensive wardrobe, since she rarely went anywhere but to the parish church or on an occasional jaunt to her elderly aunt and uncle in England. She therefore possessed but a handful of day dresses and other necessary additions to a female's wardrobe. She had only one ballgown, commissioned two years before. It did not occur to Lady O'Connell to wonder whether her daughter's ballgown was still sufficient for the upcoming grand dress ball. Nor had Megan thought about it, except in a fleeting manner that had always been superseded by more pressing concerns.

That evening as Megan tried on her old ballgown, she had cause to regret her lack of forethought. The ballgown had been let out once the previous year. There was therefore no allowance left to accommodate the maturing of her form into more womanly curves.

Megan tugged on the inadequate bodice with dismay. "It is impossible, Gwyneth," she said.

"I own, it leaves much to be desired," said Mrs. Tyler dubiously, regarding the younger woman standing at the mirror.

Megan looked at her companion's reflection. Her lips twitching on a smile, she said, "That is not in the least amusing, Gwyneth, when I am all but spilling out of the top of the thing."

"Oh! Quite so," said Mrs. Tyler, flushing and yet laughing over her inadvertent pun. "Perhaps a shawl would help. I have a lovely Norwich silk that you may borrow."

"I suppose that it might do," said Megan hopefully.

Mrs. Tyler left the bedroom to retrieve the shawl. When she returned, she said, "Here you are, my dear. I do hope that it will do the trick."

With her maid's help, Megan tried the shawl in various positions. She soon shook her head. "It's no use. It simply won't do. I look like a noddy with it tied up around my throat and if I drape it, it is likely to slither loose at the most inopportune time."

"Yes, so I see," said Mrs. Tyler.

Megan turned around and sighed. "I cannot go downstairs in this gown, Gwyneth. It is positively indecent. And yet, what can I do? My father will be highly displeased if he were to be informed that I will not make up one of the company. His lordship likes me to talk up the horses to the ladies."

Mrs. Tyler shook her head sympathetically. It was indeed a dilemma. Lord O'Connell was insistent that every member of his family be available during the houseparty. Even Celeste's present condition did not absolve her from what his lordship perceived as her duties toward the family fortunes. If Celeste was well enough to abide under his roof instead of her own, then she was well enough to comply with his wishes.

Mrs. Tyler thought for a moment, then rose to her feet. "Wait here, Megan. I shall be back presently."

"What have you got in mind?" asked Megan hopefully.

"I shan't say just yet, for I don't know whether I shall be successful," said Mrs. Tyler.

Megan watched her companion leave the bedroom for the second time. She looked at her maid. "I hope that Mrs. Tyler is able to provide a solution, Betty."

The maid bobbed her head in agreement. "Aye, miss." She eyed the outgrown ballgown with disfavor. She would not voice it out loud, but it was a terrible crime that her mistress was reduced to such pitiful straits as these.

When Mrs. Tyler returned, she brought with her Lady O'Connell's dresser. She gestured at Megan, who was still attired in the inadequate ballgown. "Now see, Simpkins. It is just as I have described to you," said Mrs. Tyler. "Can there be anything done?"

"You should not have bothered Simpkins," said Megan with a reproving frown. She was embarrassed that the haughty dresser had been brought in.

"It is quite all right, miss. Mrs. Tyler explained the problem and it would be odd, indeed, if I thought myself to be above the challenge," said Simpkins. "Now let me see what must be done."

Megan had no choice but to accept the situation. She stood docilely while the dresser poked and pulled and frowned over the ballgown. Finally the dresser shook her head and stepped back. "Even I cannot make that gown appear decent, miss," she pronounced. "I could hobstitch a length of deep lace around the borders of the bodice, but it would be an obvious addition and scarcely adequate, besides. I recommend that the thing be given away or put into the ragbag."

Megan looked at the dresser, then at Mrs. Tyler. "But then what is to be done, Gwyneth? I haven't got another gown."

"Oh, dear. I had so hoped that Simpkins—" Mrs. Tyler cut off the rest of what she was about to say. She made a determined effort to smile. "It is very bad, of course, but we shall simply have to make the best of the situation. I shall convey your regrets to Lady O'Connell with an explanation and hope that you are not missed too soon."

The dresser cleared her throat. Her expression as haughty as ever, she said, "If I may make a suggestion, miss? I have in my possession a gown that may prove adequate this once. It is a style that will be simple to alter to your figure."

"I am very willing to put myself in your hands, Simpkins," said Megan. "But will not my mother take exception to me wearing a gown that she commissioned for herself?"

"The gown is one that Lady O'Connell took an unreasoning and sudden dislike to while we were still in London. I believe that her ladyship saw one of her acquaintances attired in something very similar," said Simpkins woodenly.

"Oh, I see," said Megan. She smiled suddenly. "Thank you, Simpkins. I should like to try the gown."

The dresser nodded and let herself out of the bedroom. In short order, she returned, bearing a cascade of silk in her arms. She shook out the folds of the gown and addressed the maid. "You there, girl. Get that dress off and then help me throw this over your mistress's head."

Megan's maid nodded, not daring to say a word. The two servingwomen tossed the gown over Megan's head and smoothed it down her body. The maid hooked it up the back swiftly while the dresser began to pleat and pull at the fabric.

"Yes, I think that it can be managed," said Simpkins thoughtfully. "If we take a tuck here and here, and a third one here, the extra fullness will not be noticeable. What do you think, miss?"

Megan critically looked at herself in the mirror. She was standing in a ballgown of watered ivory silk that enhanced her red hair and fair coloring. Puffed at the shoulder, the long sleeves of the gown tapered over the hand. The bodice was cut low, but even so was not as revealing as her old gown, and the waistline was high. Rows upon rows of frothy bows and point lace decorated the bosom of the dress and the skirt.

"It is lovely, except for these bows," said Megan, touching one of the offending frills at the bosom.

The dresser nodded. "Quite right, miss. But that is a simple matter to remedy. I took the precaution of bringing along my sewing basket." As she was speaking, she brought out a pair of small sharp shears and began snipping off many of the bows. When she was done, she looked critically at the ballgown. "Aye, that will do. Now we'll simply take it in and you will be suitably attired for the evening."

Megan watched the dresser work her magic with the gown. In a matter of half an hour, the ballgown had undergone a subtle transformation. The busy look of the bows had been reduced to discreet touches. The voluminousness of the skirt had disappeared. Megan could not quite believe how sophisticated she appeared. "You are a wonder, Simpkins," she said quietly.

The dresser's face reddened, but she merely nodded.

Megan turned to the dresser. She was touched by the dresser's ministrations, for she knew that the discards from a lady's wardrobe always became the property of the lady's maid and actually constituted part of the tiring-woman's income. "I cannot thank you enough, Simpkins, especially when I know that you have sacrificed this gown for me."

The dresser gave a dour smile. She closed her sewing box. "A rare oddity I would look wearing something so akin to a bridal gown, miss."

Megan was startled. She whirled around to look again at her reflection. "Oh my word! All it requires is a lace veil and a bouquet. Gwyneth, I cannot possibly appear in this!"

"Nonsense, my dear. You look perfectly lovely. It is quite suitable for a young lady just coming out. And I have just the thing for you to wear with it for this particular occasion," said Mrs. Tyler. She unclasped the strand of pearls from around her own neck and held them out. "You will do me the honor of wearing them, Megan."

Megan felt tears come to her eyes. She accepted the pearls and allowed her maid to clasp them about her neck. "Oh, Gwyneth, I am beginning to feel like Cinderella about to go to the ball."

"A pity that there is not a Prince Charming waiting in the wings," said Mrs. Tyler regretfully. "Certainly you will turn heads tonight, my dear."

Simpkins allowed herself a small smile and let herself out of the bedroom. The dresser's formidable presence gone, the maid reasserted herself. "Now, miss, stand still so that I may fix your hair."

When Megan descended the stairs a quarter hour later, she felt herself to be almost floating. She knew that she had never appeared better. How odd that it should happen when she was wearing a discarded ballgown and a set of borrowed pearls.

She met her brother-in-law, the Honorable Patrick Kennehessey, on the landing. He looked at her appreciatively and then bowed with a flourish. "Ah, a fine-looking lass you are, to be sure," he said in a lilting brogue. He offered his arm. "Will you honor this poor soul with your company, Megan?"

Megan looked at him wonderingly, even as she placed her fingers on his arm. "Come, Patrick, what is this blarney? I have never heard you utter such an extravagance in all my life."

Mr. Kennehessey smiled, his broad pleasant face creasing. "But then, why should you? We rarely have occasion for private speech. I must say that I have never seen you appear to such rare advantage, dear sister. Why, at this moment you almost rival my heart, Celeste, in beauty."

Megan began to realize just what it was about the short placid gentleman that had so charmed her sister. She had been in England visiting her maternal relations when the romance between Patrick Kennehessey and her sister had sprung up. By the time she had returned, they had already eloped and become pariahs in her father's view. Concourse between the two households had been forbidden by Lord O'Connell for nearly two years, until he had relented upon discovering that his despised son-in-law could put him in the way of a valuable business connection. Megan had thus never had an opportunity to mingle with her brother-in-law except in such social situations as they were now preparing to attend and Mr. Kennehessey's unprecedented compliment was astonishing. "Where is Celeste, by the by? She is not ill again, I hope?"

A shadow crossed Mr. Kennehessey's freckled face. He nodded. "Aye, and a pity it is. His lordship will not care for it, but I told Celeste that I'll not be endangering any child of ours for the sake of any number of horses. I have told Celeste that she is to stay abed this evening. She fretted, of course. But I shall deal with Lord O'Connell myself."

"You are braver than I, Patrick," said Megan quietly. "I was too cowardly to remain abovestairs, even though the circumstances of an hour past seemed to warrant it."

He glanced sideways at her from out of unexpectedly shrewd brown eyes. "Courage is an odd thing, Megan. It is particularly roused when one perceives a threat to those one loves best. You have not yet experienced that."

Megan looked at her brother-in-law for a long moment. "Patrick, you have not once mentioned your crops to me."

Her brother-in-law winked at her. "No, I am saving that delicious subject for the drawing room. You have no notion, lass, how easily one may drive away unwelcome conversation with a dash of agricultural jargon."

"You are a hoodwinking rogue, Patrick!" exclaimed Megan, almost disbelieving.

"Am I, now? Or am I merely countering one sort of towering dogma with another? Certainly I am never constrained to bear with a conversation about horseflesh longer than I wish," murmured Mr. Kennehessey as they crossed the threshold.

Chapter Four

The large drawing room was full. Every chair and settee was occupied, generally by finely gowned ladies of various ages. The gentlemen lounged about, either paying court to ladies of their choice or going to stand with the group arranged before the mantel, their backs to the warm fire. The buzz of conversation slowed as heads turned to see who else was joining the company.

Raising his voice, Mr. Kennehessey said, as though continuing a long digression, "And the drainage ditches cannot be any narrower for that reason. There are exceptions, of course. There is—"

Megan's stunned expression was attributed to extreme boredom. Several individuals smiled, already well acquainted with Mr. Kennehessey's propensity to agriculture.

Captain O'Connell stepped forward to rescue his sister. "Patrick, your servant. Megan, I should like a word with you, if I may."

"Of course." Megan turned her head to say a civil word to her brother-in-law, but Mr. Kennehessey was already bowing and moving away.

"Regular jaw-me-dead, isn't he?" said Captain O'Connell, grimacing.

Megan shook her head, smiling. She wished that she could reveal their brother-in-law's astounding subterfuge, but he had not granted her permission to do that. "Patrick is a good, worthy man," she said.

"Oh, that goes without saying," said Captain O'Connell dismissively. "Let us forget him, if you please. What is this our mother has so graciously conveyed to me not two minutes before you chose to make your entrance? That I am to escort you to London to the modiste shops?"

Megan laughed. "Oh, poor Colin! It is not nearly so bad as that. I am going on a shopping trip, but I shall have Mrs. Tyler with me. You are merely to accompany us to the town house. Your duty shall end there."

"You ease my mind, dear sister," said Captain O'Connell. The rather hard glint in his eyes receded. "I was of no mind to trail behind a female while she bought a few fripperies and gloves."

"You need not fear. I would never infringe upon your good nature in such a self-centered fashion," said Megan evenly. "In any event, you would not allow me to do so, would you?"

Captain O'Connell smiled slowly. He regarded her expression thoughtfully. "I believe that I have angered you, Megan."

Megan also smiled. Her gaze was very steady, though there was a spark in the depths of her eyes. "No, why should I be? I cannot expect you to put yourself about for me. It would be the height of idiocy to think that, would it not?" She did not want to skirmish with her brother and looked about for an excuse to leave him. "Oh, there is Sophronia waving at me. Why does she need to bring those pugs along with her even tonight?"

"Look at Lionel's face for the answer to your question," said Captain O'Connell, nodding his head toward their elder brother.

Mr. O'Connell had attired himself carefully for the evening in a dark coat, frilled shirt and waistcoat, and pantaloons. His was a handsome figure, the only mar to his correct appearance being his expression. He was frowning as he stared across the room at his wife. Quite deliberately, he turned his back and began speaking to a guest.

"The cut direct," observed Captain O'Connell.

"That was very bad of Lionel," said Megan, annoyed. "That must certainly set a few tongues wagging. And I can well imagine Sophronia's feelings!"

"Do not get up in arms over it, dear sister. I doubt that Sophronia even noticed," said Captain O'Connell sardonically. "She fawns so over those pooches that one might be excused for thinking they were her children."

"Perhaps they are," said Megan quietly. "Excuse me, Colin. She is still waving at me. I think that I shall go over and just drop a word into her ear."

Captain O'Connell smiled slightly. "I suspect it will be more likely that Sophronia will drop a few words into your ear, Megan. You will hear in gruesome detail about every ill that she is suffering. I know, for I have already made the pilgrimage to greet her. Lord, what a ninnyhammer!"

Megan shook her head at him before she began to make her way through the crowd. She patiently nodded and smiled as she greeted those whom she already knew. It was several minutes before she was able to reach her sister-in-law's side.

Sophronia O'Connell was a passably pretty young woman, but there was a perpetual petulant droop to her mouth that marred her natural loveliness. She affected a languid air and always had several shawls dripping from her shoulders. That, and her constant canine companions, defined her singular style.

One of the pair of pugs cavorting at her sister-in-law's feet dared to leap up at Megan. She caught its head with her gloved hand and deflected the animal away from her silken skirt. "Down, sir!"

The pug groveled, its tail wagging. Megan bent to scratch its ears. She looked up at her sister-in-law, who sat on her chair slowly waving a fan, quite unconcerned over her pet's antics. "Really, Sophronia, must you bring them into the ballroom?"

Sophronia O'Connell adjusted her shawls. "They amuse me. Pray do not scold, Megan, for it is so tiresome. I am scarcely able to endure this squeeze and it would be utterly impossible without my dear doggies."

"Very well, Sophronia, I shan't scold. I think that you know my opinion. But how you intend to take to the dance floor with those animals nipping at your heels is more than I can fathom," said Megan, rising to her feet.

"I do not dance," said Mrs. O'Connell disdainfully. "My fragile health will not permit such exuberant exercise."

"I hope that you did not wave at me so urgently in order to discuss your pugs or the state of your health, Sophronia. For if you have, I tell you to your face that I am leaving on the instant," said Megan frankly.

"So unfeeling, every one of you," murmured Mrs. O'Connell, rearranging a shawl that one of her pugs had tugged down off of her slender shoulder. A flash of sudden temper showed in her eyes. "But you may rest easy this once, Megan. I do not intend to bore you with a cataloging of my ills."

"Thank you, Sophronia," said Megan.

Her sister-in-law chose to ignore what she considered to be an impertinence. "I merely wished to verify what I was told. Are you going up to London with Colin? If that is indeed true, I advise you strongly against it. Colin may be a gentleman born, but he is scarcely the proper person to introduce you to society. I doubt that he knows a single respectable person."

"Colin is merely providing a convenient escort, Sophronia. I am actually traveling over with Mrs. Tyler," said Megan. "She has been charged to advise me in buying a few essentials and—"

"A shopping expedition?" Mrs. O'Connell's blue eyes narrowed. Her voice sharpened. "I have not been informed of this. I suppose that it never occurred to anyone to wonder whether I should like to shop in London? I shall speak to Lionel at once!"

Megan instantly recognized the danger of her sister-in-law's envy. Not wanting to be the cause of an unwarranted and public wrangle, she said hastily. "It is not precisely a pleasure expedition, Sophronia. Mrs. Tyler and I shall not be remaining in London. We are going on to St. Petersburg. That is quite a different thing, as you will agree."

"St. Petersburg?" repeated Mrs. O'Connell blankly.

"It is in Russia," said Megan helpfully.

"I know very well where St. Petersburg is," said Mrs. O'Connell irritably. "I am not an idiot. However, I fail to understand why you are going there at all. Whatever can you be thinking? St. Petersburg is for all intents and purposes on the other side of the world! And how will you go on? Though an estimable woman, Mrs. Tyler is certainly not an entrée into Russian society! Not that I'd care for that, in any event, for I understand that they are a barbaric people."

"My mother received an invitation for me from a friend, Princess Elizaveta Kirov. The princess has offered to introduce me into Russian society," said Megan.

Mrs. O'Connell's gaze was arrested. She stared at Megan for a long moment, before a small smile touched her lips. "I see. Of course. My dear mother-in-law has always got one's interests so close to heart. Well, Megan, I do not say that I envy you. But I do wish you well."

Megan was surprised by her sister-in-law's well-wishing. "Thank you, Sophronia. It is kind of you to say so."

Mrs. O'Connell shrugged. "Not at all, Megan. Of all of the O'Connells, I find you least objectionable. It is a pity that you are to be shunted off in this paltry fashion, but I imagine that even St. Petersburg must offer more than what you would have if you remained here. Certainly you cannot expect a London Season." Her eyes wandered to her husband's stocky form and her mouth drooped in a pathetic expression.

Megan noticed. Impulsively, she said, "Sophronia, if you are so unhappy, why do you not simply leave? Why Bath? Why not London? You were used to be such a happy creature. Perhaps a change of scenery, a new existence with routs and balls and picnics and admirers would—" She brought herself up short. Her sister-in-law was staring at her in shocked incomprehension. "Forgive me, Sophronia. I am speaking out of turn. I see Lady Mansfield. I should go over and greet her."

Megan rose and quickly made her escape. She could not understand how she had come to speak so bluntly to her sister-in-law. Intimacies were not encouraged in the O'Connell household. One did not intrude upon another's private affairs, for it was an understood thing that to do so constituted a breach of the rigid propriety that was to be observed.

After a few minutes of easy conversation with the guests, most of whom were well-known to Megan from past years, she was summoned by her father with a crook of his finger. Obediently Megan crossed over to him. "Yes, Father?"

Lord O'Connell stared at her from under beetled black brows. His mane of hair was grizzled with silver and his figure, though thickened, was still that of an athletic gentleman. "Lionel informs me that you took the gelding over the Patterson fences during my absence."

Megan drew in her breath. Ever so slightly her fingers curled in the folds of her skirt. Very calmly, she replied, "Yes,

I did. I had told Lionel all week that the gelding was ready. My brother disagreed."

Lord O'Connell frowned at her. "Lionel is in charge of the stables, daughter."

Megan smiled slightly. "However competent Lionel is with the horses, you have said yourself that I often have the better instincts. In this instance, I believed in the gelding enough to give him a try."

"How did he do?" asked Lord O'Connell.

"Very well, sir. He likes to jump," said Megan.

Lord O'Connell nodded. The flicker of a smile crossed his features. "Good, good. I do trust in your instincts, Megan. However, I have set Lionel in charge of the stables when I am gone on a buying trip. In future, I ask that you abide by his authority."

"Of course, Father," said Megan unemotionally.

"I am glad that we understand one another. You may work the gelding hard after your mother's ball. We must have him ready in a few months," said Lord O'Connell.

"I am sorry, Father, but that will not be possible," said Megan. "I am going to St. Petersburg. But I am certain that now he knows of the gelding's readiness, Lionel may very well work with him."

"St. Petersburg? This is not at all convenient, Megan," said Lord O'Connell sharply. "I need you here during the selling season. You are one of my best riders."

"I am sorry, sir. Mother has accepted an invitation upon my behalf from Princess Elizaveta Kirov. I do not think it is possible to bow out without giving grave offense," said Megan. She did not say so, but she was anxious that her father not deny his permission for the journey. Now that she had made up her mind to go, she really did not want to give up the adventure that the trip to St. Petersburg offered to her.

Lord O'Connell had been scowling, but suddenly his expression turned reflective. "Kirov? Kirov? Where have I heard that name?"

"Her highness is a friend of my mother's. I met the princess very briefly two years ago in London," said Megan. "Perhaps Mother mentioned Princess Kirov to you?"

Lord O'Connell waved his hand dismissively. "No, that was not it. Lady O'Connell collects all sorts of titles. One rarely means anything more than another to me. However, the name Kirov rings a bell."

Megan waited patiently while her parent gave the matter thought. She knew that it would not be a welcome move on her part to excuse herself without permission.

His face clearing, Lord O'Connell snapped his fingers. "I have it! I thought that there was something of importance I had heard. The Kirovs are directly related to several of the nobility who specialize in breeding the Orlov carriage horses and the Kabardian trotters."

"Are they?" asked Megan with scarce interest. "I had not realized."

Lord O'Connell was suddenly all good humor. "By all means, Megan, go stay with Princess Kirov for as long as she wishes you to remain! Perhaps you may be able to arrange for the purchase of one of the Orlovs or Kabardians."

Megan was startled. "I do not think that I have either the experience or the credibility to even begin to embark upon such a task, my lord!"

Lord O'Connell waved aside his daughter's protestation. "Nonsense! My credit is well enough known, at least in Europe, so you may rely upon that. As for the rest, I trust that you have a shrewd enough head on your shoulders to know an advantageous deal when it is offered to you. It will be necessary to make funds available to you, of course." He thought for a moment, while Megan regarded him with growing astonishment. "Come to my office in the morning, Megan. I shall write out a letter of transfer for you to carry with you to St. Petersburg so that you may be able to open an account in a bank. Princess Elizaveta will undoubtedly be able to point you to a respectable banking establishment." He bent an abruptly stern regard on her. "And I expect you to spend a few pounds on yourself, too, for I wish you to make the very best appearance possible. A good appearance is imperative in business dealings, Megan. You will do me the courtesy of respecting my wishes in this matter!"

"Yes, of course, Father. I will do just as you advise," said

Megan, marveling at her good fortune. She had never been handed a virtual carte blanche in all of her life. More than ever, she was glad for the invitation to visit Russia. It promised to be an opportunity unequaled in her limited experience.

"You look very well this evening, by the way. I am glad to see that you are becoming a bit more elegant in your wardrobe. I have disliked the gowns that you have worn in the past. Not at all up to the mark. I never have cause for complaint of you in the field, though. I am always proud of how you make the horses look," said Lord O'Connell.

"Thank you, sir," murmured Megan.

Lord O'Connell's gaze wandered from her. "Ah, there is Sir Bartram. He is always good for a jumper or two. He has brought his son with him this year. Pray be a good girl and make yourself friendly, Megan. I have arranged with your mother that you are to be seated beside the son at dinner. I expect you to talk up the jumpers to him. You know the sort of thing."

"You may rely on me, sir," said Megan, stifling a sigh.

"I know that I can rely on you, Megan," said Lord O'Connell with a paternal smile. "You at least have some understanding of what is required. Sophronia is worthless at that sort of thing. Colin intends to desert me when I need him most, drat him! As for Celeste, she is a disappointment to me tonight. My son-in-law informs me that she will not be down for fear of becoming ill and making a scene before my guests. He thought it would not set the right tone."

"There is truth in that," said Megan, willing to risk a stiff setdown in order to uphold her brother-in-law. She was surprised by her father's reaction.

Lord O'Connell snorted. "Quite right! I never thought to hear anything so sensible come out of that windbag Patrick's mouth." He patted Megan on the shoulder and started off toward his quarry.

Megan had to bite back a wide smile. Patrick Kennehessey had actually managed to excuse his wife's indisposition without incurring Lord O'Connell's wrath. That was a feat indeed and Megan thoroughly appreciated her brother-in-law's ingenuity. It was the brightest spot in the whole conversation with her father. Megan was still smiling when her brother Lionel descended upon her.

"So, did Father tell you that I am to be in charge?" he asked condescendingly. He looked at her with a knowing curl of the lip.

Megan raised her brows slightly. "You may have the run of the stables with my goodwill, Lionel," she said.

She walked away, leaving her brother smiling in a satisfied way. Megan saw no reason to tell him that she did not care what he did since she would not be there to see it. Let Lionel realize it for himself, she thought. She would not demean herself by coming down to his petty level.

Megan's attention was at once claimed by Lady Mansfield, a dowager built on formidable lines. Her ladyship's autocratic face and commanding figure hid a placid nature, however, and Megan was not at all adverse to obey her penetrating summons. "My lady, you wished to speak to me?"

"I have been put in mind of something, my dear. I wish to know if it is true that Captain O'Connell is betrothed?" said Lady Mansfield, not bothering to lower her voice.

Megan glanced around, aware that there had been a ripple of interest at her ladyship's question. She shook her head, smiling. "No, he is not. Not to my knowledge, at any rate. Why do you ask, dear ma'am?" She drew the lady courteously over to a settee, which chanced to be a little removed from the crowd.

"A rumor passed on to me by m'sister in London," said Lady Mansfield, sitting down heavily. "She wrote me something about Captain O'Connell making up to some chit or other and the parents taking rare exception. I thought it might be a mistake. Your brother is not known for cutting a dash among the ladies."

"I should hope not! But I have heard nothing of this," said Megan. "Certainly Colin has never mentioned anything of the sort."

"Daresay m'sister might have gotten her stories confused, she often does, and it wasn't Captain O'Connell at all," said Lady Mansfield.

Megan agreed to it and introduced another topic. However,

she could not but wonder whether her brother had indeed stirred up some sort of gossip about himself. Her eyes sought out her brother's tall figure. He was leaning against the mantel in a casual pose, a smile on his face as he listened to another gentleman. There was no denying that Colin was devastatingly attractive, especially in his military regimentals, Megan thought. It would not be surprising to learn that he was the object of some young woman's admiration, nor that he had entered into a light flirtation. But what Lady Mansfield had related was of a more serious nature. Megan could only hope that such a story, true or otherwise, did not come to Lord O'Connell's ears.

His lordship might view his children with indifference, but he demanded a high standard of propriety. Lord O'Connell's harsh reaction to his eldest daughter's elopement had resulted in a painful and lengthy separation for Megan from her sister. Megan did not desire a similar estrangement with her brother.

When Megan separated at last from Lady Mansfield, she started to seek out her brother and ask him about the story. Before she reached him, however, Megan had thought better of it. Colin would not thank her for prying into what was essentially his private life, and he would no doubt greet her question with a chilly reserve. There was an unspoken rule in the O'Connell household. One did not involve oneself too closely into the affairs of others.

Lady O'Connell shortly announced dinner and paired up the guests. Megan smiled and graciously accepted the escort of Sir Bartram's son. She quickly discovered that he was a rather insipid young man without a single original thought in his head. He did not open his mouth except to parrot his domineering father's opinions.

Megan was excruciatingly bored, but she dutifully held up her part of the conversation as well as she was able. She was never more glad than when Lady O'Connell rose from the table, signaling the end of dinner and the departure of the ladies from the dining room so that the gentlemen could enjoy their after-dinner port in privacy.

Lady O'Connell took the opportunity afforded in a lull of conversation to murmur to her daughter, "That is not the same gown that you wore last year, surely?"

"No, ma'am, it is not. My own gown had become quite indecent and so I had to make shift at the last minute with this one," said Megan quietly. "I have already received several compliments this evening. Even my father offered a kind word for my appearance."

Lady O'Connell looked as though she wanted to inquire more closely into the gown's origins, but her attention was claimed by a guest. Megan was glad of it. She had little taste for a public discussion about the inadequacies of her wardrobe. Least of all did she want to air the fact that she was wearing a cast-down gown from her mother's dresser's wardrobe. She was thankful to be spared that embarrassment.

The gentlemen shortly joined the ladies. The orchestra was given the signal to begin and the entire company drifted into the ballroom. The night was danced away.

During the course of the evening, Megan told Captain O'Connell that, if it was convenient to him, she wanted to leave for London on the morrow as soon as she had seen their father.

"Called on the carpet, are you?" asked Captain O'Connell, smothering a yawn. "I wondered how long it would be before Lionel would get his own back. Shall I go with you and tell Father that I was as much to blame since I did not try to stop you from jumping the gelding?"

"I have already been scolded. This is a different matter altogether. And no, I do not think you should accompany me. Father has made it quite plain that he is not best pleased that your leave has not been extended this time," said Megan. "If he were to see you, he would likely say something that will set up your back. And I am of no mind to travel with you after you have been thrown into the sulks, Colin."

"Spoken like a true O'Connell," said Captain O'Connell, flashing a grin. He was not at all insulted. "Very well, then. I'll let you go into the ogre's den on your own. I made the offer with a notable lack of enthusiasm, in any event."

"As I noticed," retorted Megan. "Mrs. Tyler and I will be packed and ready to depart at any time after I have seen Father."

"That will suit me admirably," said Captain O'Connell. "I

have it in mind to go up in the morning to say good-bye to Celeste and then we can be off. I only hope she is not ill while I am in the room!"

Megan laughed and parted from her brother on good terms.

It was nearly two o'clock in the morning before the O'Connell's grand ball ended. The houseguests staggered to their rooms, the neighbors departed, and Megan was at last free to seek her own bed.

Chapter Five

The next morning all transpired as planned and the travelers took to the road before luncheon. Captain O'Connell rode, firmly declining to share the carriage with the ladies and the maid.

"I've no intention of riding bodkin between a stack of female baggage and a lachrymose maid," he said forcibly.

Megan really could not blame him. Her maid had been sniffling dolefully ever since she had learned that she was to leave Ireland. However, the woman had said that it was her duty to accompany her mistress to the ends of the earth, whether it be London or Russia. Megan almost regretted bringing the maid at all, for it was bothersome to be obliged to witness Betty's discomposure. But she and Mrs. Tyler could scarcely be expected to do without a tiring-woman.

Captain O'Connell's decision did not weigh with Megan on another count, as well. Without her brother's demanding presence, Megan could allow her thoughts to roam at will without being obliged to making conversation. She and Mrs. Tyler knew one another so well that there was no constraint between them even when not a word was spoken for several moments.

Mrs. Tyler occupied herself with embroidery while Megan divided her attention between the book in her lap and the passing miles. The journey to London was made without incident, discounting the maid's wretched bout of seasickness while crossing the Irish Sea, which made Captain O'Connell declare that he felt quite able to tumble the unhappy woman into the choppy waves.

Soon enough Captain O'Connell left the trio at the town house in Albemarle Street, expressing his relief at being able to relinquish his responsibility for them into the capable hands of Lady O'Connell's domestic staff.

* * *

The next week was very busy. Megan and Mrs. Tyler made visits to several shops to acquire everything that occurred to them which might be useful in a cold, inhospitable climate. They also visited the expensive modiste, Madame Rochet, and ordered several ensembles. Allowing themselves to be guided by the astute modiste's advice, they ended up commissioning an enormous number of gowns, day dresses, carriage dresses, pelisses, dominos, and other stylish garments. This, coupled with the purchase of bonnets, inexpressibles, innumerable pairs of gloves, hose, and other feminine fripperies, began to give Mrs. Tyler's conscience a definite twinge.

"My dear, does it not occur to you that we are taking advantage of Lady O'Connell's directive?" she asked falteringly, having caught sight of the price of a very pretty fringed shawl that Megan was just then purchasing. She had unconsciously been keeping a rough total in her mind and it was beginning to concern her. Of course, there was no knowing what the modiste's bills were, for those were to be directly forwarded to Lady O'Connell's agent, Mr. Henry.

"I have thought about it," admitted Megan. She threw a glinting glance at her companion as a small smile touched her lips. "I have discounted it, though, Gwyneth. I am spending far less than what a Season would have cost my mother and I am being gotten out of the way, as well. So there cannot really be an objection, can there?"

"Oh, my dear!" said Mrs. Tyler. She felt sorry for the younger woman. No matter how well Megan had disguised her feelings over the years, Mrs. Tyler was still aware that there was a well of hurt hidden inside the younger woman's breast. As the youngest, and quite unexpected, child, Megan had been shunted aside again and again. She had rarely been the recipient of either consideration or approval. It went against all that was natural for the daughter of a rich, established family to be relegated to the same sort of shadowy existence that was usually the realm of the indigent relation.

A sudden, unusual anger surged through Mrs. Tyler. If it was at all in her power, she meant to see that Megan was situated where she would be well and truly happy. That meant, of course, finding her a husband. In that moment, Mrs. Tyler discovered within herself a quite passionate desire to launch her protégée in style. "I quite agree with you, Megan! You must be perfectly outfitted for this extraordinary adventure. We do not know what we will find in St. Petersburg. Certainly we will not find a modiste such as Madame Rochet, nor attractive English goods for the buying. Pray do let us get whatever strikes your fancy!"

The only thing that Megan did not order was riding habits. She had brought all of her own, quite confident that nothing could outshine the outfits that had been done up at Lord O'Connell's express order. Of course, the old practice habits that she had worn on a daily basis had been consigned to the trash bin before she had left. However, she did urge her companion to order two habits.

"But you know that I do not ride," objected Mrs. Tyler. "Lord O'Connell told me once that I bounce about like a sack of flour in the saddle."

"His lordship will not be watching you in Russia. You certainly will not send me off on riding parties without proper chaperonage, so I insist that you have suitable attire for those events," said Megan.

"*Oui*, Mademoiselle O'Connell is correct, madame," the modiste quickly concurred. "It is one thing to be an ill-dressed sack of flour and quite another to be a sack of flour in the best mode!"

"Well!" Mrs. Tyler uttered, unable to keep back a laugh. "I suppose that I must, then!"

Megan informed the modiste that she and Mrs. Tyler were due to leave London shortly for an extended visit to Russia. "I trust that we shall be able to pack most of these to take with us. Any of the others can be sent along behind and I shall send payment back to you after their arrival in St. Petersburg," said Megan.

Madame Rochet promised that the orders would be ready in a week. She would personally see to it that all of her seamstresses worked around the clock to meet the obligation, for it was not often that such a large and lucrative order was placed so far in advance of the Season. She had no intention of allowing even a pence of the promised largesse to fall into delayed payment.

It was not all shopping, of course. Megan met with her mother's agent Mr. Henry for a lengthy interview, from which she emerged very well satisfied. Among other things discussed, Mr. Henry promised to procure outriders for the travelers so that Megan's last concern was laid to rest. Her journey to St. Petersburg would be attended with all the safety and comfort that one could wish.

In addition to attending to these weighty matters, Megan and Mrs. Tyler set themselves to enjoy some of the most popular destinations for sightseers, such as Astley's Circus, the zoo, and the museum. These were harmless entertainments and perhaps would be considered mundane by others' standards. However, Megan and her companion had neither one had the advantage of ever sampling the delights of London and they immensely enjoyed their excursions.

Their evenings were spent quietly at the town house. Though there were undoubtedly acquaintances of the O'Connell family in residence that the ladies could have called upon, they did not do so, preferring to keep to their own company for the short time that they would be in London.

Megan and Mrs. Tyler were thus surprised when one evening the butler came into the drawing room to inquire if they were at home to a visitor. "Why, I suppose that we are, Digby. Pray show them in," said Megan, knowing that the butler would not act without being confident that the visitor was indeed welcome.

Megan and Mrs. Tyler were astonished when Simpkins, Lady O'Connell's dresser, was ushered in. The dresser was buttoned up to the throat in a serviceable pelisse cut from excellent material and wore a plain bonnet. She clutched her reticule in tight gloved fingers. There was a heightened color to her normally pallid face that puzzled Megan until she realized that it came from embarrassment.

Tactfully, Megan dismissed the butler and waited until the door was closed before she turned to the dresser. With a smile, she said, "Pray be seated, Simpkins. I must say this is a surprise. Is my mother coming up to London so soon before the Season?"

The dresser seated herself stiffly on the settee. "I do not know what her ladyship's plans might be," she said.

"But surely—" Mrs. Tyler stopped, then looked at Megan.

"Miss O'Connell, I have followed you and Mrs. Tyler to London in hopes of entering your service," said Simpkins baldly.

Megan blinked. She exchanged a glance of open astonishment and bewilderment with Mrs. Tyler. "But, Simpkins, you are already in service to my mother, Lady O'Connell."

"That I am not, miss," said Simpkins bitterly. "Her ladyship has turned me off without even so much as a character."

Mrs. Tyler gasped. "I cannot believe it! Why, you are far too valuable to her ladyship."

Simpkins regarded Mrs. Tyler with grim agreement. "One would have supposed so, ma'am. However, her ladyship was that put out over Miss wearing her old gown, and appearing better in it than her ladyship ever did. *And* hearing so from several personages, I might add! Her ladyship flew up into the boughs and rang a rare peal over my head. It ended with my saying a few hasty words of my own, which I do not regret, never mind that her ladyship did order me off."

Megan was appalled. "I am so very sorry, Simpkins. I would never have worn the gown if I had known it would be the cause of such trouble."

The dresser nodded. "That I know, miss. But the gown was mine to do with as I saw fit and it suited me to see that you were properly attired. I was quite within my rights, which I reminded her ladyship."

"But this is dreadful," exclaimed Mrs. Tyler. "Whatever shall you do, Simpkins?"

The dresser's face paled slightly. She cleared her throat. "As I said at the outset, I hope to enter Miss O'Connell's service."

"But I am going to Russia," began Megan.

"So I had heard, miss," said Simpkins, nodding. "I thought to myself that you would be needing a proper lady's maid as would understand your requirements. Your maid Betty does very well in her own way, of course, but she might perhaps gain in skill with a little guidance. Russia is a barbaric land, so I understand, and you will not wish your dress to be overly influenced by their queer customs."

Megan thoughtfully regarded the dresser. The woman held herself with all of her customary pride, her posture erect. But Megan saw the underlying tension in the tiring-woman's eyes and face. It was patently obvious that the woman had had no other place to go. Megan felt that she could not turn her away.

"Very well, Simpkins. If you feel that you are able to make the sacrifice and leave England, than I shall be most happy indeed to engage your services," said Megan.

"Thank you, miss. You shall not regret it." The dresser's words were formal, but there was an edge of relief in her voice.

Megan put up her hand in warning. "But I must tell you that we shall be gone for an undetermined time. It might be months or even a year or more before we return to England. So pray think it over carefully, Simpkins. I would not hold it against you if you chose instead to remain in London. In which case, I will gladly pen you a reference if that is indeed what you would prefer."

"No, miss, I am quite settled in my mind. I see my duty plain. You and Mrs. Tyler need one of my talents to accompany you to these foreign parts," said Simpkins.

Megan smiled at the dresser. "I am very happy that you join us, Simpkins. You may direct Digby to see to your requirements. Tomorrow I shall advance you a year's salary so that you may purchase those things that you shall require for the journey. I understand that it is very cold in Russia, so be certain that you have a good woolen coat and boots."

Simpkins rose, her hauteur once more intact. "Yes, miss. I shall do just as you say." The dresser curtsied and left the room.

Megan and Mrs. Tyler looked at one another. "What an extraordinary thing," said Mrs. Tyler.

"Yes, and most fortunate, too, don't you think? I really do not see how we could go on better than to have Simpkins with us," said Megan.

"Nor I," agreed Mrs. Tyler. "But, my dear, how shall you afford her? She comes very dear. And Lady O'Connell is not likely to endorse her dresser's change of allegiance. Indeed, I think quite otherwise."

Megan's eyes danced. "But we are leaving England, Gwyneth. Once we are gone, no one here will give much thought to the fact that Simpkins is with me. They will assume that my mother sent her. As for funds, I shall simply inform Mr. Henry that I have acquired the services of a highly recommended lady's maid. There will be no objection, I assure you, for Mr. Henry thoroughly disapproves of this undertaking. He especially did so when he learned that you were to be my only companion. He discounted Betty, whom he stigmatized as a wilted dandelion. You will recall that he insisted upon interviewing her when I informed him that she would be accompanying us. Mr. Henry will greet the news of a staunch, loyal tiring-woman with relief."

"But the household will still know that Simpkins accompanied us," said Mrs. Tyler. "Lady O'Connell is certain to hear of it some time and then where will we be? She will likely cut off the funds that you require for Simpkins's salary."

"We will be beyond my mother's influence, Gwyneth. Once I have transferred funds to St. Petersburg, there will not be a thing to be anxious about," said Megan cheerfully.

Mrs. Tyler eyed her with open astonishment. "Transfer funds, my dear? Whatever are you talking about? That will require Lord O'Connell's signature."

"Which I possess, Gwyneth. My father was magnanimous enough to write a letter in his own hand to his banker. I have an appointment on the morrow at that establishment," said Megan.

She burst out laughing at her companion's expression. "No, I have not forged it, my dear foolish friend! My father has long desired to acquire an Orlov carriage horse or Kabardian trotter and he views my journey to St. Petersburg as the opportunity of a lifetime. He has entrusted me with his desire to acquire some of these breeds, if at all possible. I could not be expected to do so without adequate funds. His lordship also ordered me to use certain of the funds for my own needs so that I could present an excellent appearance while conducting business."

"My goodness. How things do work out for the best," said Mrs. Tyler.

"I begin to think so, indeed," agreed Megan. "Betty has been in the doldrums ever since we left, so much so that I am quite out of patience with her. We shall send her home, which ought to cheer her no end, while Simpkins makes a more than adequate replacement."

"I was thinking more of Lord O'Connell's largesse, actually. That was fortuitous in the extreme," said Mrs. Tyler. She paused, then remarked, "We shall be quite independent of anyone."

There was such immense satisfaction in her voice that Megan laughed again. "Why, Gwyneth, I suspect that you are beginning to enjoy this foray into the world."

"Why should I not? We have been kept too close, Megan. I am your companion and responsible for your well-being. Very well! I think it is high time that we kick up our heels a bit," declared Mrs. Tyler.

"I am very willing to abide by your wishes, my dearest of friends," said Megan. "But first let us get to St. Petersburg. Then we may be as flighty as we wish."

Mrs. Tyler's flare of independent spirit faltered slightly. "Remaining within the proprieties, of course."

"Gwyneth, whenever have you had cause to be anxious on my behalf?" wondered Megan.

"Not once," said Mrs. Tyler. A smile curled her mouth, however, as she affectionately regarded her companion. "That does not rule out the possibility that I shall not be made anxious in the future, however. For I know how I feel at the thought of being on our own, quite free of all the restraints of our former lives. I can scarcely credit that you are any less anticipatory, my dear!"

Megan chuckled. Her eyes danced even as she nodded in agreement. "Quite, quite true! Oh, Gwyneth, isn't it simply splendid! We shall have a wardrobe worthy of the name and go to parties and routs and do all the things that I have positively longed to do. We shall have such fun, I just know it!"

"So I hope," said Mrs. Tyler, still smiling. She kept to herself her private fears—her trepidation at the thought of stepping so thoroughly into the unknown and her utter conviction that Megan's life was about to undergo a singular change, whether for better or worse, she could not yet tell. But certainly it was all worth the risk if only to enable Megan to engage in glad hopes.

Megan unconsciously voiced something of her companion's reflections. "It is a bit frightening to think about going off somewhere, where we do not know a single person and the country might be strange to us. But I have wanted for so long to do something different, Gwyneth, that I am very ready to throw myself into any adventure!"

"Pray allow me to insert a word of caution, my dear. There are adventures and then there are adventures," said Mrs. Tyler.

"Always the cautious chaperone, Gwyneth?" quizzed Megan.

"I trust that I shall always be cognizant of my duty," said Mrs. Tyler gravely, but with a gleam of humor in her fine eyes. "I do not think that responsibility shall change overmuch, whether in London or in St. Petersburg. However, I hope that I am not so stuffy as to smother you with strictures and homilies and bind you about so tightly that you cannot breathe. I only ask that you preserve your good sense, my dear."

"Never fear. I do not allow anything to undermine my rational thoughts," said Megan cheerfully. "I have seen rather too much that passes for affection but which is not. So you need not worry. I am far too levelheaded to be taken in by some man-milliner."

"Megan! What a turn of phrase! Man-milliner, indeed," said Mrs. Tyler, shaking her head. Though she deplored the younger woman's choice of words, she was comforted by them, for she knew well enough that Megan was a sensible young woman.

Chapter Six

Megan looked around her. Slowly, she waved a fantastically painted fan in front of her face. She was standing beside a massive fluted marble column at the edge of the dance floor. The ballroom was incredibly hot, but that was characteristic of a Russian function. It was one of the things that she had had to adjust to during the months she had been in the glittering city of St. Petersburg.

"Megan, my dear sister, you do not dance?" came a light teasing voice.

Megan turned with a smile to her friend, Countess Irena Annensky. One of the things she liked best about the Russians was their warmth and their astonishing habit of addressing even near strangers as a member of their family. "No, it is too hot to dance. So I am hiding, as you see."

"What, and not one of your admirers have sought you out?" asked Countess Annensky.

"Oh, I was found only a moment before you came up. I have sent the gallant gentleman to fetch me an ice," said Megan. "I told him that dancing makes one very warm and that I would be ever so grateful for an ice."

"And so he has run off very happily to execute his important errand," concluded Countess Annensky.

Megan laughed. Her eyes sparkled. "Yes, isn't it bad of me?"

"But you are always too warm," said Countess Annensky. "It is your warmth that excites such devotion. The fire flickers in your eyes and your smile and draws the men to you. You are like a Russian firebird."

Megan laughed and shook her head. Countess Irena Annensky was a budding poetess and sometimes her extravagancies of speech were rather fanciful. "You mistake. It is not my personality, but my coloring that is so admired. I am a rarity in St. Petersburg. That is the full sum of my allure."

"Ah! But your hair is not a mere red, dear Megan. It is flickering flames of red and gold. It is no wonder that the poor moths are drawn to you," said Countess Annensky.

Megan shook her head again. She knew that her flaming tresses, pale skin, and smoke-gray eyes had excited immediate notice from the moment of her arrival in St. Petersburg and she still marveled at it. "At home in Ireland, I am considered to be very ordinary."

"Impossible!" stated Countess Annensky firmly. "You are beautiful. Everyone says so. You have turned down eleven proposals of marriage and almost had a duel fought over you. That is not ordinary."

"You have forgotten the Turkish pasha who wished to add me to his harem," reminded Megan with a quiver of laughter in her voice.

"Yes! And all of this in six months. It is enough to rouse envy in the breasts of even your closest friends," said Countess Annensky with a huge sigh and a sidelong look.

Megan laughed. "Yes, I perceive how much you envy me the Turkish pasha."

Countess Annensky giggled. "Well, perhaps not. But there is that nice baron—"

"Too old," said Megan.

"And that very handsome captain—"

"Too young," said Megan, shaking her head.

"Or that Italian count—"

"Too married," said Megan.

Countess Annensky stared at her. "No!"

Megan nodded. "All too true. I had it from Madame Riasanovsky, who had it from her maid, who was told it by the count's driver. The count has a wife and five children at home in Italy."

"No!" gasped Countess Annensky, greatly entertained. She shook her head. "Poor Megan. You have been cruelly disillusioned, have you not? The count makes such perfect love to one's fingers, kissing each tip with such reverence. Such a heartless philanderer!"

Megan shook her head in a mournful manner, though her smoke-gray eyes danced. "I am utterly cast down, I assure you. I have completely lost my trust in all the gentlemen."

"You trusted none of them from the beginning," said Countess Annensky shrewdly.

Megan's mouth curved in a smile. "Perhaps not, indeed."

The countess shook her head. "You are all fire and grace, Megan, yet you have such a coolness of head. Have none of the gentlemen touched your heart?"

"I tell no secrets, Irena," said Megan lightly. "There are too many ears to overhear. I prefer to keep my own counsel on such private matters."

"Yes, perhaps that is wisest," said Countess Annensky with another sidelong glance. "Princess Kirov makes no secret that she will be very happy to see your hand contracted in marriage before the spring comes."

"Princess Kirov has taken her role of matchmaker in too serious a vein," said Megan with a smile and a small shrug. "The princess knew of my mother's hopes for me when she invited me to come to St. Petersburg. I am proving to be a sad disappointment to her highness."

"Do you dare to go counter to your mother's and the princess' wishes?" asked Countess Annensky curiously.

"I shall not marry until it is my decision," said Megan quietly.

Countess Annensky shook her head. "I could not be so brave. I shiver at the thought of defying my father. No doubt he would beat me very hard."

"But you have no need to defy your father, for he has contracted your hand to the very gentleman that you like the best," said Megan.

Countess Annensky blushed and dimpled. "Yes, Prince Sergei suits me very well," she agreed demurely.

"Fortunate, indeed, for it saves your back," said Megan.

Countess Annensky trilled laughter. "No, no, my father is too fond of me! He would not beat me at all. That is for crude men, not great brown bears like my father. They growl more than they bite."

"I have seen many Russian bears and also many others from other countries. I have been wooed and made the object of wonderful flatteries. It is enough to turn a country girl's head," said Megan.

"But not yours," said Countess Annensky.

"No, not mine," agreed Megan. Flashing a smile, she exclaimed, "I have had a perfectly grand time. I am so glad that I came to St. Petersburg."

"I shall miss you when you return to your country," said Countess Annensky, giving the other young woman an impulsive hug.

"I am not gone yet," said Megan, laughing.

"But when the spring comes, you will leave us," said Countess Annensky positively. "It is a sad thing, and so I shall not think on it anymore. Ah! Here is Prince Vladimir with your ice."

"Thank you, your highness," said Megan, accepting the ice. "You are too good."

The youthful royalty blushed. He made an elegant bow and embarked on a tangled compliment, which Megan received with smiling good humor. Countess Annensky, standing to one side out of the prince's vision, rolled her eyes.

Prince Vladimir ended by requesting the honor of partnering Megan in the next set.

"I regret, your highness, but my hand is already claimed for the waltz," said Megan gently.

The youth's face fell. Even his extravagant mustache seemed to droop. He bowed again. "Naturally it is to be expected. There is not a gentleman here who does not recognize your worth, mademoiselle."

"You see, Megan? What did I tell you? The moths flutter and their poor wings are singed," murmured Countess Annensky.

"Enough, Irena," said Megan, giving a gurgling laugh.

Prince Vladimir looked from one lady to another. In French, he said, "Pardon, but I do not understand."

Megan had long ago gotten over her initial surprise that French was spoken as often as the native Russian language in

St. Petersburg. She shook her head. "It was nothing, your highness. Prince Vladimir, I hope that I may impose on you yet again." She was finished with the ice and set the glass down beside the column.

"Anything! But ask!" exclaimed Prince Vladimir ardently.

"Dare we request your safe escort through this crowd? I have left my dance program on my seat and I should like to retrieve it. You see, I believe that I have a country dance open, if that is agreeable to your highness," said Megan.

Prince Vladimir flushed with pleasure. Pushing out his chest, he said expansively, "You may rely upon me, mademoiselles." Offering an elbow to each lady, he slowly promenaded with them across the floor. He looked right and left, nodding regally to any of his acquaintances who were privileged to witness his elevated task.

One of Countess Annensky's acquaintances stopped their progress. After a few words among them all, the countess agreed to her friend's entreaty that she lift his boredom and join him for refreshments. With a laugh and a wave of her hand, she left Megan and Prince Vladimir. "I shall speak to you again!" she called.

Prince Vladimir brought Megan to her chair with a flourishing bow. He pressed a kiss against her gloved hand. "I thank you for the honor bestowed upon me, mademoiselle. I shall anticipate our dance together with a passionate longing."

A tall English gentleman sauntered up and presented himself. "It is our waltz, I believe, Miss O'Connell?"

Prince Vladimir straightened to his full height. He leveled a smoldering stare on the intruder. His mustache bristled with possessive outrage.

Megan rose hastily. "Indeed it is, Lord George." She turned with a smile to Prince Vladimir. "I also shall look forward to our dance, your highness."

Mollified, Prince Vladimir bowed. Before he stepped back, however, he turned a burning glance on the Englishman who was appropriating the object of his desires.

As Lord George led Megan onto the floor, he remarked, "Puppy. I thought for a moment that the boy might actually bite me."

"Truthfully, I felt much like a juicy bone in contest," admitted Megan.

Lord George barked a laugh. "That is good, 'pon my soul!"

"The prince is actually quite well-meaning and sweet," said Megan hastily.

"I am quite sure of it. He wants a little sense, of course. You are a bit too sophisticated for such a youngster as that. Now I am a different matter altogether," said Lord George, wiggling his brows meaningfully.

Megan laughed and shook her head. "We have been down this path before, my lord. And my answer is still the same. We would not suit. Friends we have become and friends we shall remain!"

Lord George heaved a tremendous sigh. "I am thrown down to the pit of despair. I am up to my neck in miry clay. I am a vessel cast adrift upon an unfriendly sea."

"My lord, how can this be? I have it on very good authority that you have formed a somewhat scandalous connection with a certain pretty widow," said Megan. "Surely Madame Lanochet is not the French version of a fishwife!"

"No, of course not! I say, where did you hear about—" Lord George broke off. He bent a reproving gaze on his partner. "Miss O'Connell, you have betrayed a knowledge that is quite beneath your notice. I am shocked, to say the least. Yes, and what's more, I am piqued that you are laughing at me. I am utterly sincere in everything that I have said."

Megan laughed in earnest. Shaking her head, "Dear Lord George, if I were to believe half of the farragoes that have been whispered in my ears over these past months, I would have gained a reputation for being a goosecap. And justly, too."

"Yes, you have never lacked for admiration, have you?" Lord George regarded her amused expression speculatively. "One wonders what goes on in that head of yours, Miss O'Connell. I could swear that your heart is as vulnerable as any other lady's, but you have not succumbed to any of our overtures."

"Not yet, in any event," said Megan cheerfully. "I am having such a wonderful time, you see. I cannot conceive of bursting my bubble with a betrothal. Such a hindrance, don't you think?"

Lord George shouted with laughter. "Upon reflection, Miss O'Connell, I do not believe that I am the man to win you. There is a better man in the wings than my poor self, one who will know just how to handle the ribbons."

"So I should hope," retorted Megan. "From what I have gathered, you made a poor showing for England last week in the sledding race."

"I am not used to a three-in-hand. Half-broken brutes and hardmouthed to boot," said Lord George, defending himself.

"And there was the snow, too," said Megan, twinkling up at him.

Lord George nodded, very much on his dignity. "Besides, I have never driven over such slick ice in my life. Sleds are different from carriages, you know. They fly. I swear it! But I shall have my revenge in England. Both Count Juarasky and Don Sevilles y Perez have pledged themselves to me for the summer. I shall show them what it is to drive to an inch!"

"I am sure of it, my lord. England's honor must be upheld at all costs," said Megan. "I trust that you are prepared to do so?"

"With my life," declared Lord George dramatically.

There was much more such lighthearted nonsense until the set was over. Lord George escorted Megan back toward her chair. "There is a rumor that you will be returning to England in the spring," he said abruptly.

Megan looked up at him in surprise. "How did that get about?"

Lord George shrugged. "Someone had it from Countess Annensky and I had it from someone else. If it is true, I shall miss you. You have been like a breath of fresh air this winter."

Megan felt her face warming. "That is very kind of you, my lord. I don't know my plans, actually. It depends upon Princess Kirov more than anything, I suppose. There was no set date for my departure."

"Speaking of the house of Kirov, here is the prince himself," said Lord George. Looking up into the Russian's handsome face, his own face broadened into a grin as he put out his hand. "Misha, you bear! Will you join me at the crossroads inn? I am leaving shortly with a party of roisterers that begs the honor of your company."

"We shall see. I am committed to wait upon the pleasure of Miss O'Connell and my mother, and the ball does not end until the morning," said Prince Mikhail Sergei Alexsander Kirov, a friendly expression lightening his ice-blue eyes.

"Oh, is that how it is? Dull duty, indeed. Well, I shall be off, then," said Lord George. He bowed to Megan, nodded to the prince, and left them.

Prince Kirov held out his hand commandingly. "Come, mademoiselle. I wish to show you the conservatory. There is a striking lily in bloom which reminds me of your extravagant beauty."

Megan opened her fan and set it in languid motion. "I am sorry, your highness. But I have made it a rule that I am never seen going off alone with any gentleman."

"I am not any gentleman. I am your devoted host. There can be no objection," said Prince Kirov with a glinting smile. His was a very charming smile, one that more often than not set female hearts fluttering and overrode gentle scruples. However, this once it failed in its objective.

"On the contrary, your highness. Mrs. Tyler is very strict in her views of propriety. She guards my reputation with intense fervor," said Megan.

"Indeed! And where is Mrs. Tyler now, Miss O'Connell?" asked Prince Kirov, making a show of his disbelief. "Surely in the eyes of such a strict guardian, it must even be beyond the line for you to acknowledge a gentleman's address without a chaperone within sight."

"Mrs. Tyler has us in her sights even now, your highness," said Megan demurely. She raised her fan slightly to point toward a small knot of ladies seated a short distance away.

Prince Kirov looked around quickly. Mrs. Tyler, mistaking Megan's gesture, waved back in a friendly way. He bowed, then turned again to Megan. "You have reminded me of my duty, mademoiselle. Naturally you are correct. It would not be seemly for you to leave the ballroom alone with me as your only escort. I shall immediately bring together a few friends so that we may all go to the conservatory and enjoy the lilies."

Megan started to laugh. "But how absurd! You should not order things tailored so exactly to your whims."

"Why should I not? How am I to take you to the conservatory otherwise?" inquired Prince Kirov in a reasonable way. He sat down beside her, half-turning in his chair so that he could observe her face.

"The conservatory must wait, your highness. I still have a very full dance card," said Megan, proffering it for his inspection. "It would be exceedingly rude of me to disappoint my admirers."

"I shall admit to it, for my name appears on that card as well," said Prince Kirov. He smiled and shrugged. "It is a pity that we are constrained by convention and by duty from what we most desire to do. But I am a Kirov. I have been raised to a full awareness of my duty to family and country. I shall not shirk either, even for the glimpse of a prized lily."

"What of those things that are of equal importance as duty, your highness?" asked Megan curiously.

"Ah, you speak of the heart. Once I believed that my duty was always to be placed above matters of the heart. I have learned that sometimes that is not entirely true," said Prince Kirov. He regarded her with lazy interest. "What of your own ideals, Miss O'Connell? Do you pay heed to the voice of duty or to the whisperings of your heart? Would you throw over all of this"—he made a sweeping gesture around at the glittering bejeweled crowd, then placed his hand against his chest—"in order to satisfy the yearnings of this?"

Megan shook her head. "I do not know. You ask me something of which I have no experience."

"I have had such experience, dear sister." Prince Kirov smiled again, but as though he was looking back over a particular memory. "It is a felicitous thing indeed when one's heartfelt inclinations come into alignment with one's duty."

"I know little to nothing of such difficult choices," said Megan. She was made vaguely uncomfortable by the prince's unusual descent into sober rumination. "However, I do know that our time together grows short, your highness. Here is Prince Vladimir to claim his set with me."

"I shall send him away," said Prince Kirov, his brows lowering as he glanced at the approaching young gentleman.

Megan laid her hand quickly on his arm. "No, pray do not. He is but a youth, easily cast down. I do not wish him disappointed on my account, for I promised the country set to him."

Prince Kirov smiled. He covered her hand with his own, warming her fingers through the thin fabric of her glove. "Your heart is soft, mademoiselle. Very well. We shall deal gently with Vladimir. I have known him since his cradle. Perhaps he will grow into a man someday, though I have heard his father often despair of it!"

Megan was grateful that Prince Kirov's statement was uttered in a low tone and so was not heard by the young gentleman. Unobtrusively she slipped free of Prince Kirov's handclasp. She smiled at Prince Vladimir, holding out her hand to him. "You are prompt, your highness. The set is not yet begun."

"How could I be otherwise when I shall lead out the most beautiful woman in the room?" exclaimed Prince Vladimir, bowing over her fingers.

"Perhaps there is yet hope," murmured Prince Kirov.

"Pardon, Mikhail? Did you address me?" asked Prince Vladimir.

"No, no, I was but contemplating a thing of astonishment that I must tell to an acquaintance of mine," said Prince Kirov.

Megan did not glance at him, afraid that if she did she might laugh. "There is the music striking up now, Prince Vladimir! We must not tarry. Prince Kirov, I shall undoubtedly speak to you later in the evening."

Megan saw Prince Vladimir slide a triumphant glance at Prince Kirov as he led her off. He obviously thought he had snatched her from under the nose of one of St. Petersburg's most respected and eligible parties. Men could be so foolish, she thought as the dancing began.

Chapter Seven

A week later, Megan was summoned to an audience with her hostess. She knew that it was for a matter of some portent since Princess Kirov, though kindly disposed toward her, was an awe-inspiring personage who did not indulge in comfortable cozes.

"I shall be down directly," said Megan to the servant who had relayed the message. The servant bowed and effaced himself from the sitting room. When he had exited, Megan turned to her companion. "Well, Gwyneth, what do you think?"

"Her highness does not dally in incidentals," said Mrs. Tyler, confirming Megan's own thoughts. "Obviously Princess Kirov has news of a serious nature to impart to you. It struck me at once that I was not included in this summons. Perhaps she has had word from Lady O'Connell? Though I cannot imagine what her ladyship might have written that would evolve into a private audience."

"Yes, Princess Kirov has always shown you a particular respect," said Megan with a small frown. "It is odd, indeed."

"You would do well not to keep the princess waiting too long," suggested Mrs. Tyler. "Hers is a formidable personality. We are both aware how thoroughly she despises tardiness in any member of her household."

Megan chuckled ruefully. "Quite true! I ran foul of her displeasure less than a fortnight ago when I returned from shopping with Irena. Her frown did not lift until we had each offered an abject apology." She rose from her chair and started across the thick Persian carpets toward the door, remarking, as she exited, "Wouldn't it be wonderful if Princess Kirov has called me to inform me that my efforts to acquire an Orlov or Kabardian have been successful?"

"Lord O'Connell would be very well pleased by that, certainly. Perhaps that is what it is all about," said Mrs. Tyler hopefully.

Megan traversed the marble-tiled, magnificently ornate halls to Princess Kirov's private apartments. She was expected and therefore ushered at once into her hostess's august presence.

Megan curtsied. "You wished to speak with me, your highness?"

Princess Kirov was enjoying a cup of extremely hot tea from the samovar, the ubiquitous wood-burning appliance that was to be found in every room of the house. She motioned for Megan to join her. "Ah, Megan! Thank you for being so prompt. You will take tea with me?"

"Of course, your highness."

Princess Kirov snapped her fingers at a servant to pour another cup of the heavily sweetened brew. When Megan had sat down and had been served, Princess Kirov said, "My dear Megan, I have requested you to visit with me because I have been giving much reflection to your situation. In a few months the snow and ice of winter will begin to warm and our roads will become impassable mires and pits. You will be unable to travel except with the greatest difficulty. Therefore I judge that it is nearly time for you to return to your homeland."

"I shall regret the necessity of leaving St. Petersburg, your highness," said Megan with sincerity.

Princess Kirov gave a thin smile. There was approval in her dark eyes. "You are gracious, Megan. I, too, shall have cause to regret our parting. But perhaps it need not be so."

"How do you mean, ma'am?" asked Megan, wondering if the princess meant to ask her to remain with her through another winter. These things were not unheard of in Russia, where the daughters and sons of minor European nobility were often made to feel themselves to be extensions of a Russian family.

If that was in Princess Kirov's mind, it would mean that Megan would not return to her homeland for a total of two years. She did not know how she felt about that. On the one hand, it would be very pleasant to stay where she was a highly regarded guest. Yet it was not the same as waking up in one's own bed of a morning. And then there was Mrs. Tyler to think of, as well as Simpkins. Megan thought that it would scarcely be fair to make such a far-reaching decision without first consulting their wishes, if such a decision was to be asked of her.

"In her letter, your mother, Lady O'Connell, confided to me her hopes for you when she gave her consent for you to come to Russia to stay with me," said Princess Kirov. "Did you know this?"

"Yes, your highness, I knew it. My mother discussed it with me before I left Ireland. And I am truly grateful for your generous hospitality and your efforts on my behalf," said Megan. "I do not believe that I could have met such a cosmopolitan set of gentlemen in any other capital."

"That is true. St. Petersburg is the richest, most glittering capital in all the world," said Princess Kirov matter-of-factly, certain in her arrogance of that truth. "But now we speak not of St. Petersburg, but of you, Megan. I would like you to remain in Russia, for I consider you almost like one of my own nieces. There is a way to possibly accomplish this purpose."

"Yes, your highness?"

"I do not wish to disappoint my dear friend Lady O'Connell," said Princess Kirov. "There have been several unexceptional offers made for your hand. Among them have been a number of good Russians. I wish you to consider well and decide which one you will accept."

"I have considered, ma'am. I shall accept none of them," said Megan quietly.

Princess Kirov's request had come unexpectedly, but it was not entirely a surprise. After all, Lady O'Connell had expressed her desire that her daughter make an alliance. With a gleam of humor as she thought swiftly of all of her suitors, Megan added, "It is no doubt because they *are* all so unexceptional."

"Nonsense. Of course you will accept one of these flattering offers. It is your clear duty, my child," said Princess Kirov. Her dark slanting eyes held a determined expression.

"I beg to differ with you, ma'am. My duty is to accept that which is most beneficial to myself and my future, and none of these offers are acceptable in that sense," said Megan. She saw that Princess Kirov was very perturbed and she smiled. "I apologize, ma'am. It is not my intent to anger you. However, in this matter I must speak my honest thoughts. I do not love any of these obliging gentlemen and—"

"Love!" Princess Kirov threw up her hands. "It is all one hears from the young. Even my Misha begins to prate of wedding for love. It is all nonsense!"

"You surprise me, ma'am," said Megan, recalling her conversation with the prince. "I had thought Prince Kirov too well-trained in the discharge of his duty to the Kirov family interests to consider an emotion such as love of any true importance."

"My son is a man of grand passion. Like all such men, there are times that he foolishly succumbs to it. But an ideal such as love is not practical, as Misha also knows," said Princess Kirov dismissively.

"Whereas I do not believe that such an ideal is impractical," said Megan.

"Megan, you must set aside this notion that love is of such importance," said Princess Kirov. "Look instead at what a man will give you: position, riches, a respected name. These are what are secure and important to a woman, for her and any children to come."

"But what of happiness, ma'am? Is that not important?" Megan asked curiously.

Princess Kirov shrugged. "Happiness is what you make of it. If it is love you want, attach a good lover. If it is style, then patronize a good modiste."

Even though Megan had learned much in the freer atmosphere prevailing in the Russian capital, she was shocked by her hostess' crude insensitivity. "You are cynical, ma'am."

"I am practical," corrected Princess Kirov. She folded her hands. "Now, you will tell me which offer you will accept."

"I have not altered my mind," said Megan. "I will not accept any of the offers which I have received thus far."

"You are an obstinate foolish girl. If you were my daughter, you would swiftly feel my wrath for your impertinence," said Princess Kirov harshly. "As it is, you are the daughter of my

Gayle Buck

dear friend and so my responsibility toward you is limited. I cannot coerce you to fulfill your duty."

Megan smiled sympathetically and shook her head. "Even my own mother could not coerce me in this, nor would she wish to do so. Her ladyship is quite content to allow me to pick my own path. Believe me, my mother will not blame you for my sad lack of cooperation."

"That is well, for I have done all that is possible. From this moment, I wash my hands of you," said Princess Kirov, suiting action to words in a symbolic manner. "I will instruct the maids to begin packing your things at once. You are dismissed."

Megan was startled. "I beg your pardon?"

Princess Kirov regarded her out of dark fathomless eyes. A small smile curved her thin mouth. "Surely you do not expect to continue to enjoy my hospitality when you have so adamantly rejected the efforts I have made on your behalf? No, it is time for you to return to your homeland."

The humor of the situation suddenly struck Megan. Lady O'Connell had sent her to Russia so that she would be relieved of all responsibility of her daughter. Princess Kirov was sending Megan back for the same reason. Megan chuckled. "No, I suppose not. I shall begin preparations for my journey at once. I will send out my regrets for those functions for which I am already engaged."

Megan rose and curtsied to Princess Kirov. "Thank you, ma'am, for an enjoyable stay in St. Petersburg. I shall remember it, and you, fondly all of my life. I assure you, I have learned much during my visit. Naturally I shall give your regards to my mother." Megan gracefully left the sitting room.

Princess Kirov stared at the closed door, her expression unreadable. Then a slight grimace crossed her face. "She is strong-willed, that one. It is a pity that she is not Russian."

Upon leaving the princess's apartments, Megan chanced to meet Prince Kirov. He stopped her with a broad smile and appropriated her hand. Ceremoniously he bowed over her fingers. "My dear sister, you are ravishingly lovely today," he said.

"You are very kind, as usual, your highness," said Megan. She smiled up at the big man. Prince Mikhail Kirov was not dark and small like his mother. He was very tall, a blond giant of solid muscle. He had ice-blue eyes that could be disconcertingly penetrating or alight with admiration, as they were now.

Megan knew very well that the prince found her attractive. He had not hidden the fact. He had always treated her with familiarity, claiming a closer relationship than was accurate simply because she had resided in his house for these several months.

Prince Kirov frowned down at her. He retained her hand. "My name is Mikhail. Have I not told you before? You are a guest in Kirov House and part of our family. I insist that you address me by my name."

"And I have told you that it would be an impertinence on my part to take such gross advantage of my position," said Megan firmly. She did not deny to herself that she was drawn to Prince Kirov. It would actually give her great pleasure to address him by his given name. But she knew to succumb to the temptation would make it very hard to keep what distance remained between them. She had no desire for a greater intimacy with Prince Mikhail Kirov than what she already enjoyed as a favored guest.

"Still so cold, mademoiselle," sighed Prince Kirov. He lifted his hand and brushed the curve of her cheek and her hair. "Fire and ice. How is it possible that they exist together?"

Megan regained possession of her hand. She stepped back the merest pace. "I do not know, your highness. You must direct your question to one better trained in philosophy than myself."

Prince Kirov's ice-blue eyes gleamed. "Ah, I perceive that you intend to shuffle me off with such a neat setdown. But it will not do, Miss O'Connell. I have seen the depths of your soul in your eyes. I have known these several weeks past that you are attracted to me."

Megan felt herself blush. "Your highness, that is a highly improper statement and completely untrue, besides. One cannot read another's soul in their eyes."

"But one can, dear sister. I have done so. Shall I prove it to you?" asked Prince Kirov.

Megan retreated another step, eyeing the prince warily. "I am not interested in your proof, your highness. It is highly irrelevant, I am certain."

Prince Kirov followed her, coming so close that she felt almost swallowed up in his nearness. "But it is not irrelevant at all, Miss O'Connell," he whispered softly. "I shall kiss you, here. And then we shall see if what I have said is not true." He touched her lips lightly with his finger.

Megan drew back. Her heart was pounding, but she did not drop her gaze from his. "Pray do not be ridiculous, your highness. I do not scheme for your kisses, nor, indeed, for any man's."

Prince Kirov smiled. "No, I know it well. I have watched you. You are toasted. Your fantastical beauty is celebrated. You are made love to with flowery compliments and poetical flights of fancy. You receive it all with smiling grace, yet your heart remains untouched. But I think, if I kissed you now, the sleeping passion would awaken. And I think that you would marry me."

Megan felt stifled by her own heartbeats. There was danger here, but heady excitement, too. "Are you making an offer for me, Prince Kirov?" she asked quietly, only the faintest tremor in her voice.

He smiled down at her with a peculiar tenderness. "No, I am not so gauche or crude, mademoiselle. You are one who desires courtship, the dance of the birds or the flight of mating butterflies. I do not charge in where delicacy is required. No, I do not offer for you today. Perhaps next week, or next month."

"Or perhaps not at all," said Megan, tilting up her head.

"That is what you will wonder from now on, mademoiselle," said Prince Kirov.

Megan shook her head. "No, your highness. I shall not wonder at all, for I shall be far too busy. I shall be making my debut in London this spring."

"What!" Prince Kirov laughed. He shook his head. "No, no, you think to tease me, mademoiselle. But I shall not succumb."

"As you will, your highness," said Megan with a shrug and a smile. "Now let me pass, please."

Prince Kirov moved aside, bowing. As she brushed past him, however, he suddenly caught her arm. Megan looked up, surprised.

Prince Kirov stared frowningly down into her face. "You do not tease, do you, mademoiselle?"

Megan shook her head. "No, I do not. I shall be leaving Russia in a few short hours."

"But this is nonsense. I have heard nothing before of this," said Prince Kirov. He glanced down the hall suddenly, realizing for the first time the possible significance of the fact that she had come out of his mother's sitting room. "Have you quarreled with my mother? Is that why you have decided to leave Russia? No, it is wrong that you should leave like this. I shall not allow you to leave in a fit of pique. I shall go to my mother at once and force her to apologize to you!"

"Your highness, I have not quarreled with Princess Kirov. We have simply come to a mutual agreement that I have overstayed my visit," said Megan. "Now it is time for me to return to my own country."

"That is utterly ridiculous!" exclaimed Prince Kirov.

"Not at all. Will you please unhand me, your highness? I have my packing to oversee," said Megan coolly.

Instead of doing as she asked, Prince Kirov shoved open a door behind them. He strode into the room, pulling Megan with him. It was the conservatory. Plants hung everywhere and there was the attractive sound of water falling into a pool. The prince shut the door. He laid his shoulder to it and crossed his arms. "Now, mademoiselle, we shall get to the bottom of this matter."

"Do you intend to keep me here against my will?" demanded Megan.

"If I must," said Prince Kirov.

"What if I scream?" asked Megan.

"My faithful Fedor saw me bring you in here. He will warn the servants away. I do not think that anyone will dare to enter until I open the door myself," said Prince Kirov arrogantly.

Megan had not seen the prince's shadow, the devoted dwarf

Fedor, in the hall; but that meant nothing. The small man could practically make himself invisible if he so wished.

Megan regarded the prince for a moment. Very quietly, she said, "I do not answer well to blackmail or to brute force, your highness. You may lean up against that door until doomsday for all the ground it will gain you." She turned on her heel and started slowly up the path, pausing now and again to sniff at an orchid blossom. She heard his bootstep on the walk behind her.

Megan half-smiled to herself. She had thought rightly. The prince was an impatient man. He would not be able to hold his pose of determined jailer for long. She turned, lifting her brows. "Yes, your highness? Was there something that you wished of me?"

"You know well that there is, Miss O'Connell," he replied, frowning.

"A civil question will gain you a civil reply, your highness," said Megan.

Prince Kirov smiled slightly. "Ah, you play me like a violin, mademoiselle. I do not believe that I have ever met your equal."

Megan almost snorted. She had heard the stories of his women and his duels. Prince Mikhail Sergei Alexsander Kirov was a well-known heartbreaker. It was why she insisted upon the formality between them. "Have you not, indeed!"

"You do not believe me?" asked Prince Kirov. He placed a hand over his heart. "My whole heart is yours, mademoiselle."

"I possess naught but a piece of it, surely," said Megan daringly. "For there have been many women who have been given bits and pieces until there is little of it left."

"Who dares to say so?" demanded Prince Kirov, drawing himself up.

"Why, it is your reputation that shouts it, your highness," said Megan.

Prince Kirov looked thoughtful. He slid a glance at her. "It is true. I have known many women. But none ever dazzled me as you have, Miss O'Connell."

Once again, Megan felt her heart thumping. There was a sheer magnetism about Prince Mikhail Kirov that was very hard to resist. She turned out her hands in a curious gesture. "So you say, your highness. But you make love so charmingly to everyone. Is it possible for a woman to trust your words? Or should I listen even more closely to the warning given me by your reputation?"

Prince Kirov closed the distance between them. "Believe this, mademoiselle." He caught up her hand and placed it firmly against his breast. She could feel the strength of his heartbeat beneath her palm. Her fingers trembled. He looked deeply into her startled eyes. "And believe this." He gathered her very gently into his arms.

Megan lifted her head to meet his kiss. She had been kissed many times since she had come to St. Petersburg, with everything from an avuncular smack to a passionate salute. But she had never been kissed by a man whom she found so compellingly attractive. His lips were firm and possessive, tasting of cinnamon and wine.

"Now, mademoiselle, I shall ask you a civil question," said Prince Kirov softly. His thumb traced her sensitized lips. "Why are you leaving Russia?"

"Your mother is displeased with me. I have refused to accept any of the offers that have been made for my hand," said Megan quietly. She felt the queerest light-headedness. She thought that if she moved she might fall.

"Ah." There was a wealth of satisfaction in his voice.

Nothing could have snapped Megan back to herself faster than that conceited inflection. She drew back, putting distance between them. A little belatedly, she realized as she stared up into the prince's smug expression. This is what came of giving in to temptation, she thought in self-disgust. "And precisely what does 'ah!' mean?" she asked.

Prince Kirov shrugged, a massive roll of shoulder. "It is just as I thought. I read your soul. You will have none other when I stand before you, mademoiselle."

Megan was instantly angered. "Indeed!" she said in her coldest inflection. "You are very taken with yourself, your highness."

Prince Kirov laughed suddenly, his white teeth gleaming.

"Your eyes shoot sparks when you are annoyed." He reached out his hand to caress her hair. "My little firebird."

"I am not your anything!" exclaimed Megan. She whirled around him and started back toward the conservatory door. "You enjoy playing with a woman's heart, but I shall not be a toy for your entertainment!"

"Megan!" Prince Kirov followed after her.

She reached the door and opened it. Her cheeks were flaming and her eyes shone with anger. "I am leaving at once! And you need not attempt to stop me, for I am very certain that Princess Kirov will be quick to remonstrate."

"You will not leave today," said Prince Kirov.

Megan's breast rose in indignation. He had thrown down the gauntlet and she snatched it up. "Won't I just!"

He shook his head and smiled. "You will dine with me tonight. Then perhaps you will leave tomorrow."

"I will not dine with you tonight. I am leaving," said Megan.

"It is Monday. We Russians are a superstitious lot. You have been long enough in my country to know this. There is not a Russian coachman alive who will begin a journey on Monday," said Prince Kirov.

Megan was furious. She had completely forgotten the Russian aversion to traveling on Mondays. She had made herself look foolish and he was grinning at her. "Tomorrow, then. I shall leave first thing tomorrow."

"And you will dine with me tonight," said Prince Kirov.

Megan did not deign to answer, but swept through the doorway with her head held high.

Chapter Eight

Megan did dine with Prince Kirov, along with several hundred others. It was a small soiree, as Russian standards went, and it ended typically. The younger members of the gathering put on their furs and ran outside to the *troikas* and the smaller *drozhkis* that had been converted to sleds for the winter.

Megan had meant to get into the same *troika* with her friend, Countess Annensky, the countess's brother, and her betrothed. Instead, Megan found herself lifted into one of the small light *drozhkis* by Prince Kirov. He climbed in after her. They were fitted so snugly together that he had to drape his arm over her shoulders in order to sit down. Megan realized that the prince had deliberately maneuvered to be in the *drozhki* with her to take advantage of this forced intimacy. She should have been furious with him, but she was not.

All of the coachmen started off at a gallop, arms outstretched straight in front of them with a rein in each hand, shouting "*Beregis! Beregis!* Take care! Make way! *Padi! Padi!*"

The *drozhki* flew through the iced streets. The cold wind whipped Megan's cheeks, but she was warm in her sable furs and the close embrace of the big man seated beside her. She loved the speed and the frosted night. "It is wonderful!" she exclaimed, looking up at the moon, shining clear and glacial and the stars scintillating like winking jewels.

The snow sparkled like pulverized marble and the bells on the horse's harness sounded a high, sweet accompaniment to their shimmering, rapid progress. The coachman broke into song. Even though sung in Russian, it was a familiar carol. Megan and her companion smiled at one another. Megan was astonished and delighted when Prince Kirov threw back his head and added his strong baritone to the song. Megan hesitated only a moment before she, too, joined in the caroling.

The *drozhki* and the others of their group whizzed across the frozen Neva River to the islands upon which half the city was built. A sleepy tavern was roused. Inside the huge parlor the samovar was heated to prepare the strong sweet tea; iced champagne was opened; plates of caviar, ham, herring, and little cakes were arranged on the long heavy table. The lively group of young men and women put off their furs. For more than an hour they chatted and laughed and joked over the impromptu meal. Then the furs were put on again.

"Where are we going now?" asked Megan, pulling on her fur-lined gloves.

"The ice hills!" exclaimed Countess Annensky, her eyes shining with excitement.

Megan looked at her friend in dismay. Since she had been in Russia, she had heard much about the ice hills. She had seen the high snow hills constructed up to the very eaves of the houses in St. Petersburg and marveled at the spectacle of children and servants climbing out of opened windows to slide down the packed ice on mattresses. She had seen, too, the huge ice hills that had been erected to enormous heights for the amusement of the entire population of St. Petersburg. The platforms at the top of the hills were gaily decorated open pavilions, complete with fluttering flags. Little fir trees marked the sides of the course. The mirrorlike slide was wide enough to allow as many as thirty sleds at a time and stretched the length of several city blocks.

Megan had been fascinated by the sight of the flying sleds, and particularly admired the brave souls who stood perfectly upright as they came down on wooden skates. She had envied their soaring fun, but the thought of actually riding one of the sleds was faintly terrifying. She had never seen a collision, though at the end of the ride people sometimes tumbled over each other. However, she was absolutely certain that accidents must occur. It was just that no one discussed the accidents.

"You do not admire our ice hills, Miss O'Connell?" asked Prince Kirov softly.

Megan glanced at him quickly. Never would she let him see her consternation. "They are wonderful, of course," she said.

Prince Kirov nodded. "Good! I am glad that you enjoy them." He handed her into the *drozhki,* got in, and signaled the coachman. Again the full-tilt ride across the Neva River and a return to the city.

Megan did not know what to say. She didn't want to go down the ice hill, but she was trapped. Prince Kirov obviously expected her to do so and so did all of her friends. It would be difficult to excuse herself from the treat without giving offense.

The ice hill was reached. The party tumbled out of the *troikas* and *drozhkis,* all speaking with great excitement and hilarity. Torches lit the scene, striking glistening silver from the snow. Megan was carried along on the tide, wanting to say something, anything, but unable to do so. Prince Kirov had his hand under her elbow, conveying her toward one of the waiting sledmen. For a few *kopecks,* the sledman agreed to guide them down.

Megan climbed up the ice hill with the prince and the sledman, who was pulling the sled. At the top, when she looked down the dizzying winding distance to the bottom, she balked. "I—I do not think that—"

Prince Mikhail looked down into her face. "You are afraid!" he declared.

Megan flushed. "A little, yes," she admitted.

"Then you must not go down with the sledman," he said firmly.

Megan let out her breath in a relieved sigh. "Thank you."

"You will go down with me," said Prince Kirov. He turned to the sledman and there arose a heated discussion. The sledman was objecting to the commandeering of his craft, while the prince stubbornly insisted that for his lady's peace of mind he must have it.

"Please, your highness, do not force the issue on my account," said Megan. She was already appalled at the thought of going down on the sled, but going down without the expert guidance of the sledman was even more foolhardy. She drew a breath. "I shall go down with the sledman."

Prince Kirov flashed a grin. His ice-blue eyes were alight. "Very well, mademoiselle. You are brave. You will adore the ice hill, I promise you."

The sledman positioned the sled. It was flat and shaped like a butcher's tray, but fantastically ornamented with red, yellow, and blue carvings. The man seated himself on it, very far back, his legs extended perfectly straight. He let it be known that the lady could seat herself.

Without consciously realizing it, Megan was clutching Prince Kirov's arm. He glanced down at her, then covered her gloved hand with his own. "Never fear, my firebird. I shall not let harm come to you."

He stepped over to the sled and seated himself in front of the sledman, stretching out his own long legs. "Come, Megan. You will be safe enough," he said, holding out his hand to her.

Megan shook her head, a smile trembling on her lips. She seated herself in front of the prince, positioning her body as had the two men behind her. Her boots dangled over the front edge of the sled. She tucked her skirts securely under her.

"Are you ready, mademoiselle?"

Megan moistened her lips. "Of course."

Prince Kirov laughed. His arms came around her from behind and pulled her securely back against him. Megan started to stiffen, but then the sled slipped over the summit of the ice hill and she spared not another thought for the prince's assumption of intimacy. Instantly the speed and the icy wind ripped over her and she felt as though she was soaring. She was glad for the prince's secure hold.

Megan gasped. Passing through the cutting air was extremely painful. Shards of glass seemed to be thrusting into her nostrils and lungs. Her skirts billowed and whipped, threatening to tear free, and she pressed her legs tighter against the sled bottom.

The descent seemed to last forever, yet was over in the blink of an eye.

At the bottom, Prince Kirov hauled Megan to her feet. "Let us go again, Megan!"

Megan was speechless. She could hardly suck in the cold air, it hurt so much. She shook her head, but the prince seemed to misunderstand her. She was clinging to his arms because she could scarcely stand and he probably thought that she was dizzy. And well he might, thought Megan dazedly.

Before she quite knew what was happening, she was once more positioned on the sled at the summit of the ice hill. Again the dropping descent, the burning in her lungs. Again the sensation of leaving her stomach behind as she soared away. Then a peculiar thing happened. The pain went away and instead an exquisitely pleasurable feeling enveloped her. Her senses became heightened. Megan felt herself to be intoxicated on the rush of frigid wind. She had never felt such a thrill in all of her life.

At the bottom she staggered upright. Prince Kirov caught her in his arms before she fell into the snow. Megan started laughing and flung her head and arms back in abandon. Prince Kirov laughed, too, his eyes alight as he straightened. He was still supporting her in his arms. "You see, Megan, I told you that you would adore the ice hills," he exclaimed.

"Yes, I do! I adore everything about them! The rush of ice and wind, the moment's terror, everything!" said Megan breathlessly. "Let us go up again!"

Prince Kirov lowered his head and snatched a quick kiss. "I have unlocked the passion in you, my dove. You will never, never be the same again," he breathed softly into her startled face. "You will remember this night forever."

Megan suddenly stood up on her toes and kissed him. Then she whirled out of his arms and raced away, laughing back over her shoulder. "You have called me a firebird, Misha. Do not your legends say that a firebird cannot be possessed?"

Prince Kirov quickly recovered from his astonishment. He strode after her and had almost caught up to her when she joined a group of their friends on the ascent to the summit of the ice hill. He longed to pull her back into his arms, as she undoubtedly knew, judging from the luminous glance that she tossed him from out of the corners of her eyes, but it was impossible to extricate her without exciting the interest of many eyes.

For himself, he did not care. But for her, he would exercise restraint. A quickly snatched kiss in the exhilaration of the ice

hill was one thing and could be easily excused as a spontaneity
of the moment. A deliberate separation of man and woman
from the company could only be construed as something far
different. He was too wise in affairs of the heart to want there
to be whispers about the woman he was going to make his
wife.

Prince Kirov stopped short, absolutely stunned by his
thoughts. He realized that he had been thinking of Miss Megan
O'Connell in that way for some time. He had entered into a
flirtation with her from the moment of her arrival at Kirov
House; but just when that light flirtation had begun to turn into
a serious, honorable pursuit he could not say. It was enough to
know, however, that he had at last found a woman he wanted
to wed.

He threw back his head, bellowing laughter into the cold
clear air. His breath frosted white. He felt a surge of joy and
well-being. Never had he experienced it to such a degree.

A heavy hand clapped him on the back. "Misha! You are
happy, brother?"

Prince Kirov swung around to face his friend, Prince Sergei
Rushevsky. Still grinning broadly, he said, "Yes! I am glori-
ously happy. I have discovered a pearl beyond price and I will
make it mine."

Prince Sergei laughed. "You are drunk, Misha. There are no
pearls in the snow."

"There you are wrong," said Prince Kirov, looking up to
find the boisterous group climbing toward the top of the ice
hill. The slimmer figures of the women flitted among the
bulkier frames of the men.

Prince Sergei's eyes followed the direction of his gaze.
"Ah! Now it is explained. You have fallen in love again. Who
is it, Misha? Perhaps the little dancer from the ballet, eh? Or
the exotic flower from the Caucasus?"

Prince Kirov shook his head. "No, brother, I do not tell. I
will not hold her up to gossip, for the lady is the last to ever
hold my heart. I am a willing prisoner of her beauty, a pen-
sioner for her smiles, a captive of her charm!"

Prince Sergei hooted. "How many times have you claimed
to be in thrall to a new passion, Misha? There is always a

whirlwind of courtship, a passionate love affair! Then the glorious haze fades and you come again into your right mind."

"It is different this time," said Prince Kirov quickly.

"Yes, yes, Misha! It is always different," said Prince Sergei, thumping him on the back again. "Come! The ice hill waits. Let us go, for the night is still young!"

Prince Kirov wanted to protest his fidelity to the newfound emotion that filled his heart. He wanted to swear to his steadfastness and his unshakable conviction. But he did not. All of his friends had heard the same things too many times. Prince Sergei had laughingly brushed off his declaration and so would the others. It would take action to convince them, and perhaps even himself, that this time he was well and truly falling in love.

"Yes, the ice hill waits! A race, Sergei! A race! I challenge you, brother!" exclaimed Prince Kirov, breaking into a run for the top.

Prince Sergei called out and started after him. "I am stronger, Misha! It is I who shall win!"

"We shall see, Sergei!" Prince Kirov suddenly swiveled and broadarmed his friend into the snow. Then he bolted upward again.

Prince Sergei came up out of the snow with a roar, his long arms and legs pumping. He caught up with the fleeing man and tackled him. The two men rolled over and over into the snow, shouting good-natured threats as they grappled.

At the top of the ice hill, the rest of the group had noticed. Pointing and laughing, they watched the impromptu wrestling match. "What is happening?" asked Megan. She had never seen such a contest before.

Countess Annensky gave a happy laugh. "It is the winter, Megan. The winter is a boisterous child. We play, we sing, we dance. We celebrate it in living."

"And the men fight," said Megan, marveling. She started laughing. "Look! They are both so covered with snow that they look like walking snowmen!"

"Snowmen? What is that?" asked the countess. Megan told her and Countess Annensky clapped her hands in delight. "That is wonderful! I shall tell my nephews so that they may construct one. Now, let us not linger any longer. Let us go down the ice hill. Sergei and Misha will tire soon and follow us."

Megan agreed and turned away, still smiling. She thought she would always remember the sight of two princes at play in the snow like overgrown boys. Russia was a strange and odd place, but there were many things that she would miss.

Megan and Mrs. Tyler left St. Petersburg three mornings later. It had been impossible, after all, to leave the city without first saying good-bye to all of their new friends and acquaintances. Countess Annensky was especially devastated that Megan's visit was to be cut short. "You will not be here for my wedding," she said, shaking her head sorrowfully. "I had hoped that you would be one of my wedding party."

"How I would like that!" said Megan. "But it is not to be. Princess Kirov frowns whenever she sees me now. I have become a pariah to her and so it is best that I go home."

Countess Annensky sighed. "Yes, that is true. It is for the best. But how I shall miss you!" She threw her arms around Megan. "You must come back to visit us. And you will stay with Sergei and me this time."

Megan returned the tight embrace, laughing but with tears pricking at her eyes. Never had she had such a friend as the countess. It was indeed difficult to leave her. "I shall, I promise! And perhaps one day you and Sergei will come to London and I can meet you there, too."

The two friends parted with mutual promises to write to one another between visits. Megan found it hard to take leave of her other friends, as well. She was actually rather astonished at how well accepted she had become in Russian society during her short stay. It gave her a warm feeling to know that her absence would be regretted and missed.

On the crisp morning that Megan and Mrs. Tyler had chosen to leave, they were seated cozily in the packed sled, covered by fur rugs. A second sled held most of their baggage and Simpkins, their dresser. An armed escort of Cossack horsemen assigned to protect the travelers was already mounted. A gossamer curtain of snow was falling.

Prince Kirov came out of the house to see them off. He held Megan's hands a moment longer than was protocol. "I will follow you soon, my dove," he said solemnly.

Megan smiled and shook her head quickly. She gently pulled free her gloved hands. "You think so now, your highness. But you will not. I am but a passing fancy, as you will discover."

"No, I tell you, no!" he exclaimed fiercely. "You have captured my heart."

Megan looked up into his face. His blue eyes blazed with conviction. "If that is indeed true, then I shall see you again in London. But I shall not hold it against you if you do not come, your highness," she said in a low voice.

"You try me almost beyond endurance," he snapped.

She smiled again. "I am a woman, your highness. Is that not excuse enough?"

His countenance changed and he laughed. "Yes, mademoiselle, you are right. Very well, then. I let you go still doubting me. But first"—he stripped a heavy ring from his hand and placed it in her palm, closing her fingers around it—"this is my pledge to you, my dove. I shall claim it again."

Megan's cheeks were flushed. "I shall treasure it always, your highness." She got into the sled. The glistening gold ring went into her reticule.

The sled took off over the ice. Megan glanced back once. Prince Kirov stood watching her drive away. A swirl of snow obscured his figure, making him appear ghostlike. A smile touched Megan's lips. Just so would she remember him. A fantastical, unattainable lover.

She was too levelheaded, and now even a little too worldly, to really believe that Prince Kirov would follow her to London for the purpose of declaring himself. He was a prominent man, much courted. Megan had not a sliver of doubt that Prince Kirov would manage to forget her within a fortnight. She raised her hand in farewell.

The sled whipped swiftly out of St. Petersburg and into the surrounding forests. There was a fairy-tale quality to being whisked over the snow, the sled throwing sprays of white in its wake, but with only the jingling of the horses' harness bells and the driver's pleasant monotone singing to break the cold clear silence.

For several miles, the ladies were silent, busy with their own thoughts. Megan smiled without consciously realizing it as she recalled all the enjoyment and the discovery of new things that she had experienced over the months.

"It's a pity to be leaving Russia so soon," said Mrs. Tyler, voicing her own regret.

"Yes, it is. I have enjoyed myself very much," said Megan. "It has been a perfectly magical time. But now it is time to return to reality. I shall be glad to see our own shores again."

"And I," agreed Mrs. Tyler. She curiously observed Megan's serene profile. "I overheard you say something about London to Prince Kirov. Do you plan a shopping expedition before we return to Ireland?"

"Actually, I have decided to remain in London for the Season," said Megan. She flashed a glance at her companion. "I cannot endure the thought of sinking back into obscurity now that I have been brought out into society, Gwyneth."

"No, indeed," agreed Mrs. Tyler emphatically. "But, my dear, what will her ladyship have to say to this decision?"

Megan laughed. "My mother will be quite displeased," she acknowledged. "But I am determined to carry the day. Gwyneth, I intend to make the most of the Season and find a suitable husband. I do not wish to moulder away in my father's house the remainder of my days."

"I understand perfectly, my dear. And naturally you have all of my support. However, I rather thought that you would make a match of it with Prince Kirov," said Mrs. Tyler. "Do you not harbor some feelings for him?"

"Oh, the prince is the stuff of which a maiden's dreams are made!" said Megan, laughing lightly.

"My dear, I know you too well to be put off with such froth," said Mrs. Tyler gently.

Megan glanced at her companion, hesitating before she answered. "Perhaps I do, Gwyneth. However, it makes very little difference now. I am leaving Russia and will likely never see the prince again. I will never know whether the emotions I feel could ever grow into anything warmer or of permanence. So I have determined to put aside those things and instead cultivate a comfortable relationship with a fellow countryman."

"But my dear!" Mrs. Tyler stared at her in astonishment. "How can you say such a thing? Why, Prince Kirov gave you his own ring as a pledge."

"Gwyneth, I hope that I am too practical to place much construction upon a generous, spontaneous gesture," said Megan. She shook her head. "No, Gwyneth. Though Prince Kirov thought himself completely sincere in uttering his promise, he will not follow me to London in order to court me. I would do far better to set aside our flirtation as a pleasant memory and look to the settling of my future."

"I have never heard anything so baldly cynical in all my life!" exclaimed Mrs. Tyler.

Megan laughed. She looked at her companion with sympathy. "Poor Gwyneth! Have I shocked you so terribly? But I am not of a particularly romantic nature, you know. Oh, I should very much like to be swept off my feet by an adoring gallant whom I held in equal esteem. But that is not at all likely to happen, is it? And so I have set my sights much lower. I will settle for a good, kind husband who will show me gentle courtesy and lend a polite ear to my chattering."

"One may surely aspire to both romance and practicality!" said Mrs. Tyler with asperity.

"My dear Gwyneth, I fear that you are a hopeless romantic," said Megan tolerantly.

Not another word would she volunteer about Prince Kirov, no matter how often or how persuasively Mrs. Tyler presented the advantages of the prince's possible suit. Megan merely laughed and passed them off, likely as not countering by introducing another topic. The verbal sparring continued in the same way for the length of Russia.

By the time that Poland's borders were crossed, Mrs. Tyler had exhausted every argument that she could muster on Prince Kirov's behalf. "Very well, then! I shall not say another word about the prince," said Mrs. Tyler, closing her lips tight. She folded her hands and stared determinedly out at the wintery landscape.

Megan merely glanced at her with quiet amusement. She

knew it would be but a matter of time before Mrs. Tyler would summon new arguments to her command and begin all over again.

The first opportunity arose when they stopped at an inn to exchange their sleds for carriages and their sable furs for warm wool. Mrs. Tyler managed to bring Prince Kirov's name into the conversation several times as she reminded Megan of various amusing experiences they had had in Russia. The departure of their Cossack escort brought even more poignancy to Mrs. Tyler's reminiscings.

However, as Europe rolled away under their wheels, Mrs. Tyler's thoughts became increasingly centered on their destination. She began talking about London and what they might expect there during the Season.

Megan was grateful for it. She had not allowed herself to betray how arduous it had been to listen while her companion extolled Prince Kirov's several virtues. She entered gladly into discussions of how best to handle Lady O'Connell's undoubted opposition to their intention to enjoy the London Season, hoping at last to be able to put away all lingering thoughts of Prince Mikhail Kirov.

Chapter Nine

The shadows were long when the mud-spattered carriage drew up in front of the elegant town house. The driver climbed off of his box to let down the step and opened the carriage door. Out stepped a stylishly dressed young lady. She paused for a moment on the walkway while another lady was assisted down from the carriage.

Two gentlemen perambulating down the walkway noticed the elegant young lady at once. They slowed in mutual appreciation and curiosity. When she glanced around, the two gentlemen were favored with the sight of a lovely countenance framed by an elegant confection of straw and feathers and ribbons on her head. In hopes of discovering a clue to her identity, the two gentlemen slowed their steps as they passed. They touched their beavers and bowed to the young lady, and were gratified when she favored them with the slightest of bows.

When the other lady had joined her, the young lady said, "Here we are at last, Gwyneth. Let us see if Mother is at home." She started up the steps to the town house, her skirt lifted gracefully in one gloved hand.

The gentlemen were startled by what they had overheard. The town house belonged to Lady O'Connell. They had never heard of a daughter, but here was this pretty creature claiming kinship and banging the knocker.

A haughty woman had also descended from the carriage and began directing the driver in the placement of the baggage on the walkway.

The door was opened. Megan smiled at the porter's astonished face. "Good afternoon, Geoffrey. I trust that we are welcome."

"O' course, miss! I shall notify Mr. Digby at once," said the porter, ushering in the ladies. With a quick look down the steps, he saw that there was a well-loaded carriage at the curb and that a superior female was dealing with the driver. Leaving the front door open, he hurried down the hall to alert his superior.

A moment later, the butler returned with the porter. His dignified expression relaxed into the shadow of a smile. "Why, miss, the last we heard of you was that you and Mrs. Tyler were still in Russia."

"Well, we are here now," said Megan cheerfully. "We have a great deal of baggage coming, Digby. Simpkins is already giving instructions to our own driver, I know."

"Of course, miss. I shall send out some men to bring it in," said the butler. He snapped his fingers at two footmen, who at once leaped into action. "Did you say that there was another carriage, miss?"

Simpkins appeared in the front doorway. "Indeed there is. I shall go up directly to make ready for the deposition of our baggage. You will naturally direct your people here, Mr. Digby."

The butler nodded. "Of course, Miss Simpkins. The second housemaids are at your service."

Megan was busy pulling off her gloves and putting off her pelisse, as was Mrs. Tyler. She listened with a good deal of amusement as her dresser climbed the stairs and overawed the under-staff trailing in her wake.

Megan turned back to the butler. "Digby, is her ladyship at home?"

"Indeed she is, miss. Lady O'Connell is presiding over tea in the front sitting room," said the butler, ushering the two ladies upstairs. "And very surprised her ladyship will be to see you and Mrs. Tyler."

"Yes, no doubt," said Megan. She swept into the sitting room with Mrs. Tyler close behind.

Lady O'Connell was entertaining her callers. Tea and biscuits and cakes had been served to the ladies while they exchanged mutual pleasantries. Lady O'Connell looked around at the opening of the door, a polite smile on her face, expecting some others of her acquaintance. She was stunned by the sight of her daughter and her daughter's companion coming into the room. Her mouth opened but no sound came out.

Megan smiled and swooped down on her mother to greet her in the Russian manner. After kissing her mother on each cheek, she stepped back. "Mother, what an utterly ravishing dressing gown. You look extremely well in it."

"Megan?" faltered Lady O'Connell, still startled and off balance.

"And who is this? Surely this cannot possibly be your daughter, Agatha," said one of the visitors, raising a lorgnette to her rather protuberant eyes.

"My daughter? Oh! Yes, this is my daughter, Miss Megan O'Connell," said Lady O'Connell, her ingrained social training enabling her to recover sufficiently to make coherent introductions. "Megan, Lady Stallcroft and her daughters, the Misses Stallcroft." She gestured to her other visitors. "And this is Lady Bishop and Mrs. Hadcombe."

Megan greeted the starchy lady and the other ladies with a murmured word and a handshake. She nodded in a friendly way to the two misses who sat beside their mother on the settee, regarding her like wide-eyed barn owls. "Lady Stallcroft, Lady Bishop, Mrs. Hadcombe, it is a pleasure, I assure you. Goodness, I have only been back in England for two days and already I am beginning to feel quite at home. Allow me to present my dear friend and companion, Mrs. Tyler."

Mrs. Hadcombe and Lady Bishop murmured polite greetings to Mrs. Tyler. "Pray join us," invited Mrs. Hadcombe, indicating a space beside her on the settee, "You will want tea, of course. Lady O'Connell, I shall do the honors, if you have no objections."

"No—no, not the least in the world," stammered Lady O'Connell.

"Thank you, ma'am," said Mrs. Tyler quietly, seating herself. With a soft word and smile, she accepted the tea that Mrs. Hadcombe handed to her.

Lady Stallcroft spared Mrs. Tyler only a prim dismissing nod before she turned back to Lady O'Connell's daughter. Pinning a sharp gaze upon Megan's face, she said, "You have but recently returned to England, I believe you said? Have you come from Ireland, then?"

Lady O'Connell was staring as though she still could not quite grasp the fact that her daughter stood in the same room with her.

Megan chuckled as she seated herself. She also accepted tea poured by Mrs. Hadcombe. "Oh, no. I have been in St. Petersburg these several months past. Mother, I must at once convey Princess Kirov's fond regards. She sent me away with deep expressions of regret, for she quite considered me one of the family, a favored niece, in fact. I must admit, it was difficult to tear myself away from St. Petersburg, for I had made so many friends and I still had so many engagements. However, the London Season has already begun and so I shall not repine too terribly much."

"St. Petersburg? Russia? You have been to Russia!" exclaimed the eldest Miss Stallcroft, her soft gray eyes lighting up. "Oh, how I do envy you!"

Lady Stallcroft sent a steely glance in her daughter's direction. "That will be enough, Annabelle. I am certain Miss O'Connell is quite willing to expound without the encouragement of your histrionics."

Miss Stallcroft's face flamed and she lowered her eyes. "Yes, Mama." Her sister's hand stole into hers to give her fingers a light squeeze. Miss Stallcroft glanced in gratitude at her sister.

Megan decided at once that she did not care for Lady Stallcroft. The woman was obviously a bully of the worst sort. "Yes, well, it was wonderful, of course. There were balls and routs and soirees and sledding parties every day of the week. I met ever so many personages, including the czar. Czar Alexander is quite an extraordinary gentleman. I found him to be rather enigmatic, but—"

"I am certain that he is. However, one must naturally make allowances for the deficiencies of foreigners in comparison to our own countrymen," said Lady Stallcroft, bestowing a patronizing smile on Megan.

Megan returned the lady's smile. Flatly, she said, "I am certain that I do not know what you mean."

Lady Stallcroft's expression stiffened.

Mrs. Tyler was sipping at her tea and she spluttered, drawing all eyes to her. "So sorry," she gasped. "I—I seem to have choked somehow."

"Quite all right," said Lady Bishop, slanting a glance in Megan's direction. She turned to the elder of the travelers. "Did you also enjoy St. Petersburg, Mrs. Tyler?"

"Very much, indeed," said Mrs. Tyler, glad to turn attention from Megan's less than subtle snubbing of Lady Stallcroft. "It was vastly different, of course. All that ice and the furs one had to wear and the sleds racing up and down the streets with their bells merrily pealing! And the plethora of languages one heard! Why, I have never seen so many different nationalities gathered in one place in my life. It was quite exhilarating, actually."

"Yes, no doubt," said Lady Stallcroft repressively. She set down her teacup and saucer and rose to her feet. "I fear that I must be going, Lady O'Connell. It has been a delightful visit, as usual. You must come take tea with me one afternoon. Come along, girls."

Lady O'Connell rose to accompany her guests to the door. "Yes, of course. How delightful that you could call, Lady Stallcroft. I shall certainly come to tea." She exchanged a few more pleasantries with Lady Stallcroft and waved good-bye.

When she returned it was to discover that her daughter was deep in friendly conversation with Mrs. Hadcombe and Lady Bishop. Indeed, it appeared that the two ladies were highly amused and even mildly scandalized. Lady O'Connell realized with a start what her daughter was saying.

"It was the Italian count who so sadly disillusioned me, however. I discovered quite by accident that he was safely wedded and the proud papa of six hopeful heirs," said Megan, shaking her head. "Imagine my pique when this most faithful of swains was revealed for a philanderer!"

"Megan!" exclaimed Lady O'Connell, shocked.

Megan turned an inquiring expression. "Why, it is perfectly true, Mother. You may ask Gwyneth if it is not," she said, not at all abashed.

Mrs. Tyler sighed and nodded her head. "Indeed, it is all perfectly true. The count was a consummate gallant. He deceived us all with his pretty protestations and his finger-kissing."

"Finger-kissing?" asked Lady Bishop, fascinated.

"Oh, yes. It was quite his trademark," said Mrs. Tyler. "I do not believe that there was a single lady whose fingertips he did not mumble over."

Mrs. Hadcombe turned an amused expression to Lady O'Connell. "I am highly diverted, my lady. You must bring Miss O'Connell and Mrs. Tyler to my ball and supper next week so that I may hear more of their sojourn in St. Petersburg. I am persuaded that their recollections will be quite the highlight of the evening."

Lady O'Connell summoned up a polite smile. "That is extremely kind of you, Mrs. Hadcombe. However, I scarcely think—"

"I do realize that it is short notice when Miss O'Connell and Mrs. Tyler have but just returned. But they cannot yet have a full calendar, so I shall expect them," said Mrs. Hadcombe. She was still smiling, but there was a determined expression hardening her eyes.

"Oh, in that case!" Lady O'Connell managed a laugh. "I had not immediately perceived that your lists were so flexible, Mrs. Hadcombe. Naturally I shall be only too glad to accommodate your wishes." Despite her ladyship's attempt at complaisance, however, she could not quite disguise her reluctance to fall in with the suggestion advanced and it was visible to everyone.

Lady Bishop raised her brows. A smile quirked at the corner of her mouth. There was nothing she enjoyed more than encouraging a stir, and certainly there was something curious about Lady O'Connell's reaction to an advantageous invitation for her daughter. It would be most interesting to observe what might develop. "I, too, should like to put in my own invitation before the rush. You must both come to a small soiree that I am giving this Friday evening. Lady O'Connell is attending and I assure you of the same warm welcome."

"Thank you, my lady. And you, Mrs. Hadcombe. I shall be delighted to accompany my mother and attend both evenings," said Megan. She slanted a glance brimful of mischief at her companion. "Gwyneth?"

"Oh, yes, it sounds quite delightful," said Mrs. Tyler with a smile.

"Then it is settled! I shall expect you next week," said Mrs. Hadcombe, rising. She held out her hand to her hostess. "I did not anticipate to be so wonderfully entertained during a simple call, my lady."

"Nor I," said Lady Bishop, also preparing to take her leave. She said good-bye to her hostess. Then she nodded graciously to Miss O'Connell and Mrs. Tyler, offering her hand to each of them. "We shall leave you now, for I know that you will have much to talk over with your delightful daughter."

"Of course," said Lady O'Connell helplessly. "Thank you for coming. It was wonderful to see you both, as always."

Lady O'Connell showed out her callers. When the door had safely closed behind them, she turned back to her daughter. All of her bewilderment and consternation showed on her face. "Megan, whatever are you doing here? I had no notion that you were not still in Russia. It was such a shock when you suddenly just appeared in my sitting room."

"I have not simply appeared, Mother. The journey was actually quite long and tedious," said Megan. She rose from the settee. "In point of fact, I am rather fatigued. Since I know that you will dine out, I shall go lie down for an hour so that I will be ready to accompany you this evening. Gwyneth, do you go with us?"

"I think not this evening," said Mrs. Tyler quietly, glancing at Lady O'Connell's astounded expression. She knew that it was rather cowardly of her, but she didn't relish the notion of bearing with Lady O'Connell's inquiries and complaints the first evening that they arrived in London. "I would prefer taking supper in my room before retiring, I think."

Megan hugged her companion. Her eyes twinkled in complete understanding. "Poor Gwyneth! I am frightfully selfish to have dragged you all over the Continent and then expected you to dine out on your first evening home! I will allow you to bow out tonight, but I shall insist upon your company later this week, so be warned."

"That will not be a burden, Megan. I suspect that I shall enjoy a little of our English society," said Mrs. Tyler, smiling. She left the drawing room.

Lady O'Connell barely absorbed the meaning of their exchange, being more nearly concerned with her own immediate interests. "Megan, you cannot possibly go with me tonight," said Lady O'Connell. "It is a dress function, a soiree, in fact. You have not the wardrobe for it and have not been invited besides."

Megan smiled at her mother. "But I do have a few gowns that I am certain must be suitable, Mother. I brought back a very extensive wardrobe from St. Petersburg. Princess Kirov was kind enough to enlarge upon my own collection since I was expected to attend every function that she deemed appropriate. I have even a court dress. It is quite mouthwatering, I assure you. You will be quite in alt at sight of it when I am presented to the queen. As for an invitation, I am certain that your credit must be high enough to carry off an addition to your party."

"Of course it is," said Lady O'Connell with automatic vanity. Then realizing what she had said, she added hastily, "But that is quite beside the point, Megan! You will not know a single soul, except Sophronia, of course, and I do not wish to be forever introducing——"

"Sophronia! Is she in London, too?" asked Megan, surprised.

Lady O'Connell frowned slightly, at once sidetracked. "Yes, and has been this last month. Really, I do not know what has gotten into her lately. I assure you, Megan, you would not recognize your sister-in-law. Why, I wrote to Lionel about her just this week. The Season has scarcely begun and already Sophronia is to be seen everywhere. She has put off her shawls and her die-away airs. I do not mind that so much, but everyone is forever pointing her out as though she has become a society belle."

"And has she?" asked Megan, fascinated.

"It is most annoying," said Lady O'Connell, scarcely heeding. "I have been on the town for any number of Seasons. I have always enjoyed a well-deserved recognition. It is the outside of enough when I am suddenly introduced as Sophronia O'Connell's mother-in-law! Such impudence!"

Megan burst out laughing. At her mother's affronted expression, she swiftly sobered. "I do apologize, Mother, but it just seems so fantastic. Almost unbelievable, in fact!"

"Yes, and so I think, too," said Lady O'Connell, mollified.

"Is Sophronia abovestairs? I should like to visit with her," said Megan, already moving toward the door.

"Here?! Of course not! Why, do you think that I should allow Sophronia to behave so shockingly were she to reside under my roof? She has acquired her own house, if you please!" said Lady O'Connell on a fresh note of disgruntlement.

"I am positively unmanned," said Megan. She looked at her mother with a teasing light in her eyes. "Can a female properly be said to be unmanned, Mother?"

"What? Whatever are you talking about?" asked Lady O'Connell, confused.

"Never mind, Mother. It was a rhetorical question, at best. Certainly I must see Sophronia's wondrous transformation for myself," said Megan. "Wild horses could not keep me from accompanying you this evening, dear ma'am. Has she given up the pugs, too?"

"Yes, nasty creatures! At least, they do not accompany her everywhere as they were wont to do. Very well, Megan, you may accompany me. You always seemed to be on a more friendly footing with Sophronia than anyone else. Perhaps you may talk some sense into her and persuade her to return home to Lionel. She will not pay the least heed to me!" said Lady O'Connell.

"Will she not?" asked Megan, greatly appreciative. "I begin to wonder just what I wrought when I chose to go off to Russia."

"Whatever do you mean? What a nonsensical thing to say! As though you have done anything to the purpose!" said Lady O'Connell. "Sophronia has merely taken the bit in her mouth. There! I am so overwrought that I am using disgusting horsey phrases just like your father. If only Lionel had managed

Sophronia differently! But stupidity seems to run in the males
of our house. All they think about are those silly horses."

"Is it so surprising, Mother? And not without cause, perhaps. None of us would be able to dress or live in the style to
which we are accustomed without the income from the
horses," said Megan coolly. She discovered that she had no
patience for such deluded talk. "It is a pity that I must write
my father and tell him that I failed in my commission. The
Russians do not let go of their breeding stock, except to give
them to those with family connections. Believe me, I discovered that there are quite a number of personages in this world
who are just as fiercely possessive of their horses as my father
ever was. And certain members of their families are just as in-
ordinately obsessed with what they can provide for us as are
we."

Lady O'Connell stared at her daughter, quite taken aback.
"What extremely odd things to say, Megan. You have never
spoken to me in that tone before. Yes, almost as though you
were delivering a lecture!" Her bruised emotions caught up
with her. She glared at her daughter, affronted. "And I do not
think that I care for it at all, miss!"

Megan smiled at her mother. "Forgive me, ma'am. I spoke
out of my private thoughts. I shall go upstairs at once and
make ready to accompany you." She whisked herself out of
the sitting room before her mother could formulate either a
reply or an objection.

Chapter Ten

A few hours later Megan and Lady O'Connell were ushered into the elegant ballroom. Her ladyship was greeted at once by various acquaintances. When one or two openly asked Lady O'Connell the identity of her youthful companion, Lady O'Connell introduced Megan with grudging civility, calculated to deflate any pretensions that her daughter might have.

Megan merely smiled. She was all too aware of her mother's disgruntlement at having her hand forced that evening. She had listened to such strictures and complaints on the drive over that it was all that she could do to hold her tongue between her teeth. However, it was no plan of hers to come into direct conflict with Lady O'Connell, at least not just yet, and so she had preserved silence. Now she politely replied to all statements directed to her, neither putting herself forward nor shrinking back. Eventually her presence was accepted without further curiosity and she was at last free to take stock of her surroundings.

After a few minutes of observing the crowded company, Megan caught sight of her sister-in-law. She glanced at her mother. Lady O'Connell was deep in conversation. Megan doubted that her mother would notice whether she remained at her side or not.

Megan murmured a low excuse and detached herself from the circle. There were a few glances thrown her way, even a polite smile, but no one decried her desertion.

Megan crossed over to greet her sister-in-law. "Sophronia, how are you?"

Mrs. O'Connell turned quickly. "Megan!" She looked at Megan with astonishment.

"Yes, it is indeed I," said Megan with a laugh, aware that her unexpected appearance must be startling.

Mrs. O'Connell caught Megan's hands. "What a start you gave me! But how glad I am to see you!"

Megan was astonished by her sister-in-law's friendly reception. "Why, thank you, Sophronia."

Mrs. O'Connell had been conversing with several other ladies and introduced Megan to them, before saying, "Come, let us go over to that alcove where we may be private." She excused herself lightly to her friends and separated herself and Megan from the crowd. Megan allowed herself to be led away, curious about what her sister-in-law might say to her.

Their progress was impeded several times by acquaintances who wished to address her sister-in-law. Mrs. O'Connell's light rejoinders and her obvious popularity were not lost on Megan. Gone was the sulky, petulant expression, the shawls, the languid movements, and complaining discourse.

When they had entered the alcove and seated themselves on the small settee, Megan felt compelled to make comment of her sister-in-law's transformation. "I scarcely know you, Sophronia."

Mrs. O'Connell laughed. A faint tinge of color came into her cheeks. There was a quicksilver quality to her animated glance and sparkling eyes. "I am different, am I not? And I owe it all to you, Megan."

"To me! Why, I did nothing but advise you to seek a healthier climate," said Megan, shaking her head.

"No, Megan. You made me see what a total disaster I was making of my life," said Mrs. O'Connell. "After you left, I could not put out of my mind what you said to me at the grand dress ball. And I realized that you were quite right. I should leave Lionel. So I did."

"But that is not what I said at all," said Megan, appalled. "I meant leave Ireland to enjoy a few weeks of shopping and theater-gazing and forming new friendships. I never meant that you should leave Lionel!"

"Leave Ireland or leave Lionel, they are one and the same really," said Mrs. O'Connell with a shrug. "Lionel does not exist separately from the lands." Her eyes suddenly hardened.

"Has Lady O'Connell asked you to attempt to persuade me to go back? Ah, I can see from your face that has! Let me save us from a bothersome argument, Megan. My mind is quite made up. I shan't return to Ireland. There is little in the way of happiness for me there."

"I am sorry," said Megan quietly. "I wish very much that the circumstances had been different. But surely Lionel objected to your decision?"

A flicker of a melancholy smile crossed Mrs. O'Connell's face. "Lionel was not the least bit distressed when I informed him that I wished to remove to London. He quite willingly bought a town house for me and gave me adequate funds to do whatever I wished. It seems that I had made myself so abhorrent to him that he was glad to foot any bills which I might incur."

Megan heard the undercurrent of pain in her sister-in-law's self-mocking voice. Impulsively she reached out and squeezed the other woman's fingers. "I am sorry for you and, yes, Lionel, too. I know that he would think differently if he were to see you now."

"You are kind, Megan. Far kinder than I deserve, for I was a poor sister to you," said Mrs. O'Connell.

"You must not say such things," said Megan.

"But it is true, Megan. I could have made a push to see that you were brought out last Season. I could even have chaperoned you. But I did not because I was so wretched myself that I could not see beyond my own nose," said Mrs. O'Connell. She shook her head. "It is strange. Once I came to London, I could see things ever so much more clearly. After I lost the baby and Lionel turned from me, it was as though I existed in a deep well. And the more I tried to claw my way out, the worse matters became. It did not matter what I did to reclaim Lionel's attention. He did not want me. All he wanted was to breed horses."

"Sophronia, I do not know what to say," said Megan hesitantly. She had never been the recipient of such a personal confidence from her sister-in-law. It felt extremely awkward. "I never understood, or otherwise I might have been kinder, more obliging toward you."

Mrs. O'Connell gave a watery chuckle. "How could you understand, my dear, when I did not myself?" Suddenly she reached out and clutched Megan's fingers. Her expression intent, she said, "Pray say that you can forgive me, Megan. I am so exceedingly sorry! I had the power to help you, but I did not."

"Of course I do, Sophronia," said Megan, embarrassed. She was not embittered by her sister-in-law's lack of interest. She had simply assumed that Sophronia had been like everyone else—totally consumed by her own desires to the exclusion of all else. It was eye-opening, indeed, to be the recipient of a repentant outpouring. "You had more pressing concerns than to be thinking of a young girl's come-out."

"Thank you, Megan," said Mrs. O'Connell quietly, releasing Megan's hand. "That means more to me than I can say."

"But, Sophronia, what will you do now? You cannot stay in London forever. At some point you must talk to Lionel about how you feel." Megan hesitated, then said, "You do still have some feelings for him, do you not?"

Mrs. O'Connell gave a hiccuping laugh. She turned her head away to hide her expression. "You see far too much, my dear. Oh yes, I still harbor feelings for Lionel. I always shall. But it is not likely that he will ever know it, and nor would he care."

"My mother seems to believe that Lionel will care at least to a small extent. She told me that she wrote to him last week about you," said Megan.

Mrs. O'Connell's eyes rose to Megan's, then slid away. She carefully pleated her skirt. "An unprecedented action, certainly."

"What if Lionel should come to London after you?" asked Megan, curious.

"I should lead him a fine dance," said Mrs. O'Connell promptly. She straightened, lifting her chin to a proud angle.

"But why?" asked Megan.

"Oh, so that Lionel would understand that he must prove his devotion to me. For I will never follow him about begging for his attentions again," said Mrs. O'Connell. Then she laughed, the somber mood falling away from her. "But enough of this! I wish to hear about you. I was quite under the impression that you were settled in Princess Kirov's household indefinitely."

"No doubt that is what my mother hoped," said Megan with a quick smile. She was perfectly willing to follow her sister-in-law's lead. Such confidences were uncomfortable when they had never really been close. "But I managed to upset the apple cart quite unintentionally. Her highness sent me home in disgrace for abusing her hospitality."

"Nonsense! You would never do so!" said Mrs. O'Connell roundly. As she looked at Megan's pensive countenance, she became concerned. "Megan, you are jesting! Are you not? I cannot believe that— Megan, whatever did you do?"

Megan's smoke-gray eyes danced, but her expression was perfectly sober as she replied. "It was what I did not do! You see, I was totally insensible to my duty. I turned down eleven suits for my hand."

Mrs. O'Connell's eyes widened. "Eleven?!"

At her sister-in-law's awed expression, Megan began laughing. "It was not actually as impressive as it sounds, Sophronia. I suspect that the gentlemen were suffering from moon madness or otherwise why this strange attraction to me? I am quite an ordinary female, after all."

"I am all agog, my dear Megan. You must tell me all that happened," said Mrs. O'Connell.

"And so I shall, some rainy day when neither of us has anything better to do," said Megan, shaking her head.

"Unfair, my dear. I shall badger you unmercifully until you satisfy my curiosity." Mrs. O'Connell's amused expression altered suddenly. "Megan, does Lady O'Connell know of this?"

"Not yet. There has not been an opportunity to talk. I have but just arrived in London and when I heard that you were here, I insisted upon accompanying her tonight so that I might visit with you," said Megan. "I was delighted to learn that you, too, were in London. Though now I wish, just a little, that I had not said anything at all to you."

Mrs. O'Connell shook her head. "You merely inspired me to act upon my own behalf, my dear. I do not hold it against you and certainly you must not hold it against yourself. We each make our own choices, after all. And speaking of which,

I am perfectly willing to ally myself with you this time, Megan. I shall speak to Lady O'Connell about allowing you to remain in London at least for a few weeks. That will be better than nothing and perhaps, if I prove myself an adequate chaperone, her ladyship can be persuaded to extend that time."

"That is very kind of you, Sophronia. However, there is not the least need to put yourself out for me. I have already decided to remain in London for the entire Season," said Megan cheerfully. "My mother does not yet realize it, of course, but I have already cast her into the role of duenna."

Mrs. O'Connell leaned back so that she could regard her sister-in-law more fully. Slowly, she said, "You have changed, Megan. You were not used to be so decisive."

"Was I not? I suppose that broadening my horizons has had more of a beneficial effect than I thought, then," said Megan.

Mrs. O'Connell agreed, then regarded her sister-in-law with curiosity. "But however shall you manage it, my dear? Lady O'Connell is so very used to shuffling you off somewhere or anywhere as it suits her."

"I am no longer a green girl, untried and lacking confidence, Sophronia. I have been introduced into society and that cannot be changed however much Mother may balk at recognizing the fact. I have a fair acquaintance of my own now, also," said Megan quietly.

"Oh, you are talking about that set we always entertain during the winter months," said Mrs. O'Connell, waving her hand dismissively. "*That* will not help you, Megan. You may depend upon it. None of those personages will put themselves out for you in the least."

"Oh, I know that perfectly well. I have something quite different in mind," said Megan.

"What do you mean? You must tell me, for I count myself as one of your friends now," said Mrs. O'Connell.

"Before I left St. Petersburg, I secured several letters of introduction to a number of hostesses here in London from mutual acquaintances," said Megan. "I anticipate that shortly Mrs. Tyler and I shall be exceedingly busy making the social rounds. My mother will not be able to stop me from enjoying a

Season without risking grave insult to some very prominent personages."

Mrs. O'Connell's mouth dropped open in momentary astonishment. Suddenly she laughed. "How utterly delicious! But will it answer, I wonder? At all events, I shall enjoy watching your progress, Megan. I hope that it all falls out just as you wish. And Megan, should Lady O'Connell cut up too stiff, you and Mrs. Tyler are welcome to come stay with me at a moment's notice."

"I do appreciate that, Sophronia," said Megan. "Do you know, I am so very glad to have discovered you here in London, too!"

"Yes, it is most fortuitous, indeed!" said Mrs. O'Connell.

The two exchanged an affectionate hug, then agreed that it was past time to return to the party. As they rose, Mrs. O'Connell said with a mischievous light in her eyes, "I am determined to do my part for you, Megan. Pray allow me to introduce you to all my friends."

"I should like that very much," said Megan.

Mrs. O'Connell was as good as her word. She at once made the rounds with Megan, introducing her to everyone of her own acquaintance. In a very short time, it was known that Sophronia O'Connell's sister-in-law had come to London for the Season and Megan found herself the recipient of a number of invitations. Several gentlemen expressed their hopes to better their acquaintance with Miss O'Connell and asked permission to call upon her, which Megan readily gave.

"Now it will be a bit more difficult for you to leave London without creating a stir," said Mrs. O'Connell on a note of satisfaction.

Megan saw a few familiar faces, as well. Lady Bishop and Mrs. Hadcombe both recalled Megan and added their endorsement. Lady Mansfield, whom Megan had last seen at her mother's grand dress ball, was sitting with a lady who bore an uncanny resemblance to her. Megan had no difficulty in recognizing her as Lady Mansfield's sister before they were even introduced. Lady Mansfield cordially recommended that Megan call upon them and waggled her fingers in a friendly wave as Megan and Mrs. O'Connell passed on.

Lady Stallcroft was also in attendance at the soiree with her two daughters. Lord Stallcroft was not in evidence, which Mrs. O'Connell whispered to Megan was not unusual.

Megan was pleased to see the Misses Stallcroft again. While Mrs. O'Connell engaged Lady Stallcroft in conversation, she took advantage of the situation to address the girls privately, ending, "I appreciated the warm interest that you showed in my travels, Miss Stallcroft. Are you desirous of traveling?"

Miss Stallcroft cast a glance toward her mother as though afraid to be overheard. "Oh, yes, indeed! It is something that I have always longed to do. But Mama is so set against it that she will not hear of a holiday in foreign parts."

"Mama believes that the Cotswolds are foreign parts," said Miss Phoebe with almost a snort.

"Hush, Phoebe," said Miss Stallcroft, soft color coming into her face. "You should not be so critical. You will give Miss O'Connell a strange notion of us."

"I am not so Gothic," said Megan, smiling. "Nor am I easily shocked at the vagaries of people, as you will discover if you become at all acquainted with me. I suppose that arises out of my own upbringing. I am accustomed to all sorts of eccentricities."

"Your father is Lord O'Connell, is he not?" asked Miss Phoebe.

"Yes," said Megan, surprised. "Do you know him?"

"Oh, no. But I am slightly acquainted with your brother, Captain Colin O'Connell. Captain O'Connell told me once about his lordship and the magnificent horses that he breeds," said Miss Phoebe.

"You are acquainted with Colin?" repeated Megan. She looked with renewed curiosity at Miss Phoebe Stallcroft. She wondered whether her brother could possibly have an interest in that direction. But then she decided that such a young miss could not possibly hold Colin's wayward attention. It was more likely that Miss Phoebe had seen him, perhaps even been briefly introduced, and she had developed a tendre for him. Her brother did look exceedingly handsome in his regimentals, Megan thought. "I had no notion."

"Phoebe, pray remember what Mama said," murmured Miss Stallcroft in warning.

Miss Phoebe flashed her elder sister a glance and tossed her head. "I recall perfectly well what she said to me, Annabelle. You need not remind me. And I am not at all breaking my promise by speaking to Captain O'Connell's sister. That is nonsensical, as even Mama would agree!"

Megan looked from Miss Stallcroft's blushing face to Miss Phoebe's animated expression. With amusement, she said, "I see that I have stumbled upon a private matter. And I suspect that Colin is at the heart of it, isn't that so?"

Miss Stallcroft nodded, obviously embarrassed. "It was only a schoolgirl's crush, but Mama would"—she caught herself up—"that is, Mama read Phoebe a little stricture on appearing too encouraging to a gentleman."

"Oh, Annabelle, why wrap it up in clean linen?" said Miss Phoebe. "The truth of the matter was that Mama cut up stiff over what was a perfectly innocuous kiss."

Megan was taken aback. She had not expected such a confidence. Of a sudden, she recalled Lady Mansfield's inquiry, months past, about her brother. At the time she had wondered if there had been any truth at all in the rumor and if Colin had indeed become embroiled with some female. Now it was confirmed that he had been. However, Megan was shocked to discover that Colin's flirt was a young girl scarcely emerged out of the schoolroom.

Megan's expression had betrayed her astonishment, and Miss Stallcroft immediately discerned it. "No kiss is innocuous," uttered Miss Stallcroft, mortified. "Now do be quiet, Phoebe."

"Oh, very well. I shall not say another word. But not because you say so, but because Mama is looking at us. How I wish she would not keep us so close!" said Miss Phoebe in a fierce whisper.

Lady Stallcroft had started toward her daughters, Mrs. O'Connell with her. She bestowed a frosty smile on Megan. She had not forgotten the snub that she had been dealt at the younger woman's hands. "My dear Miss O'Connell, I trust that my silly daughters have not been boring you."

"Not at all, my lady," said Megan quietly. "It is a pleasure to converse with two such obviously well-bred young ladies. They are a credit to you, ma'am."

Lady Stallcroft looked at once surprised and gratified. She unbent a little. "Well, that is gracious, indeed! Girls, you must thank Miss O'Connell for such a pretty compliment." Her daughters obediently did as they were commanded. Miss Stallcroft's eyes were cast down, but Miss Phoebe's gaze was brimful of conspiratorial laughter.

"Mrs. O'Connell has requested the pleasure of your company tomorrow when she makes her morning calls, Annabelle. I have accepted her kind invitation on your behalf," said Lady Stallcroft.

"Thank you, Mama. I shall look forward to such a treat," said Miss Stallcroft, looking up. She directed a shy smile in her benefactress's direction. "I appreciate your kindness very much, Mrs. O'Connell."

"Think nothing of it, my dear. I have assured your mother that I shall be glad to help bring you out a little," said Mrs. O'Connell pleasantly. "I have a very large acquaintance and I am persuaded that I may be able to introduce you to a few personages who perhaps have not yet come in your way."

"You will behave with proper dignity, Annabelle, and not bore Mrs. O'Connell with any of your silly prattle," admonished Lady Stallcroft.

Miss Stallcroft looked faintly crushed. "Yes, Mama."

All of Megan's sympathy was roused. She wished very much that she could administer a well-deserved setdown to Lady Stallcroft, or at least console Miss Stallcroft for having such a dragon for a mother. However, all she could do was to stand by while the odious woman delivered another of her heavy and unnecessary corrections.

"Mama, may I accompany my sister?" asked Miss Phoebe, coming fast on the train of her mother's injunction to the elder daughter.

"Certainly not, Phoebe! You are to attend me, if you will recall, and write out my invitations. Your copperplate is much better than my secretary's," said Lady Stallcroft.

Miss Phoebe did not appear particularly gratified by her mother's compliment. Instead, there was a mutinous expression in her clear blue eyes. However, she cast down her gaze and said nothing further.

"Megan, you are to come, too. That will make us a delightful party," said Mrs. O'Connell.

"I will be happy to join you, Sophronia. I am certain that my mother will be able to spare me," said Megan.

"Oh? Is her ladyship already so accustomed to your presence that she is content to leave you to your own devices?" asked Mrs. O'Connell with a wicked gleam in her eyes.

"Quite," said Megan dryly.

"Such slack supervision is abhorrent to me," said Lady Stallcroft. "But I am not one to criticize. However, one must be grateful for a sister-in-law who is willing to step into the office of chaperone, Miss O'Connell."

"Indeed, I am," said Megan. "I am trusting to Sophronia to guide me in all the proprieties whenever my mother is unable to do so."

Lady Stallcroft bestowed a small prim smile on her. "You speak just as a sensible young woman should. Phoebe, you might take a page from Miss O'Connell's book. I warrant, I am pleasantly surprised to discover a young miss so amenable to taking direction from their elders. You are in a fair way to winning my approval, Miss O'Connell."

"You are kind, Lady Stallcroft," murmured Megan.

"I see that Lady O'Connell is waving to get my attention," said Lady Stallcroft. "Come along, girls. We shall go over to greet her."

"I shall follow you in a moment, my lady. It grows late and my mother may wish to depart," said Megan, who rather thought that it was to her that Lady O'Connell was signaling.

"Very well, Miss O'Connell. How refreshing it is to see a young lady so considerate of her mother's wishes," said Lady Stallcroft. She surged off, Miss Stallcroft in her wake and Miss Phoebe trailing reluctantly behind.

Megan turned to her sister-in-law. "I look forward to seeing you again on the morrow. Will you call for me?"

"Indeed I shall. Of course, we will not be entirely alone; but

I know that you won't mind Annabelle Stallcroft. She is some sort of cousin to me and I pity her. She is such a gentle creature," said Mrs. O'Connell. "Not at all like Phoebe. Phoebe is made of sterner stuff."

"Your cousin? Then you are related to Lady Stallcroft?" asked Megan, faintly appalled.

"Lord Stallcroft, actually. He is my father's first cousin. I have known Lady Stallcroft all of my life. I have never liked her," said Mrs. O'Connell, making a face. "She treats those girls abominably."

"So I have noticed," said Megan. "I really cannot abide a bully."

Mrs. O'Connell regarded her from out of cool, knowing eyes. "That is why you do not care overly much for Lionel, isn't it?"

Megan was taken aback for a moment. Her innate honesty compelled her to tell the truth, but she felt that she could not. After all, Sophronia was married to Lionel and had admitted to still having feelings for him. "Lionel and I never had much to do with one another, except when it came to a question of the horses. There are so many years between us, so perhaps that accounts for it. Let us say only that he and I do not see eye to eye on occasion," said Megan tactfully.

Mrs. O'Connell gave a low laugh. "Yes, I am quite sure of that. I do not mind, Megan, really. Lionel is who he is. I hope one day that he may change and for the better." She gave her hand to Megan in leavetaking. "I shall see you tomorrow about ten o'clock. Lady O'Connell is approaching and so I shall be off. I avoid her ladyship as much as it is possible!"

Megan watched her sister-in-law disappear quickly through the crowd. Then she turned to go meet her mother, a smile still on her face. How wonderful it was to have made a friend of her sister-in-law.

Lady O'Connell came up, but her eyes were not on Megan. She frowned after her daughter-in-law's graceful, retreating form. "What does Sophronia mean by it, pray? She must have known perfectly well that I wished to have a word with her before I left."

"Oh, are we leaving?" asked Megan quickly, wanting to divert her mother's attention from her sister-in-law. She took hold of Lady O'Connell's arm. "I am quite willing to fall in with your wishes on that head, Mother. I am more fatigued than I knew."

"It is just such a dreadful bore tonight," complained Lady O'Connell. "I have not enjoyed myself at all. First there was my responsibility to chaperone you. Then Sophronia, who actually snubbed me. Me! And now Lady Stallcroft has informed me that she is inviting you to her alfresco party on Saturday. You have quite won her over, Megan. I do not know how it is that you have insinuated yourself into my life all of a sudden, but you have done so and in the process have thoroughly cut up my peace!"

"It is bad of me, of course. But you will have the pleasure of washing your hands of me before much longer," said Megan consolingly.

Lady O'Connell nodded. "Indeed I shall! As soon as Mrs. Hadcombe's dinner ball and Lady Bishop's soiree are over, I will be free to send you back to Ireland."

Megan did not reply. She smiled graciously at their hostess as she and her mother took their leave. It was certainly not the appropriate time to inform Lady O'Connell that she was remaining in London for the Season. Megan rather thought that little detail was something that should gradually be borne in Lady O'Connell's consciousness.

Chapter Eleven

Mrs. O'Connell called punctually at ten o'clock at the town house. She knew quite well that Lady O'Connell would still be abovestairs, so she did not hesitate to come inside to the drawing room while a footman went up to inform Miss O'Connell of her arrival. She had Miss Stallcroft with her.

A light misting rain was falling that morning. When Megan entered the drawing room, the two ladies saw that she had attired herself suitably in a pomona green walking pelisse and kid half-boots. Her upstanding bonnet was adorned with two smartly curling plumes and Miss Stallcroft regarded this elegant headgear with a twinge of envy. She was not allowed by her mother to aspire to a more daring style and her own bonnet was a neat gray affair trimmed with a bit of ribbon.

Mrs. O'Connell greeted Megan kindly and said at once, "I did not think to include Mrs. Tyler in my invitation yesterday evening. Would she perhaps care to join us, Megan?"

"The same thought occurred to me, but Gwyneth begs to be excused from our outing this morning. I left her just now planning a lengthy visit to the bookshops. She missed her novels while in Russia and she is determined to lay hold at once on everything that she missed during our absence," said Megan, smiling. She nodded a greeting to Miss Stallcroft. "We shall undoubtedly return hours before she does."

"I did not know that Mrs. Tyler was so fond of reading," said Mrs. O'Connell, surprised.

"Colin would no doubt call her a regular bluestocking," said Megan, smoothing on her gloves.

"Oh, Colin! He would think that of anyone who read more than the racing sheets," said Mrs. O'Connell dismissively.

Megan laughed, agreeing that was probably true. She exchanged a few easy words with Miss Stallcroft, making that damsel feel herself to be favored indeed. Megan left a message for her mother with the butler and left the town house with her companions. They walked down the steps to the carriage.

Megan was touched and amused when Miss Stallcroft at once begged to be allowed to take the seat with her back to the horses, leaving the preferred seat to Megan and Mrs. O'Connell.

"Thank you, Miss Stallcroft," said Megan with a friendly smile. "That is very kind of you. But are you certain that you would not prefer—"

"Oh, no, no! I am perfectly comfortable, I assure you," said Miss Stallcroft hastily. "I am used to it, you see. Mama always sits with her friends on the forward-looking seat."

Megan met Mrs. O'Connell's eyes before turning back to the younger woman. "If that is indeed the case, I yield the point to you, Miss Stallcroft."

The ladies entered the carriage and the door was closed by the driver. Megan smiled at Miss Stallcroft. "It seems so silly to stand on formal terms. May I call you Annabelle?" she asked.

Miss Stallcroft pinkened. "Pray do," she said quickly.

"And I urge you to call me Megan. I hope that we will become good friends," said Megan.

The carriage started out. The three ladies called on several personages known to Mrs. O'Connell, many of whom already knew Miss Stallcroft or her mother and had met Megan the previous night. There were also a few that Megan had not yet had the opportunity to meet, but they greeted her cordially and with curiosity.

At Lady Bancroft's, Megan was surprised to run into her brother Colin. Captain O'Connell was sitting with her ladyship and the daughter of the house, Miss Bancroft, when Mrs. O'Connell and her party were announced. He rose to his feet to greet the newcomers. After Lady Bancroft had welcomed the three ladies to her drawing room and had introduced her daughter to Megan, she said, "And I fancy that you know this gentleman, Miss O'Connell!"

"Indeed I do. How are you, Colin?" said Megan, smiling up at her brother's astounded expression.

"Megan, I can scarce believe my eyes. I thought you still in St. Petersburg," he said, taking her hand for a brief moment. He searched her face as though he had difficulty absorbing the evidence of his own eyes.

Lady Bancroft and Mrs. O'Connell laughed. "Megan surprised us all, Colin. And I suspect that she will continue to do so," said Mrs. O'Connell. She turned to Lady Bancroft. "I am sorry to have missed you at the soiree last night, Maria. You and Priscilla would have enjoyed it very much, for it was a very decent squeeze. I trust that your son Edgar is feeling more the thing this morning?"

"Yes, he is on the mend at last. The physician was in earlier this morning, in fact, and said that the fever has been completely broken. I appreciate your friendly inquiry on his behalf. But now, you must tell me all about the soiree, Sophronia," said Lady Bancroft, patting the sofa beside her.

Miss Bancroft, who had greeted Miss Stallcroft with every appearance of pleasure, at once commanded her friend to join her. "So stuffy to be obliged to stay at home and miss the soiree," she said. "It is a pity that Mama decided that I could not go without her."

"But you would not have enjoyed yourself knowing that your brother was still ill," said Miss Stallcroft.

Miss Bancroft flashed a saucy grin. "I would have tried to, however!" Miss Stallcroft gave a small laugh and sat down. The two girls immediately put their heads together to exchange confidences.

Captain O'Connell seized the moment to take Megan aside. He took her over to the window, saying, "Your appearance this morning shocked me, Megan. How does it come about that you are in London?"

"I came back to England to enjoy the Season," said Megan. "I have already made a number of acquaintants, thanks in large part to Sophronia, and accepted several invitations. I have letters of introduction to others, as well. In short, I am in a fair way to committing myself for weeks to come."

"Hasn't our mother had anything to say against this little scheme of yours?" asked Captain O'Connell.

"We have not had the opportunity to discuss the matter," said Megan. Her eyes glinted with mischief. "And I trust that I shall be able to avoid it until some future time."

Captain O'Connell laughed. "I wish you good fortune, dear sister. I at least do not begrudge you a few parties. I see that Sophronia has taken Miss Stallcroft under her wing. That is a task worthy of Hercules. The lady almost disappears in company."

"I think that the result of her mother's brutal handling. With the proper encouragement, Annabelle could blossom into an accredited beauty," said Megan.

"Her?" asked Captain O'Connell in open astonishment. "Why, she shrinks whenever one even addresses a polite pleasantry to her and tosses a scared look at her mother. For my part, I prefer a miss who is able to hold her own whatever the circumstance."

"Yes, I have met Phoebe," said Megan dryly.

Captain O'Connell looked down at her, his eyes narrowed. "Have you, indeed."

"I liked her very much," said Megan, glancing up at her brother. In light of what she knew, she was curious to see whether he would volunteer anything to her about Miss Phoebe Stallcroft.

Captain O'Connell appeared about to say something more, but at that moment Mrs. O'Connell rose to take her leave. Miss Stallcroft and Megan added their assurances of pleasure to their hostess and Miss Bancroft. Captain O'Connell said that he had to be going also and offered to walk out with the departing ladies.

When they had emerged from the Bancroft town house, Captain O'Connell said, "Well, Sophronia, I never thought to see you looking so well. Congratulations are in order."

"Thank you, Colin," said Mrs. O'Connell with a cool smile. She allowed him to hand her up into the carriage.

Captain O'Connell offered his hand to Miss Stallcroft. She blushed, murmured something unintelligible to his polite good-bye, and hastily entered the confines of the carriage.

Captain O'Connell grimaced and turned to Megan. He lingered for a moment, looking down at her with a frowning expression. "I wish I knew what was in your head, Megan."

"Why, I have told you, Colin. I am going to enjoy the Season," said Megan.

He shook his head. "No, I suspect that there is more to it than that. You came back from Russia without notice to anyone, apparently. There is something here that I don't yet understand."

"I told you not long ago that I am as selfish as anyone else, Colin," said Megan quietly. "Is it so strange that I should at last be looking out for my own interests?"

Captain O'Connell grinned suddenly. "Lord, I should like to see our gracious mother's face when you inform her that you are staying the Season!"

"You are not very chivalrous, Colin," chided Megan, but with a smile of her own. "Pray call on me one day. I should like to see you again. Now I must go, for I have been keeping Sophronia's horses standing about for too long already." Her brother saw the sense in that and handed her inside, shutting the door after her and giving the signal to the driver.

When the carriage had rolled away from the curb, leaving Captain O'Connell behind, Megan requested that they stop briefly at Countess Lieven's residence. Her sister-in-law and Miss Stallcroft regarded her as though she was mad. She gave a laugh at their expressions. "I merely wish to leave my card and a note. I have a letter of introduction to Countess Lieven from a mutual acquaintance in St. Petersburg. I hope to meet the countess one day," said Megan.

"Countess Lieven is very haughty and exclusive. Do not be surprised if even your friend's letter does not open her door to you," said Mrs. O'Connell, nevertheless giving her driver the address.

However, it was Mrs. O'Connell who was surprised. When Megan sent in her card and the note, the butler returned with word that the countess was in and would see her. Megan thanked him and stepped inside, accompanied by Mrs. O'Connell and Miss Stallcroft.

Countess Lieven greeted her unexpected visitors, if not with warmth, at least with distant cordiality. She dismissed Mrs.

O'Connell and Miss Stallcroft with a few short words before turning to Megan. "You will join me at the window, Miss O'Connell," she said, drawing her arm through the younger woman's.

Megan cast a glance back at her sister-in-law and Miss Stallcroft, who had been left standing beside the settee. Mrs. O'Connell gave a small nod of encouragement.

Countess Lieven drew back the heavy velvet drape and looked down onto the busy thoroughfare. The sunlight was a watery hue due to the light rain. "London is nothing like Russia," she remarked distantly.

"No, my lady," agreed Megan. "I very much enjoyed my stay in St. Petersburg."

Countess Lieven turned a considering gaze on her. "It is remarkable that you procured such a letter, my dear Miss O'Connell. My friend speaks most highly of you. I value her opinion, and so I have decided to do something on your behalf. I am a patroness of Almack's. I shall sponsor you. I will send you vouchers this same afternoon."

Megan blinked in astonishment. It had never crossed her mind that such an advantage could possibly come to her. She had merely been intent on establishing herself with another prominent personage in society. The more she was known to be in town, the less likely it was that Lady O'Connell could comfortably insist that she return to Ireland before the Season was finished. "My lady, you are too good. It never occurred to me that you might do this for me. I thank you very much."

Countess Lieven smiled. "Miss O'Connell, I am granting you my favor. We shall pretend that I am naive enough to believe in your polite protestation. Shall we return to your friends?"

Megan found herself with nothing left to say. The countess obviously had the fixed notion that she had come to call for the express purpose of gaining this particular objective. Megan did not believe that she could disabuse the countess of her cynical mistake, so she did not make the attempt. Doing so would merely have made her look ridiculous.

The countess said good-bye to her callers. Megan thanked

Countess Lieven again and the three ladies were ushered out of the town house.

After they had been handed back up into the carriage, Mrs. O'Connell asked with lively curiosity, "What did the countess wish to say to you, Megan?"

"Countess Lieven is sponsoring me to Almack's. She is sending round the vouchers this afternoon," said Megan, still disbelieving of her good fortune.

Miss Stallcroft uttered in awe, "Oh!"

"My word!" Mrs. O'Connell stared at Megan. "You do run in exalted circles, do you not?"

"I merely handed her a letter of introduction from a well-known St. Petersburg hostess. Countess Lieven took it upon herself to do the rest," said Megan.

"I begin to wish that I had accompanied you to St. Petersburg," said Mrs. O'Connell. "Whom else are you planning to become acquainted with? Any of the royals, perhaps?"

Megan laughed and shook her head. "What nonsense, Sophronia! I know no one at court. At least—no, I am persuaded that I do not. But you look. I have all of my letters here." She undid her reticule and brought out the packet of letters.

Mrs. O'Connell quickly flipped through them, occasionally making an approving comment. When she was done, she handed the packet back to Megan. "It is utterly amazing what you have accomplished, Megan," she said.

"Do you truly think so? I so wish to remain for the Season and I thought that if I could make myself known a little—"

Mrs. O'Connell chuckled. "Oh, Megan, it is better than you could ever wish! Once you have contacted these, my dear, you will be extremely well-entrenched. There is nothing that Lady O'Connell will be able to do except to allow you to remain. Make the most of it, Megan, for her ladyship will be fit to be tied by the end."

"I fully intend to do just that, Sophronia, for I've no wish to sink back into oblivion," said Megan, tucking away the letters. "I hope to have contracted an eligible match before the Season ends."

She realized that Miss Stallcroft was listening to their conversation in wide-eyed amazement. Megan smiled at the other girl. "Do forgive us, Annabelle. We are airing some private linen without giving a thought to your sensibilities."

"Oh, no! It is quite all right," said Miss Stallcroft quickly. "I understand perfectly. And you may rest assured that I shall not breathe a syllable to anyone."

Mrs. O'Connell laughed and reached out to pat her cousin's knee. "It is not an evil conspiracy, Annabelle, you may be assured of that much! Megan has been kept so close for many years without even a hope of a come-out. Now she has the opportunity to make something grand happen in her life. And all through an exile to St. Petersburg! That is what is so marvelous to me, Megan."

"Yes, and to me, too," admitted Megan. "Princess Kirov opened the world to me. I could never express all of my gratitude to her highness."

"Well! I suggest that we make a few more such worthwhile calls," said Mrs. O'Connell. "Let me see the directions again, Megan."

"But do you not wish to make your own calls first?" asked Megan.

Mrs. O'Connell laughed. "My dear Megan! I may call on my own friends any day of the week. It is not often that I have the entrée to such as Countess Lieven. Besides, I shall enjoy helping you."

"I know that Mama will be very impressed that I have met Countess Lieven," said Miss Stallcroft. "Perhaps some of your other contacts will be just as notable."

"There! Annabelle has hit on the very best argument. Megan, you simply *cannot* be so selfishly shabby as to deny us this treat. Why, who knows to what new heights Annabelle and I might not soar on your credit?" said Mrs. O'Connell teasingly.

"Now you are being absurd!" said Megan.

"Oh, no, no," said Miss Stallcroft, quite seriously. "My cousin is perfectly correct. I do not run in such circles, but it would be such fun to pretend just this once."

Megan looked at Miss Stallcroft, then at her sister-in-law.

Mrs. O'Connell was smiling at her. "You see, Megan."

"You persuade me, Annabelle," said Megan. "Very well, let

it be as you wish, Sophronia! But do not eat me if we are treated with chilly reserve or denied the door!"

"Oh, I do not mind a snub or two!" said Mrs. O'Connell. She got her driver's attention and let him know the next address. When she settled back into her seat, she said, "This will be a truly edifying experience. Let it be a lesson to us, Annabelle. One must never look askance at opportunities to travel. One's horizons are certain to be broadened, don't you think?"

"Oh, quite. I have always longed to travel, but I daresay this will be almost as good!" said Miss Stallcroft happily.

The remainder of the day was spent in visiting with various personages. Contrary to Megan's warning, not once were the three ladies denied the door. Nor were they snubbed. They were received everywhere with cordiality and several magnificent invitations were issued to them.

It was a heady and dizzying experience for Miss Stallcroft. She ended by falling into a blissful state, only breaking her silence once with an uncharacteristically gleeful comment. "Mama will be unable to scold me for days, I daresay!"

Mrs. O'Connell let Megan off at Lady O'Connell's town house. "I shall not come in. I have no desire to incite a scold down on my head by my very presence. There is Annabelle to consider, too. I do not wish her bubble to be burst so rudely."

Megan laughed. "No, indeed! Take her home and give her into the offices of her maid, for I doubt that anyone else will know what to do with her for a while. I suppose that you will talk with Lady Stallcroft?"

"I shall give her every detail of our triumphant progress," said Mrs. O'Connell. "Annabelle is quite right. Her ladyship will be hard put to find anything to scold her about once she is informed of all of the exalted invitations that are shortly going to rain down on their heads."

"I am glad!" Megan said good-bye and lightly trod up the steps to the town house. The porter opened the door at her knock. She entered, a smile still on her face.

"Oh, miss, it is good to have you returned!" blurted the porter.

Megan regarded the man with surprise. "What is it, Geoffrey? What is wrong?"

"Such a rumpus we have had, miss! But I should be letting Mr. Digby tell you," said the porter, shutting the door. "If ye'll wait a moment, miss, I'll be getting Mr. Digby directly, miss."

Megan walked into the drawing room, her brows contracted. She had scarcely had time to put off her bonnet and gloves when the butler entered. As he closed the door, she inquired, "Digby, whatever has happened? I have never seen Geoffrey thrown into such a fluster."

"It is her ladyship, miss. She has discovered that Miss Simpkins is in the house and is in your employ," said the butler.

"I see." Megan drew a breath. She looked at the butler and put a blunt question. "Is her ladyship greatly agitated, Digby?"

"For the last hour and a half, miss," said the butler. He covered a discreet cough. "I may add that Miss Simpkins is at present closeted with the housekeeper, having suffered mild hysterics."

"Oh, dear! Poor Simpkins. I must do something at once," said Megan. She stood for a moment, thinking. Then she started moving toward the door. "Thank you, Digby. I shall go up to her ladyship. Is she in her own apartments?"

"Yes, miss," said the butler, bowing and opening the door for her.

Megan passed through the doorway, then paused. "Digby, pray be kind enough to convey a message to Simpkins from me. Tell her that I shall require her services as usual this evening."

"Yes, miss," said the butler, his wooden expression easing just a fraction. "I will be happy to do so, miss."

Megan crossed the marble-tiled hall and started up the stairs, catching up the hem of her pelisse in one hand. She did not pause at her own bedroom, but passed on down the hall. Before she ever reached her mother's door, she could hear Lady O'Connell's shrill voice. Megan lifted her hand and knocked firmly on the door, before turning the knob and going inside.

Chapter Twelve

Megan gained a singular victory with her mother. When it was explained to Lady O'Connell that it would scarcely rebound to her credit for it to become known that her daughter had removed herself to the protection of Mrs. O'Connell's house because she did not want to give up her dresser, Lady O'Connell managed to control her spleen. She could well imagine that Mrs. O'Connell would delight in making such a ridiculous story known all over London.

Lady O'Connell abandoned her demand that the dresser be immediately turned off. Her ladyship even went so far as to try to cajole Simpkins back into her own service. The dresser politely declined. This so piqued Lady O'Connell's temper that she thereafter uttered catty remarks about the dresser's waning talents. Her ladyship laid the blame at her daughter's door, for if it had not been for Megan's effrontery in making use of Simpkins's services in the first place, there would have been none of this unpleasantness.

Lady O'Connell retaliated by adopting a distant and chilly civility toward Megan in the mistaken belief that she was punishing her daughter. Her ladyship went about her own affairs, avoiding her daughter as much as possible. While she was out making her courtesy calls or taking tea with various of her friends or shopping, she assumed that Megan was languishing at the town house with only Mrs. Tyler for company.

Of course, Lady O'Connell had no choice but to lend her countenance to Megan's appearance at Lady Bishop's soiree and Mrs. Hadcombe's ball and supper. It was quite an inconvenience, but at least Mrs. Tyler was present, as well, and could be trusted to chaperone Megan properly so that she herself was freed to enjoy the entertainments.

Lady O'Connell begged off from Lady Stallcroft's alfresco party and sent Mrs. Tyler in her stead. "For I know that you will not mind going, Gwyneth. It is more your style of thing," she had said.

"I do not mind in the least, my lady," said Mrs. Tyler quietly.

"I knew that you would oblige me," said Lady O'Connell with a nod. "It is a pity that I am so engaged or otherwise I might see more of Megan. I trust that you are keeping her tolerably well entertained."

"We enjoy one another's company, my lady," said Mrs. Tyler.

Lady O'Connell had smiled and dismissed her cousin, thinking that, really, she must do something to reward Mrs. Tyler for her loyalty. The next instant she had forgotten the vague thought and was absorbed in choosing her toilette for that evening.

Mrs. Tyler had gone away with the comfortable conviction that they might never have to confess to Lady O'Connell that they were remaining in London. As long as Lady O'Connell continued to go off and leave them to their own affairs, they would do very well. She and Megan had formed the habit of walking in the park each afternoon and it was amazing how much one was able to intermingle with society by taking one's exercise. They also made morning calls on everyone who was kind enough to acknowledge them and soon became prime favorites with several hostesses.

Cards that came to the town house for Megan and her companion were discreetly funneled directly into their hands by the obliging staff. Lady O'Connell never saw them and for a fortnight remained in happy ignorance of her daughter's burgeoning social life. Acquaintances were made aware that Miss O'Connell and Mrs. Tyler could be found at home only on certain days, and those days were carefully chosen to coincide with Lady O'Connell's own absences.

Megan and Mrs. Tyler accepted those invitations that might conceivably be thought by Lady O'Connell to be too stuffy or too beneath her notice to attend. There was also Megan's entrée to Almack's to put to good use. Lady O'Connell rarely attended the assemblies at the exclusive club. If she had done so that week, she would have seen her daughter enter the very cream of the *ton* and receive the nod from no less a personage than Countess Lieven for permission to waltz.

As for the sort of entertainments which Lady O'Connell always attended, Megan said nothing to her mother about them. She simply appeared at the functions with Mrs. Tyler and Mrs. O'Connell. Without argument or cajoling, Megan had made her debut.

If it was wondered at that Megan was seen in her sister-in-law's train rather than her mother's, the question was dismissed rather easily. Lady O'Connell's character was well known. It was widely assumed that her ladyship preferred to leave her daughter's come-out to Mrs. O'Connell's management.

"Depend upon it, Agatha did not wish to be tied down by the responsibility of bringing the girl out. That is why she is taking full advantage of Mrs. O'Connell's good nature," said Mrs. Hadcombe.

"Oh, undoubtedly! Though I hardly think it is such a burden upon Sophronia O'Connell's shoulders. Miss O'Connell has taken to society quite well," said Lady Bishop, watching the young lady in question waltzing with a gallant gentleman. "I am very impressed with her poise and grace."

"Are you thinking of her for your son?" asked Mrs. Hadcombe with a glance. "She hasn't anything but a small portion, as I understand it."

"True, but I would prefer Miss O'Connell over that twitty Henrietta Beaseley. My word! What Eugene sees in her is beyond my comprehension. It is enough to send me into palpitations, I assure you," said Lady Bishop.

Mrs. Hadcombe laughed. It was well known that the Honorable Mister Eugene Bishop was making up to that confirmed bluestocking, Miss Henrietta Beaseley. Of course, Mister Bishop was also of a scholarly bent; but that did not excuse his unfortunate passion for a lady who had the bad taste of actually quoting Plato in company.

Lady O'Connell came up to the two ladies. There was an agitated expression on her face. "My dears! I cannot begin to tell you of my mortification. It is enough that Sophronia is so lost to propriety as to bring Megan and Mrs. Tyler tonight. But Megan to dance the waltz! It is bizarre behavior, indeed! Whatever shall I do?"

Mrs. Hadcombe stared. "My dear Agatha, what can you mean? Miss O'Connell's manner is quite unexceptional, I assure you."

Lady O'Connell practically wrung her hands. "You do not understand! I never gave her permission to dance, nor indeed did I sanction this appearance tonight!"

"Come, Agatha! These are the merest qualms of the nerves. Countess Lieven herself has conveyed her approval on your daughter. What more can you desire?" asked Lady Bishop, who had been at Almack's with her son and seen the honor conferred on Miss O'Connell.

"Countess Lieven!" Lady O'Connell looked from one to the other of her friends. Their surprised expressions were beginning to turn to curiosity. Her ladyship saw the danger of confiding too much and sharply turned about. Hastily, she said, "Oh well, then! What can I have to be anxious about?" She gave an unconvincing laugh.

"You surprise me, Agatha. I had not thought you to be such an anxious parent," said Lady Bishop, regarding her with an amused smile. "Surely Miss O'Connell's debut into society is coming along just as it ought. Of course, she has had the advantage of having been brought out already in St. Petersburg. That was wise of you, Agatha. It has given Miss O'Connell a confidence that I feel certain she might not have had otherwise."

Lady O'Connell felt herself momentarily bereft of speech. Her stunned mind grasped two facts, however. One was that she must speak to her daughter. The other, and far more important at that moment, was that she must at all costs preserve her dignity. "I did not realize—that is, I am just so overwhelmed! One does not appreciate these things until one is faced with them."

"You are fortunate that you have Mrs. O'Connell to help you take her around," said Mrs. Hadcombe. "I understand that she has introduced your daughter as widely as possible."

"Of course! Of course!" said Lady O'Connell, reflecting that was another lady that she very much wanted to have a word with. In fact, there was nothing to prevent her from taking her daughter-in-law to task that very moment. "Pray excuse me. I wish to—to *consult* with Sophronia on a certain matter. You will understand, I know!"

A few moments later, it could be observed that Lady O'Connell and Mrs. O'Connell were in the midst of a difference of opinion. Lady O'Connell's glacial expression was in direct contrast to Mrs. O'Connell's heightened color.

Mrs. Tyler was one of those who witnessed the ladies' meeting, and that it was an unhappy one was all too obvious. "Oh, dear! I knew that it was too comfortable to last," she murmured.

"What was that you said, Mrs. Tyler?" asked Lady Mansfield.

"I was just reminded of something that I wished to ask Megan. Pray excuse me, my lady," said Mrs. Tyler, hastily taking her leave. She made her way at once over to Megan, who was just returning from the dance floor. Mrs. Tyler nodded to the gentleman who was escorting Megan back to her chair and as soon as he bowed himself off, she said, "Megan, there is trouble! Lady O'Connell and Sophronia are exchanging words."

Megan turned around and at once perceived the accuracy of Mrs. Tyler's warning. "I shall go over at once. Poor Sophronia! I know that she is catching cold at my expense."

With Mrs. Tyler following her, Megan quickly went over to join her mother and sister-in-law. Before she ever reached them, she overheard enough to have her suspicions confirmed. Lady O'Connell was indeed accusing Mrs. O'Connell of overstepping her bounds where Megan herself was concerned. She interrupted without ceremony. "Nonsense, Mother! Pray do not say another word against Sophronia. You are quite out, you know."

"Megan!" Mrs. O'Connell turned to her with relief. Her blue eyes were ablaze with anger. "I am so glad that you are here."

"Exactly where she should not be!" exclaimed Lady O'Connell. "I take extreme exception to—"

"Mother, pray suspend this wrangling until we have departed. I cannot imagine that any of us wishes to make any more of a spectacle of ourselves than we already have," said Megan.

"I for one shall be happy to leave this unfortunate scene!" exclaimed Mrs. O'Connell. "I am sorry for you, Megan. But I shall not remain another instant in her ladyship's presence, for fear of what I might say!" She swept away.

"Well! I have never known such rude treatment at anyone's hands," said Lady O'Connell. She turned a rigid countenance to her daughter. "As for you, Megan, I should like an explanation, if you please!"

"With my goodwill, Mother. However, I think not here," said Megan, quite unflustered. "Gwyneth, let us collect our wraps. We will not be returning home in Sophronia's carriage, of course. I hope you do not mind that we ride with you, Mother."

Lady O'Connell gobbled a furious rebuke. Her ladyship was not attended to either by her daughter or Mrs. Tyler, since those ladies actually had the effrontery to walk away from her in the most unfeeling way imaginable. Lady O'Connell had no choice but to follow hurriedly after them. She put as good a face on as possible as Megan and Mrs. Tyler took leave of their hostess, and added her own short and untruthful praises for the evening.

However, once the carriage had been called and the ladies had embarked in it, the tirade broke over their heads. Megan preserved silence during the drive home. Lady O'Connell scolded and accused and complained all the way to the town house.

Megan and Mrs. Tyler descended from the carriage. Lady O'Connell got out, exclaiming, "It is beyond anything when you do not stand still as I am speaking to you, Megan! Yes, and you also, Gwyneth. I am of half a mind of letting you go, for you have proven yourself to be unfit for your position!"

Megan turned suddenly, her eyes blazing. "Do not dare to threaten Gwyneth!" While Lady O'Connell stared at her, quite taken aback, she said, "We shall discuss everything once we are inside, Mother!"

The ladies were admitted to the town house by the porter. The manservant took one look at her ladyship's face and prudently faded out of the hall. The butler met the ladies and asked if there was anything that they required.

"Yes, Digby, we shall have tea in the drawing room," said Megan, beginning to pull off her gloves.

"You make yourself mightily free in my house, daughter!" said Lady O'Connell.

Megan looked at her mother, slightly raising her brows. "Would you prefer something else, ma'am?"

Lady O'Connell waved one hand dismissively. Very much on her dignity, she said, "Tea will do well enough, I suppose! Now let us go in, for I have a great many things to say to you, Megan. And to you, Gwyneth! Digby, the door!" The butler leaped forward to open the door.

Megan and Mrs. Tyler followed her ladyship into the drawing room. The door was barely closed behind them when Lady O'Connell seized the opportunity to launch into a new tirade.

"I think you should know that I am staying out the Season," said Megan, raising her voice to be heard over her mother's furious squall.

Lady O'Connell was aghast. "What did you say? Why, you unconscionable girl! It is all a plot to cut up my peace! I do not know at all why you came back from Russia! I wish you had not!"

"My lady!" exclaimed Mrs. Tyler reprovingly.

"It is quite all right, Gwyneth. It is only what I expected," said Megan. "The truth of the matter is that I came back because Princess Kirov wanted me off her hands. She took offense when I turned down eleven offers for my hand."

"Oh, Megan," said Mrs. Tyler, shading her eyes with one hand and sinking onto a settee.

"Eleven offers?" Lady O'Connell stared in stupefaction at her daughter. "But I do not understand. Megan, why?"

"None of them appealed to me," said Megan on a small laugh.

"Unnatural girl!" gasped Lady O'Connell.

"I returned to England and have launched myself on a Season with every expectation of successfully contracting an offer," said Megan calmly.

"I forbid it! I shall not allow you to wreck all my pleasure this Season. I shall not have you here in this house another hour! You are returning to Ireland this very night!" exclaimed Lady O'Connell, going to the bellpull and giving it a yank.

"You may force me from the house, Mother, but not from London, for I shall go directly to Sophronia," said Megan.

"I shall cut off your pin money!" said Lady O'Connell.

"You may do so, of course. But Sophronia has her own independence. And I trust that I would not be a large charge on her since I am already in possession of a very adequate wardrobe," said Megan.

"You are completely selfish and unfeeling," complained Lady O'Connell. "Only think how it would look if you were to remain in London under Sophronia's roof! I would be talked about by all the vulgar gossips."

"I do sympathize, Mother," said Megan.

"If that were true, you would instantly comply with my wishes!" said Lady O'Connell bitterly. "But instead, you have set yourself against me."

"Well, yes, that is true," said Megan, a smile touching her face. "But I am only following your own directive to make the most of my opportunities. I have a full calendar of commitments and I have every intention of meeting them. It would be thought very strange indeed for me to leave just now."

"What are you talking about? You know no one! How can you have accepted any invitations?" said Lady O'Connell, at once diverted.

"Megan is speaking the truth. She brought letters of introduction with her from Russia. Princess Kirov is known in all the best circles and her credit has been of immense value. That was why Countess Lieven gave Megan vouchers to Almack's and any number of others have already solicited her presence to their entertainments," said Mrs. Tyler. She gave a tiny smile at Lady O'Connell's astounded expression. "I am also in demand, my lady. It is a heady experience, indeed. We are committed for every evening for the next two months at least."

The door opened and the butler looked in. "You rang, my lady?"

"Tea, Digby! And my smelling salts! At once, you dense man!" exclaimed Lady O'Connell, stumbling to the settee. "I am feeling very unwell. My head is pounding. I am certain that I feel a spasm coming on."

"Perhaps you should call her maid to her, Digby," said Megan quietly. The butler nodded and exited. Megan turned back to her mother. "I hope that you are better directly, ma'am. I think, once you have had an opportunity to adjust yourself to the notion, that you will become quite reconciled to having me here this Season."

"Go away!" begged Lady O'Connell. "Just go away!"

"At once, ma'am," said Megan. She and Mrs. Tyler left the drawing room. Behind them, they could hear Lady O'Connell begin to indulge in a mild fit of hysterics. As they climbed the stairs, a maid flew past them in the opposite direction with a bottle of smelling salts clutched in her hand.

"We brushed through that fairly easily, I thought," said Megan.

"Indeed! It was not half so bad as I imagined," agreed Mrs. Tyler.

Chapter Thirteen

Lady O'Connell was prostrated by the successive shocks of the night before and she kept to her bedroom all morning, rejecting even a cup of weak tea and toast with loathing.

A gentleman's card was carried into the sitting room, where Megan was keeping company with Mrs. Tyler. It was not an unusual occurrence now for admirers to send up their cards and Megan thought nothing of it. "Thank you, Digby," she said.

She glanced at the name on the card. Color flew into her cheeks.

Mrs. Tyler noted the phenomenom with lively curiosity. "Why, who is it, Megan?"

"It is Prince Kirov. He has come to London," said Megan in a strangled voice. She did not seem to know what to do with the calling card, but stared at it as though she had difficulty bringing it into focus.

"But how delightful! Digby, pray show the gentleman in. He is a friend from St. Petersburg," said Mrs. Tyler.

"No!" said Megan, turning sharply. But the butler was already retreating. She looked almost wildly at Mrs. Tyler. Her usual self-possession was nowhere in evidence. "Gwyneth, how could you? What am I to say? I don't know what to say!"

"You will say just what you ought. I have every confidence in your good sense," said Mrs. Tyler comfortably. She was privately delighted by Megan's reaction. "Er—it might be best if you were to compose yourself on the settee. You do not wish to appear too eager."

"No, no, of course not!"

Megan hastily seated herself, arranging her skirts with a slightly trembling hand. She was glad that she was wearing

one of her prettiest gowns, a simple muslin day dress trimmed
with knots of blue satin ribbons. Her thoughts were in a whirl,
at once chaotic and strangely focused. Fear and pleasure
warred within her breast. Why had Prince Kirov come to London? It could not be just because he had vowed to follow her.
But what if he had? What if that was the sole reason that he
had come here today? But no, he could have planned all along
to come to London on business and this would be no more
than a polite courtesy call.

By the time the door was opened, Megan's nerves were
stretched taut. However, she managed to school her expression
so that there was no hint of her inner turmoil. When Prince
Kirov strode into the room, she looked up at him and was at
once struck by his appearance. He was dressed in a tailored
coat and buckskins, his boots shined to a mirror finish. Megan
had almost forgotten how large he was, how magnificent his
physique. She offered a pleasant smile of greeting. "Your
highness! This is a welcome surprise. I had not looked for you
in London."

"Had you not, Miss O'Connell?" There was a glint in Prince
Kirov's blue eyes as he raised her fingers to his lips.

Megan's breath caught. That simple question, uttered with
intimate disbelieving amusement, had put her already agitated
mind into complete disarray.

Prince Kirov turned from her to greet Mrs. Tyler, leaving
Megan feeling that she had been spared a second or two to recover. "Dear Mrs. Tyler! You appear delightfully English, like
a fragrant, delicate rose. I salute you, ma'am." And he did so,
bussing her on both cheeks.

Mrs. Tyler emerged from the prince's embrace, blushing
and slightly disheveled. "My goodness! I had forgotten how
demonstrative you Russians can be. How very gratifying, to be
sure! But it will not do, your highness. You will shock all of
our acquaintances if that is how you mean to go on."

Prince Kirov snapped his fingers. "That for the stiff English
proprieties! Am I to withhold a gesture of affection for my
friends for fear of offending some personage I do not know
and do not wish to know? I am a Kirov and I define mine own
honor."

The prince's arrogant declaration settled Megan's composure as nothing else could have done. "Just so, your highness. Who could argue the point?" she said, lightly teasing.

He flashed a smile at her. His blue eyes were twinkling. Prince Kirov spoke amiably to the two ladies for a few minutes, describing portions of his journey to them and also his impressions of London since he had arrived. He had particularly high praises for the park, which he declared to be delightful.

"I have already developed the habit of riding there each afternoon, for I do not like to be idle. I have been very busy, as you may imagine, in establishing myself comfortably. My maître'd is at this moment negotiating terms for a suitable residence," he said.

"I wish we had known earlier of your arrival, your highness. It is so disagreeable for you to be obliged to put up at a hotel," said Mrs. Tyler. "I am positive that Lady O'Connell would have asked you to stay here if she had but known."

Prince Kirov bowed his appreciation. "That would have taken quite an unfair advantage of her ladyship, however. Naturally I would have waited upon you sooner, but it was not convenient until today."

"Then I am glad that we were at home when you chanced to call," said Megan, unaccountably piqued. She had gathered the impression that he had been in London long enough to have called on them several days earlier. Perhaps he had come to England on a business matter, after all. "We might possibly have missed you otherwise, for we are not usually so quiet."

Mrs. Tyler did not dare to turn her head, for fear of directing such a look of reproach at Megan that it could not possibly have been misinterpreted by their guest.

"I do not doubt that you have many social commitments. It was to be expected," said Prince Kirov.

"How was dear Princess Kirov when you left? My, it seems ages ago since we were in St. Petersburg," said Mrs. Tyler.

"Yes, it does indeed," agreed Megan. "No doubt that is because we have been so very busy also. Did Fedor accompany you?" She ignored Mrs. Tyler's quick reproving glance and instead smiled brightly at their guest.

Prince Kirov gravely responded. "My mother was well,

though she was angry that I left her so soon after your own departure. I thank you for your inquiry, Mrs. Tyler. As for my
good Fedor, I left him at the hotel today to oversee my personal affairs." He turned to Mrs. Tyler with a winning smile.
"I know that it is a forward request in England, but for the
sake of the friendship forged among us in Russia, I ask your
permission to speak to Miss O'Connell in privacy."

Mrs. Tyler rose immediately from her chair. "We became
such good friends while in your house that I confess to stand
on ceremony now seems absurd. I am confident that I may entrust my dear Megan to you for a few moments, your highness."

"Gwyneth!" exclaimed Megan, at once annoyed and amused.
There was a shiver of anticipation, too, for she had seen a flash
of deep satisfaction in Prince Kirov's eyes.

"Thank you, Mrs. Tyler," said Prince Kirov, bowing over
the lady's hand before he escorted her gallantly to the door.

Mrs. Tyler directed a meaningful smile at Megan before she
left the room.

Megan turned away and moved toward the pianoforte. She
well knew that her companion thought a budding romance was
being well-served. However, Megan was uncertain what she
wanted Prince Kirov to say to her. He had uttered his undying
devotion to her, but Megan hoped that she was not setting too
much store by that. Yet it would be very pleasant to be told
that she was indeed the reason that he had come to London.

Megan heard the door shut and then the prince's quick step.
She did not turn around but waited until she knew that he had
drawn close. Megan slipped onto the pianoforte seat and began
softly pressing the keys

"Allow me to turn your music, mademoiselle." The prince's
large well-kept hand came into her view and opened the
sheets.

Megan felt heat in her face. She had no need of the sheet
music and she knew that he was well aware of it. The pianoforte had simply been used as a stratagem to avoid looking
at him. He obviously knew it and was amused by it. Megan
wanted to retain a polite constraint between them, afraid that if

she did not, something that she was unprepared for might happen. "Thank you, your highness."

"In St. Petersburg you began to call me Misha," he said quietly.

Megan's color heightened. So much for keeping matters on a formal footing. She had not taken into account the prince's regrettable lack of convention. "A slip of the tongue, surely."

"Perhaps. Then again, perhaps not." He turned the next sheet of music. The sweet notes of the air filled the moment of silence.

"You also kissed me," he said softly.

Megan turned swiftly on the seat, abandoning the keyboard. Her smoke-gray eyes flashed up at him. "Ungentlemanly of you, sir! You took that kiss by overcoming my resistance."

"Oh, the conservatory! No, dear Megan, I was referring to the ice slide," said Prince Kirov with a slight smile.

Megan's face flamed. She quickly rose from the pianoforte and retreated from him. "Oh! I had forgotten. But that was because you caught me unawares. It was such a silly moment. The exhilaration of the sledding and—and—the moon!"

Prince Kirov caught one of her hands. He turned it over and pressed a kiss into her warm palm. "Forgotten, mademoiselle? No, not forgotten. Not by me; nor by you. I can feel the fluttering of your heart in your wrist."

Megan snatched her hand away. She put her hands behind her back. She managed a breathless laugh. "You are nonsensical, Mikhail!"

He reached out and caressed her cheek with a feather touch. "You see? I read the mysteries of your soul in your eyes. I awakened the passion in you. It is impossible to pretend that you have turned cold toward me."

Megan was fast losing perspective. "You go too fast for me," she whispered.

He nodded in reluctant agreement. "Yes, you are one who deserves all the extravagances of elegant courtship." He gave the flicker of a smile. There was a banked heat in the expression in his eyes. "Do not fear, my dove. Though you are mine to possess, I shall not rob you of that homage which every beautiful woman desires." He possessed himself of her hands and bent to kiss her fingers in a formal salute.

Megan pulled her hands free. "How dare you?" she choked.

Prince Kirov straightened in surprise. He was startled at the infuriated expression on her face. He took another step toward her. "Megan—"

"No! Do not come near me," commanded Megan, throwing up her hands.

The prince stopped, his heavily marked brows lowered a fraction. "What is this nonsense? I do not find it amusing."

"You are quite right, your highness. It is not at all amusing!" Megan's eyes were alight with sparks. "I am not a mare to be possessed at your whim, your highness!"

"Come, Megan, this is ridiculous. I told you in Russia that I love you more than any other woman," began Prince Kirov.

"And just how many women do you presently love, your highness?" asked Megan, her voice dripping ice.

"None! You have my heart and no other! Did I not swear to it and give you the ring from off my own finger? Did I not vow to follow you to London? Have I not proven my love for you?" asked Prince Kirov, his voice rising with each question. His expression was one of virtuous outrage.

"Do not dare to yell at me, Misha," said Megan.

"No, you are right! I should not yell. I should shake you instead!" He started to close the distance between them. His intent was evident in his expression.

Megan whisked herself behind the settee. "I do not believe you. You only say that you love me. You think that I am a ripe plum ready to fall into your hand whenever you should hold it out to me. But I am not! I do not belong to you, sir!"

"I do not think that you are a plum! You do not resemble any fruit at all, for you are too thin," said Prince Kirov unthinkingly.

"Too thin? How dare you insult me in such a fashion!" gasped Megan.

Prince Kirov raked a heavy hand threw his blond locks, roaring his frustration. "Megan, I say it again! I love you! I love you! Why do you deny me?"

"I received eleven requests for my hand. Not one of those honorable proposals was from you, Misha. Instead you snatched kisses from me in the conservatory and seduced me with the ice hills. And now you announce that I am yours to take whenever it should suit you!" said Megan.

There was a short silence. Prince Kirov stared at her, his eyes narrowed beneath his heavy brows. "Not once did it cross my mind to make you my mistress," he said stiffly.

"Liar," said Megan softly.

He was startled. Then, slowly, he began to grin. "Yes, I am a liar. I thought it many times. But you held me at arm's length all those months. You insisted upon a formal address even when I made you free of my name. You would not allow any familiarity. Is it any wonder that I should begin to think of you in my arms?"

Megan's face was flaming. "You are a wicked, wicked creature."

He threw his head back and bellowed in laughter. When he had expended it, he looked at her with warm amusement. "Not so wicked, after all. My thoughts changed, my dear delight. That night on the ice hill, when you kissed me of your own will, I wanted to catch you up and carry you off into the night. But I did not. Do you know why, Megan?"

Megan shook her head, her heart beating remarkably fast.

"I did not wish anyone to speak evil about the woman that I would take to wife," he said.

"Oh!" Megan did not know what else to say. She could scarcely breathe. She felt confused, about his feelings for her and about her own.

Suddenly fear rose up. If she melted into his arms now, would she ever know whether he truly loved her? She had heard enough from Princess Kirov to know that her son had an obligation to marry well. Megan did not believe that an Irish miss of minor nobility and modest portion was exactly what Princess Kirov had in mind as a daughter-in-law. That is, if he actually married her. It was one thing to say that one was thinking of marriage, but Prince Kirov had never actually voiced a proposal to her. And if he did marry her, would she be able to depend upon his fidelity? His reputation, as well as his own mother's observations concerning her son's passionate nature, shook Megan's confidence.

Prince Kirov seemed to be able to read something of her thoughts, for he smiled and shook his head. "I shall not press you now, Megan. I see that I have been unbelievably clumsy—"

"Arrogant," corrected Megan.

Prince Kirov lowered his brows and finished, "—in my dealings with you. You are a woman. Naturally you do not think clearly, for a woman thinks with her heart. I will give you time. When your head and your heart have come together, you will be willing to accept me."

"I am situated in London for the Season," said Megan.

"Of course," said Prince Kirov in surprise. "Where else would you be?"

Megan smiled. She could have told him, but he knew little of the life she had led before her arrival in St. Petersburg. "I shall have many engagements."

"I shall escort you," said Prince Kirov, waving his hand as though it was a matter of little moment.

"I shall have many admirers and entertain their suits," warned Megan.

"I shall kill them all," said Prince Kirov amiably, but with a somewhat wolfish grin.

Megan laughed and came out from behind the settee. She held out her hand to the prince and he took it, clasping it loosely as he smiled down at her. "We have reached an understanding, Misha. I am glad. I have missed you, my dear friend." She stressed the words.

Prince Kirov grimaced. "You are hard, Megan. That is not the relationship that I would claim, as you know."

"No, I know well that it isn't," agreed Megan, her eyes gleaming. "But I think it wisest for my peace of mind."

"Then I bow to your wishes, mademoiselle," said Prince Kirov, suiting action to his words and making a formal bow over her hand.

The door opened and Mrs. Tyler entered. When Prince Kirov straightened and turned, she said, "Oh, are you taking your leave so soon, your highness? I had hoped to offer you tea."

Prince Kirov shook his head. "Thank you, but no, Mrs. Tyler. I have outstayed my time and I have other engagements. Perhaps I shall call again later in the week."

"Pray do so," said Mrs. Tyler cordially, offering her hand to the prince. She slid a glance at Megan, attempting to read something in her expression. "Our doors, or rather Lady O'Connell's, will always be open to you."

Prince Kirov gravely expressed his appreciation and left.

Mrs. Tyler at once turned back to Megan. "Well, my dear? What did he say?" she asked in highest hopes.

"Prince Kirov said that I was his to possess whenever he chose to do so and that I was too thin to be a proper fruit," said Megan baldly.

Mrs. Tyler stared at her, nonplussed. "Well! How very odd of him, I must say. What—what did you say?"

"I raked him over the coals, naturally. Prince Kirov is far too self-assured and charming. He is a danger to the female, whomever she might be. But I hope that I am too sensible to lose my head over an accomplished flirt," said Megan.

"Quite frankly, my dear, it does not sound to me that the prince is any hand at all at flirtation," said Mrs. Tyler roundly.

Megan laughed. "No, he is not quite like your romantic heroes who are all perfection, Gwyneth. He says stupid things. He does not understand me. And I am not certain that I entirely trust him."

"My dear!" exclaimed Mrs. Tyler, shocked.

Megan flushed. "But it is true, Gwyneth! Prince Kirov vows that he loves me, but does he really? I am sure you heard as much about his celebrated reputation as I did while in St. Petersburg."

"He followed you all the way to London," said Mrs. Tyler.

"Oh, Gwyneth! I might be only one of so many other reasons why he chose to come to London this spring. I know, for instance, that the Kirovs have always had business interests in England," said Megan. "Until I know for certain what is in his heart, I do not know whether I can trust my own heart. Can you not understand that?"

"Yes, I suppose that I can." Mrs. Tyler looked at her with mingled sympathy and perplexity. "But, my dear, what will you do?"

"Sophronia said something to me once. She said that if Lionel were ever to come to London for her, she would lead him a dance. I wonder whether that might not be the answer in my own situation," said Megan slowly.

Mrs. Tyler regarded her with strong misgivings. "What are you thinking, Megan? I've seen that expression before! Oh, I should so dislike it if you were to do anything that you might regret!"

"Never fear, Gwyneth. I am an excellent rider," said Megan, turning to the door.

"Whatever are you talking about?" asked Mrs. Tyler, completely bewildered.

"Only that I am going riding, Gwyneth. I am getting up a party with Colin and as many of his friends as can be persuaded to join us," said Megan cheerfully. "I am going to the library now to write a note to Colin."

"Oh. Well, I am certain that there is nothing untoward in that," said Mrs. Tyler, somewhat relieved. She picked up her embroidery hoop as Megan left the sitting room. However, there was something about Megan's last glance, brimful of mischief, that Mrs. Tyler could not quite put out of her mind.

Chapter Fourteen

Prince Kirov left the town house with mixed feelings. He knew that Megan was strongly attracted to him. He was too experienced not to recognize what was in a woman's eyes. He would have liked to have swept her off her feet and carried her back to Russia that very day. But he knew that was an impossibility. Megan was resisting her feelings for him.

"This I do not understand," he stated to the sunlit air. He, Mikhail Sergei Alexsander Kirov, had never found it difficult to charm his way into a woman's heart. Indeed, he had enjoyed many satisfying relationships. He had toyed with the thought of marriage more than once since becoming head of his family, but there had always been another woman whose eyes promised more than the last and . . .

Prince Kirov's thoughts came to an abrupt halt, as did his long strides. He stood still on the walkway, a huge handsome rock in the stream of saunterers. Prince Kirov had complete disregard for the passersby and their curious glances. He thought over his interview with Megan again, carefully. He began to smile. "Ah, my wise little dove! Now I know what is in your mind. You fear that you are not my last love. But I shall prove it to you."

With renewed purpose, Prince Kirov strode to the curb to signal his carriage. He had ordered the driver to walk the horses up and down the street while he was visiting at the town house. Then he had chosen to walk while he sorted out his thoughts. Now the time for reflection was over.

The driver had been awaiting the prince's signal and handily negotiated passage through the oncoming traffic. The carriage slipped over to the curb.

"Take me to the hotel!" Prince Kirov pulled open the door

and sprang inside. When he was seated, he began to plan in his mind almost a military strategy. He would lay siege to Megan's heart and woo her and win her. She would surrender to him before many weeks were gone. He was confident enough of that. In the meantime, there was much to be done.

When Prince Kirov reached the hotel, he at once rang for his maître'd, the head of the huge retinue that he had brought with him to London, and his faithful companion, Fedor. He questioned the maître'd first. "Has a suitable residence been acquired?"

The maître'd answered in the affirmative. "The house is even now being made ready for you, your highness. I estimate that in two days' time you shall be able to remove from this place."

"Very good, Frederick. I wish to begin entertaining immediately, in the manner to which I am accustomed. I know that I may rely upon you in all things. Spare no expense. You may go," said Prince Kirov. The maître'd bowed himself out, armed with a directive worthy of the scope of his talents. Prince Kirov turned to his remaining companion. He threw himself into a chair, one leg slung over the arm. He addressed the dwarf in Russian. "Well, Fedor? We are returned to London. Is it to your liking?"

The dwarf looked at the prince. He shrugged. "It is better at home, your highness."

Prince Kirov flashed a smile. "I, too, shall be glad to return to Russia. But I do not return without a bride, Fedor."

"No, my lord," said the dwarf, his black eyes never leaving his master's face. He was completely and utterly loyal to the prince. If he had been ordered to plunge his long dagger into the heart of an enemy, he would have done so without hesitation or regret.

"Fedor, there are things that I wish to know about Miss O'Connell's family. You know the sort of things that I mean. I wish to make a very good impression. I charge you with the task of gathering that information for me," said Prince Kirov. "Also, when the jewels that I commissioned have arrived, I wish to be notified at once."

"Consider it done, my lord," said Fedor quietly. He bowed and went to the door. Without sound he exited, quietly shutting the door behind him.

Prince Kirov stood up and stretched. The first concerns had been dealt with to his satisfaction. He could trust his household to do all that was necessary. He need not think of those matters again.

Restlessly, he paced the drawing room while he turned over in his mind his next steps. At last he went over to the desk and pulled out the chair. Seating himself, he pulled a sheet of paper to him and dipped a sharpened pen in the inkwell. He had not brought his secretary with him because the man had had the audacity to fall ill just hours before they were to leave St. Petersburg, so he was reduced to writing his own correspondence. It was a task that he viewed with impatience. However, it was necessary until his maître'd had engaged the services of an English secretary.

Prince Kirov grunted and set pen to paper. In the short time that he had been in London, he had already established his presence in English society to a limited extent. Now it was time to enlarge his exposure.

The first letter that he penned was to Lady O'Connell, expressing regret that he had missed her when he had called at the town house. Prince Kirov made known his intention to wait on her ladyship at her earliest convenience, hinting that he had something of moment to convey to her ladyship. He confidently relied upon the friendship between her ladyship and his mother, Princess Elizaveta Kirov, to smooth his path.

Prince Kirov sanded the sheet. He fully intended to insert himself firmly into Lady O'Connell's good graces. Her ladyship would then naturally grant him favor when he made known to her that he wished to court her daughter. He had already won over Mrs. Tyler. The first rule in war was to subvert any possible support which the enemy might rely upon. By the time he was finished, thought the prince, his lovely Megan would be unable to hide from his overtures behind either her mother's authority or her chaperone. And that was just where he wanted her.

The other letters that he wrote were to various hostesses and acquaintances he had met during his previous visit to England or whom he had met abroad. Soon there would be a deluge of invitations coming to him and he would become a prominent figure on the social rounds. In this way, he could make himself available to Megan as her faithful escort. Also, and his fingers clenched a little as he thought it, he would be in a position to frighten off those impudent dogs who might challenge his own claim to her hand.

Prince Kirov had no intention of losing Megan by default. She might not know her own mind and heart. She might doubt his loyalty and steadfastness. However, she would be left in no doubt of whose hand commanded her destiny.

Prince Kirov was utterly convinced that he was head and shoulders above any other gentleman worthy of the name. As such, he meant to constitute himself as Megan's protector. Any gentleman who dared to pronounce himself a suitor for Megan's hand would have him, Mikhail Kirov, to deal with.

He also wrote out a lengthy list of names for the first entertainment that he planned to host. It was necessary to acquire the services of a hostess, of course, since no function was complete without one. However, Prince Kirov anticipated no difficulty in overcoming the handicap of his bachelorhood. He knew a handful of respectable widows, any one of which would be delighted to fill this position for him. This lady would also be able to write out the invitations for him and make any last-minute adjustments to the guest list that might be required. He need not concern himself further.

When he was done, Prince Kirov shouted for a servant. He gave the sealed letters into the man's hands with instructions for delivery. When the servant had bowed himself out, the prince leaned back in his chair, feeling very well satisfied with himself. He smiled, thinking of his coming triumph. Megan was already his. Shortly he would claim her.

It was just as well that Prince Kirov was not aware of his lady's own designs or he would not have been so complacent. Megan was equally determined that Prince Kirov would not have things all his way. She wanted above all things to be utterly convinced that he was in love with her and no one else.

To that end, she devised a plan that was guaranteed to throw as many rubs in the prince's way as possible.

The first salvo in her campaign was a note sent around to her brother, Captain O'Connell. Megan requested that he get up a small party of accomplished equestrians from his fellow officers at his earliest convenience.

It chanced that Captain O'Connell was returned from his duties when the note was delivered. He read it with mingled surprise and curiosity. His sister had rarely importuned him for anything, the last time being when she had asked him to lengthen his stay in Ireland for her sake and he had refused. He still felt a twinge of guilt for his refusal to oblige her and that, coupled with his curiosity, was enough to cause him to answer her in the affirmative. He suggested that very afternoon. After all, it would cost him nothing but an hour or two to comply with his sister's request and the time would be spent in the company of convivial friends.

Megan received the captain's scribbled reply with satisfaction. Even if she was unable to drum up enough ladies to make up a respectable party, her purpose would still be accomplished. Prince Kirov would be given the opportunity that very day to see that she was already acquainted with several gentlemen. Megan at once dashed off another note to her sister-in-law, begging her to procure Lady Stallcroft's permission for the Stallcroft girls to go riding. She also asked that Mrs. O'Connell solicit Miss Bancroft and whomever else her sister-in-law might interest in the impromptu outing, ending with the assurance that the ladies would have adequate escort.

She was interrupted in her task by the sounds of an arrival. Curious, Megan laid down her pen. She opened the library door and looked out into the hall. She was astonished by the sight of her eldest brother giving over his beaver and gloves to a footman. The butler was directing another footman where to take Mr. O'Connell's portmanteau and valise. Megan stepped into the hall. "Lionel?"

Mr. O'Connell turned. "Megan!"

The ludicrous look of astonishment on his face made Megan chuckle. She advanced on him with her hand out. "Good morning, Lionel. I trust that your journey was comfortable and uneventful?"

"Megan, what on earth are you doing here?" Mr. O'Connell took her hand and continued to stare at her. "You are supposed to be in St. Petersburg."

"That is what everyone has been telling me," said Megan with a small laugh. "Have you come to London to see Sophronia? You will be greatly surprised by the change in her. She is become quite the social creature, I assure you."

"Yes. That is, I came to—I cannot believe, however—" Breaking off, Mr. O'Connell frowned and, realizing that he was still holding his sister's hand, abruptly let it go. "I am not here to see Sophronia. I came to see our mother. Is her ladyship at home?"

"She is still in her apartments, I believe," said Megan, glancing toward the butler for confirmation. Digby gave the smallest of nods. She looked again at her brother. "I should perhaps warn you that her ladyship is not in best form at present. However, I am certain that your arrival must gladden her spirits."

"Meaning precisely what?" asked Mr. O'Connell suspiciously.

"Mother has been rather preoccupied with Sophronia's dashing popularity. She has taken it in rather bad part, I am afraid. And, of course, she has grave qualms over my comeout," said Megan calmly.

Mr. O'Connell's frown deepened at his sister's description of the situation, particularly in regard to his wife, but he seized upon the other information that she had given to him. "Your come-out! I know nothing of this."

"How could you, indeed, when you thought me to still be in St. Petersburg?" asked Megan. "Now do go up and see our mother, Lionel. I know that she will be utterly delighted to tell you all about it!"

The butler gave a discreet cough. "Her ladyship has been informed of your arrival, sir. She is most desirous of seeing you and requests that you step up directly."

"I shall talk with you again later, Megan, for I mean to get to the bottom of all this," said Mr. O'Connell as he started toward the stairs.

"Just as you wish, Lionel," said Megan, already making up her mind that the less she saw of her brother the better she would like it. She really did not understand why she had come out of the library to greet him at all. Lionel's belligerence was distasteful to her and aroused some very unkind thoughts toward him. It was a pity that they could not seem to get along, but always seemed to come to loggerheads.

Megan turned back into the library and added a postscript to the note to her sister-in-law. Sophronia would want to be informed that Lionel had indeed come to London. As Megan sanded the sheet, she wondered what would come of it all, for Lionel had not seemed to be in a particularly conciliatory mood. However, that was not her concern, but Sophronia's business. She gave the note to a footman with directions that it was to be delivered directly into Mrs. O'Connell's hands.

Then she returned to the sitting room, where she was reasonably certain of still finding Mrs. Tyler. "Gwyneth, the most extraordinary thing! Lionel has arrived and is closeted with my mother at this moment," she announced.

"My word! Lionel here, in London! But what does it mean?" said Mrs. Tyler, looking up from her embroidery.

"Do you recall that I related to you that my mother wrote to him about Sophronia?" asked Megan. "He has come up because of that. He is staying here, I think."

"Oh, dear," said Mrs. Tyler with dismay. "We shall see some unpleasantness, then."

"So I should suppose. But it is Sophronia's business, after all. And I suspect that she is well able to handle Lionel," said Megan.

"That may be," retorted Mrs. Tyler. "Nevertheless, I do not care to be caught in the crossfire when those two meet, as inevitably they must. Nor do I wish to look across the breakfast table at your brother's black-browed face each morning. It is too bad that Lionel is not putting up at a hotel!"

"You are hard, indeed, Gwyneth!" said Megan, her eyes gleaming with amusement. She was not at all surprised by her companion's blunt opinion, for her eldest brother had at best treated Mrs. Tyler with indifference and at worst with a sort of bullying condescension.

"You must forgive me, Megan. However, I intend to make every effort I can to avoid Lionel while he is with us," said Mrs. Tyler. "I am enjoying the Season and I do not wish it to be marred by unpleasantness. Fortunately, I am pledged to Lady Mansfield for a drive in the park this afternoon, so I need not hide in my rooms until dinner for fear of running foul of Lionel's surliness."

"I do not blame you in the least, for it is very much what I have decided, too," said Megan. "I am myself going out riding with Colin and some others. I have sent a note to Sophronia begging her company, as well."

"That is a very good progam," approved Mrs. Tyler. "I cannot be said to be shirking my duties as your chaperone when you are with your brother and Sophronia."

Megan did not reveal to her friend the true motive behind the outing, instead agreeing that it was all very unexceptional. "I suppose that since you are going out with Lady Mansfield you might possibly run into her nephew, Mr. Bretton?"

Mrs. Tyler pinkened becomingly. She gave a rather vigorous tug of her embroidering needle. "It is not outside the realm of possibility," she said. "Lady Mansfield is most sincerely attached to the gentleman. And for his part, Mr. Bretton is very kind and considerate toward her ladyship. He visits her nearly every day. It is wonderful, indeed, to see the affection between them."

Megan hid a smile. She knew that from the moment of introduction to the gentleman some days previously, Mrs. Tyler had been at great pains to cover her interest in him. "Well, I shall leave you now. I suspect that if I do not leave the house quite soon that I shall receive a summons from Lionel. He told me that he means to get to the bottom of everything that has been happening. He is particularly exercised by astonishment at my come-out."

"Why did you not say so at the outset!" exclaimed Mrs. Tyler, setting aside her embroidery. "We must both make ourselves scarce at once, Megan. I have no wish to be called upon to explain my part in your come-out. And it would be just like Lionel to do so, too."

"Yes, he is rather officious, isn't he?" agreed Megan. "I thought I would call on Annabelle Stallcroft and Maria Bancroft to see if I might persuade them to go shopping. Do you wish to go with us, Gwyneth?"

"That will suit admirably. Then you may set me down at Lady Mansfield's before your return here," said Mrs. Tyler, rising with energy. "I shall be ready in ten minutes, Megan. Have you requested a carriage already?"

"Yes, when I sent the note off to Sophronia. I shall meet you belowstairs," said Megan as she followed her companion out of the sitting room.

Megan managed to avoid her brother Lionel for the rest of the morning with the shopping expedition. When she returned shortly before the agreed-upon time for the afternoon ride, she quietly repaired to her rooms until she was informed that her party had arrived.

She returned downstairs dressed in one of her most becoming riding habits. It was cut from green velvet with a tight-fitting bodice and sleeves, a flowing lace cravat, and a sweeping skirt. On her head was a matching beaver, decorated with a black curling feather. The ensemble was in striking contrast to her pale coloring and bright burnished locks. She pulled on her supple riding gloves, her whip under her arm, and left a message with the butler. "Pray tell Mrs. Tyler when she returns from her drive where I have gone."

"And her ladyship, miss?" asked Digby suggestively.

Megan looked up quickly, meeting the butler's gaze. She suddenly chuckled. "Yes, if her ladyship should inquire!"

Hearing Megan's voice, Mr. O'Connell emerged from the drawing room just as she turned to the front door. "Megan! I should like a word with you."

Megan raised her brows at her brother's peremptory tone. "Do you, Lionel? I am so sorry! It is not convenient just now, for my friends are waiting for me. Perhaps when I return." She swept out of the front door.

Behind her, Mr. O'Connell turned back into the drawing room, his expression one of exasperated temper.

Chapter Fifteen

The equestrians awaited Megan at the bottom of the steps. Captain O'Connell had brought a handsome hack for her use, as she had asked him to, and Megan thanked him with a quick smile as she mounted with the help of a groom.

Captain O'Connell saluted her with lazy affection before introducing her to his friends. He was surprised when three of the gentlemen claimed previous acquaintance with Megan, greeting her with the gallantry reserved for eligible and lovely young ladies.

Lord Dorsey and Sir Lawrence were members of the Lifeguards, for like Captain O'Connell, they were well over six feet in height and sat their horses as though they were one with the magnificent animals. Lord Haven and the other two sporting gentlemen were slightly raffish fellows, dandified in high shirt points and elaborately cut coats. These high-spirited gentlemen made a practice of enjoying life as hard and fast as they possibly could. Their conversation was larded with references to gaming and sporting events and social functions.

Casting a glance about at the escort her brother had provided, Megan thought she could not have done better herself in gathering together such a splendid example of hedonistic gentlemen.

Mrs. O'Connell was with the gentlemen, mounted on a fine bay hack. Her habit was celestial blue, trimmed with quantities of gold lace that complimented her blond hair. She greeted Megan with an amused expression. "My dear! You should have warned me. I had no notion that I would be taking my reputation in my hands with a simple ride in the park."

"Unfair, Mrs. O'Connell! We are the very pink of gentility," exclaimed Lord Haven.

This roused laughter and sallies from the other gentlemen.

Megan took the opportunity to inquire the whereabouts of the Misses Stallcroft and Miss Bancroft. "They will be meeting us at the park," said Mrs. O'Connell. "I suggested to Lady Stallcroft that it might be preferable for Annabelle and Phoebe to meet Miss Bancroft before going to the park. They would then have the benefit of an extra groom in attendance."

"I am glad that her ladyship consented to allow Annabelle and Phoebe off the leash, if only for a little while," said Megan.

Mrs. O'Connell laughed. "If her ladyship had known what sort of party it was to be, nothing could have persuaded her to allow those two girls to come out, even if it is under my aegis. My dear, whatever were you thinking of to ask Colin to provide our escort? Surely you must have known the sort of gentlemen that he would bring!"

Megan laughed. "Of course I did. What could be more entertaining than riding with a set of sad rattles?" She said nothing more, believing that it was not the right moment to divulge to her sister-in-law the little scheme that she had revolving in her head. There were too many ears that could catch a careless word.

One of the dandies, Mr. Peasbody, took instant good-natured exception to her description of himself and his companions. "I say, Miss O'Connell! I may be a rattle but I am rarely sad! Now Newton here can fall into the mopes easy as falling down."

The other dandified gentleman shook his head in a mournful manner. "Miss O'Connell, I crave your opinion. I ask you, can one regard that cravat without one's sensibilities suffering?"

"Here, now!" protested Mr. Peasbody, raising his fingers gently to his exquisitely tied neckcloth. "I'll have you know that it took me two hours and half a dozen destroyed neckcloths to achieve this."

Mr. Newton shook his head. "You see how it is, Miss O'Connell. But one must make the best of it when one's friend has done his poor best."

The raillery continued with much laughter and exchange of

outrageous insults, which amused Mrs. O'Connell and Megan very much.

The riders approached the gates of the park. Just outside waited the other ladies of the party, accompanied by a trio of grooms. Fresh introductions were made. Miss Stallcroft regarded Captain O'Connell with dismay and she cast a glance of reproach at Megan and Mrs. O'Connell. "Oh, Mama shall be so displeased!" she murmured.

"Never mind, Annabelle. I shall make all right," said Mrs. O'Connell reassuringly.

Without seeming to do so, Megan watched curiously the meeting between Miss Phoebe Stallcroft and her brother. Miss Phoebe colored prettily as she nodded to him, while Captain O'Connell made a stiff bow from his saddle. Neither spoke a word to the other. Megan noticed that Miss Phoebe was not as reticent with any of the other gentlemen, greeting them easily and with a bright smile; nor was Captain O'Connell backward with either Miss Stallcroft or Miss Bancroft. It was apparent to Megan that there was indeed something of moment between her brother and Miss Phoebe.

When the party started through the park, their close formation relaxed so that the riders were not so bunched together. Mrs. O'Connell seized the first opportunity and offered to hold a few private words with Megan. "My dear, I must thank you for the warning that you gave me," she said in a low voice. "I at once issued directions to my staff that I was not receiving. I was in a positive quake that Lionel would come to the town house and he did! I saw him from the window. He was very angry to be turned away, let me tell you!"

"So that was why he was in a black temper when I left," said Megan cheerfully. "But then, Lionel is scarcely ever in good humor. I have often wondered whether he suffers from biliousness."

Mrs. O'Connell glanced quickly at Megan. "Was Lionel at the house just now? Do you know if he saw me from the window? He is quite capable of following us if he did."

"No, I do not think that he did. He came out of the back drawing room to speak to me," said Megan. She cast a curious glance at her sister-in-law. "Why ever did you not let him come up to see you this morning? Surely you intend to talk to him, now that he has come to town for that purpose."

Mrs. O'Connell flushed. "You will think me a coward, Megan, but I do not feel able to do so just yet." She looked away to stare between her horse's ears as she frowned over her thoughts. "It is difficult to explain. But before I condescend to speak privately to Lionel, I wish him to see me in society first. I want him to see me as I am now, not as the same woman that I was before I left. Does that make any sense at all?"

"Yes, of course it does. I do not blame you in the least, Sophronia. Lionel is used to dealing with you in a certain way. It will do him a world of good to realize that he must learn new habits," said Megan warmly.

"That is it precisely," said Mrs. O'Connell with a quick smile.

At that moment Mrs. O'Connell's attention was claimed by Sir Lawrence and she dropped behind. Her place was taken by Captain O'Connell, who sidled his horse up beside Megan. He wore a frown and his voice was clipped. "You did not tell me that the Miss Stallcrofts would make up part of the party, Megan. I would not have consented to it if I had known."

"Why, what is there in that, Colin? Do you not like Miss Stallcroft and Miss Phoebe?" asked Megan, glancing at him.

He shook his head impatiently. "It is not that! Perhaps you are not aware that— But that is neither here nor there! How did you come to meet them, Megan?"

"They are Sophronia's cousins. I do not think that any impropriety or surprise can be attached to Sophronia inviting them to accompany her on an outing such as this," said Megan calmly. "But perhaps you are put out because you and Miss Phoebe have been the subject of gossip?"

"So you have heard that, have you?" Captain O'Connell regarded her grimly, his blue eyes hard. "Just what is in your head, dear sister? I warn you, I shall not have you or anyone else interfering in my affairs."

"Is it an affair, Colin?" asked Megan quietly.

"Megan! I should say not!" exclaimed Captain O'Connell. His gloved hand had jerked on the bridle and his horse tossed its head in protest. "I scarcely know the girl! What happened was blown completely out of proportion. It was merely the impulse of the moment that led me to— Nothing would have come of it, except that Lady Stallcroft chanced upon us at that moment."

"That was careless of you, Colin. Completely bacon-brained, in fact, and quite unlike you. Surely you knew how closely Lady Stallcroft watches over her daughters. Of course you did! And yet you were caught in the very act of kissing her daughter. What might one suppose from that, Colin?" said Megan, looking over at him and smiling a little.

"It was an unfortunate thing all around. That is all!" snapped Captain O'Connell.

"Oh, I think it a bit more. I think that you engineered your own fall from grace so that you would have an excuse for keeping away from Phoebe. In the process, you also held Phoebe up to public censure, which I think is quite despicable. However, all must be sacrificed to your own self-interest, must it not?" said Megan.

She did not wait for her brother to shake himself out of his astonishment and reply, but set heel to her horse. The mare bounded forward to catch up with the lead riders.

"That is absolute rot!" exclaimed Captain O'Connell hotly to his sister's back. He started to say more, only catching himself back when he saw a couple of interested glances thrown his way by his cronies.

"Anything wrong, Colin?" asked Lord Dorsey.

Captain O'Connell shook his head. He made a remark about Tattersall's next auction, calculated to draw interest away from himself and so it did. For the next several minutes there grew a heated debate among the gentlemen about a certain celebrated team that was said to be going on the auction block. Even Lord Haven and his companions, who had been paying extravagant compliments to Miss Bancroft and Miss Phoebe, suspended their delightful byplay to offer their opinions.

"Monty would never be selling them unless he was completely rolled up," said Lord Haven positively.

"He would if they've slipped their wind," suggested one of his friends.

There was a general outcry at this, most of the gentlemen coming down heavily on the side of the theory of the Honorable Montebatten Swail's pecuniary circumstances as having been the reason for his getting rid of such a fine team.

"The man is a hardened gamester and his luck has been fairly out this last month," observed Lord Dorsey. "I've heard that he is pretty heavily into dun territory."

"He always seems to come about, though," said Captain O'Connell with a shrug.

"Look! There is Monty himself. Why don't you ask him about his team?" challenged Sir Lawrence.

"You're mad! The man takes a distempered freak if one chances to look at him in the wrong way," muttered Lord Haven.

The gentleman in question, himself mounted on an elegant hack, slowed when he saw the riding party. "Ah, O'Connell! Dorsey, Lawrence and Haven, as well!"

"Hallo, Monty!" said Captain O'Connell, reaching over to shake the gentleman's hand. "Let me make you known to my sister, Miss Megan O'Connell, and the Misses Stallcroft. You will know everyone else, of course."

"I am well-acquainted with Mrs. O'Connell. How do you do, ma'am? And Miss O'Connell! Enchanting! Did you say Stallcroft? But of course! I am delighted, Miss Stallcroft, Miss Phoebe. Ah, Miss Bancroft, your obedient servant," said the Honorable Montebatten Swail, bowing with a flourish from his saddle. He stayed a few moments, talking easily to various of the gentlemen. His unreadable gaze dwelled thoughtfully on Miss Bancroft and Miss O'Connell. He declined an offer to join the party, but set himself to call upon the ladies at some future date.

"Mister Swail seems a nice enough gentleman," ventured Miss Stallcroft.

One of their escort chuckled. Sir Lawrence said earnestly, "You stay as far away from Monty Swail as you can, Miss Stallcroft. He is well enough, but not of the best *ton*."

"Oh, has he a wicked reputation?" asked Miss Bancroft innocently. "I mean, besides that of being a hardened gamester?"

"Just so," said Lord Dorsey with a smile. "I would not wish

any young lady to fall captive to Swail's importunities, Miss Bancroft."

"Do you mean that he is on the lookout for an heiress, my lord?" asked Miss Bancroft with a hint of mischief in her expressive eyes. "Then certainly I, for one, shall be very careful of him!"

"Oh, I don't know! It might be rather fun to be the object of interest to such a desperate character," said Miss Phoebe contemplatively, watching the gentleman ride away. "Not that it should ever come my way, for I am scarcely an heiress, after all!"

The gentlemen all laughed at Miss Phoebe's merry declaration, the sole exception being Captain O'Connell. He scowled and looked at the young miss with a hard glint in his eyes.

"Phoebe!" uttered Miss Stallcroft. She had seen the captain's glance and read condemnation in it.

"You embarrass your sister, ma'am," said Captain O'Connell shortly.

Miss Phoebe tossed her head. Her blue eyes flashed. "I am tired of such a snail's pace. May we not exercise the horses a little?"

"Indeed we may," said Mrs. O'Connell cordially. "There is a short green up ahead that will do very well. But mind, Phoebe! It must not be a race!" Heedless of the admonishment, Miss Phoebe set heel to her horse and bounded swiftly away.

"Yoiks!" exclaimed Lord Haven. "It's a race! Tally-ho!" He and three of the other gentlemen set themselves to catch up. Captain O'Connell muttered something under his breath and spurred his own animal.

"Forgive me, Megan, but I must not let Phoebe out of my sight. Drat that girl!" exclaimed Mrs. O'Connell, also taking flight. One of the grooms also kicked his horse forward.

Megan laughed and watched what was assuredly beginning to assume a mad scramble over the green.

"I do envy Phoebe her liveliness," said Miss Bancroft, also laughing.

"Miss Phoebe is an engaging romp," agreed Lord Dorsey. "However, I fear that I am more inclined to favor a more restful style." Miss Bancroft cast down her eyes demurely, quite content to bask in his lordship's admiration.

Miss Stallcroft, thoroughly mortified by his lordship's speech, sent an agonized glance in Megan's direction. "Mama will be so very angry," she whispered.

"Your mama will know nothing about it," said Megan firmly. "Her ladyship will ask Sophronia for a report and that will be the end of it, for Sophronia stands your friend, as I think you already know."

"Yes; I do know it." Miss Stallcroft breathed a sigh of relief. She raised an uncertain gaze to Megan. "You must think me a regular noddy for caring so much, but— "

"Nonsense, I understand perfectly," said Megan gently.

"My word, who is that magnificent horseman?" exclaimed Miss Bancroft.

Megan looked around quickly. Coming toward them was a very large gentleman on a powerful chestnut stallion. Beside him rode a diminutive man, equally well mounted. She felt her heart give a great leap in her breast.

"Whoever he is, Miss Bancroft, he has excellent taste in horseflesh. Where the devil did he get that animal, for I swear I've not seen its like before," said Lord Dorsey, his gaze fixed on the prancing stallion.

"Why, he is coming straight over!" Miss Bancroft looked quickly toward Megan, to whom the gentleman had touched his beaver. "Do you know him, then, Miss O'Connell?"

"Indeed I do," said Megan. She smiled and reined in as Prince Kirov stopped before them. "Prince Kirov, it is delightful to see you again."

Prince Kirov bowed from the saddle. "Mademoiselle O'Connell, well met. You will remember Fedor, whom you kindly asked about at our last meeting."

"Of course I do." Megan greeted the dwarf with polite friendliness. She saw that Miss Bancroft was agog with curiosity. "Allow me to introduce you to some of my friends," she said, performing the office quickly. She watched in amusement as the prince set himself to charm Miss Bancroft and Miss Stallcroft. The two ladies succumbed almost immediately to his glinting smile and polished compliments.

Lord Dorsey was equally impressed, but more with the horse than the man. Almost at once he launched an easy discourse about the stallion. His lordship was greatly astonished that Prince Kirov had actually brought the horse all the way from St. Petersburg. "I wonder that you should have exposed him to the rigors of such a long journey, your highness," he said.

Prince Kirov flashed a gleaming smile. "But I had no choice, my lord! I could not be assured of finding another mount in England that suits me as well."

"That is true," agreed Lord Dorsey, shrewdly weighing the prince's large frame with his eyes. "I imagine it is difficult to find a horse that is up to your weight."

"Prince Kirov is related to some of the most famous horse breeders in Russia," said Megan, smoothly breaking into what was promising to degenerate into a sporting conversation. She could tell that Miss Bancroft, for one, was becoming slightly bored. "The rest of our party is unfortunately not with us just now, Mikhail, or I would make you known to them as well. There was got up an impromptu race across the green and we four have been quite abandoned."

"A race!" Prince Kirov's brows rose. "Here, in proper England? You astound me!"

Miss Bancroft giggled. Lord Dorsey gave a hearty laugh, saying, "Yes, you may well say so, your highness! But there was no stopping it once Miss Phoebe took it into her head to set spur to her mare. It was a challenge not to be easily overlooked!"

"My sister is impulsive and young, your highness," said Miss Stallcroft with quiet dignity.

"Then I shall like her very much, Miss Stallcroft. I, too, can be impulsive, although I have long since outgrown my foolish youth," said Prince Kirov.

He slid a glance in Megan's direction. "I am well able to set my mind with purpose to a difficult task and accomplish it. I do not know that I have ever failed in my objectives. I sweep all before me, in fact."

He was satisfied when he saw a faint tinge of color come into her cheeks, even though she did not look at him but instead seemed intent on the twitching of her horse's ears. "My Lord Dorsey, do you not find it to be the same for you? Do not the years prove to be a tempering force upon one's character? One comes to know one's own mind better than ever before."

"That is undoubtedly true," agreed Lord Dorsey. "A certain steadiness of character is inevitable as one grows older."

"Precisely what I was saying to Miss O'Connell earlier," said Prince Kirov promptly. "She takes exception, however, and maintains that one who was volatile can never become more steadfast or faithful of purpose."

Megan knew that she was blushing hotly. She sensed the curiosity roused in her companions by the prince's comments. Smiling, with a sparkling challenge in her eyes, she said, "You choose to tease me, your highness. But I am not to be so ignobly baited."

She addressed her companions, giving a light explanation of the familiarity between herself and the prince. "Princess Elizaveta Kirov was my hostess while I was in St. Petersburg. Mrs. Tyler and I came to know Prince Kirov quite well. He was very attentive to see to our enjoyment of his country."

"Ah, some of our racers return," said Lord Dorsey. He hailed the first to reach them. "Well, Haven, who took the honors?"

"Oh, Lawrence did, of course. That great brute of his has the longest stride I have ever seen," said Lord Haven cheerfully. He caught sight of the stallion bestrode by a stranger. "I say, there's a beast that could give your Rufus a go, Lawrence!"

"This is Prince Mikhail Kirov," said Megan, performing introductions quickly.

As she had expected, the high-spirited gentlemen quickly accepted the prince as one of their own. They were making exactly the impression she had hoped, as evidenced when Prince Kirov at length drew alongside her and commented, "You have a lively set of friends, mademoiselle."

Megan agreed with a smile. "Yes, they are all very kind."

"Particularly the gentlemen?" he inquired softly.

She laughed and shook her head. "I have not said so, nor shall I! You must draw your own conclusions, Mikhail."

The prince smiled. "I rest easy, Megan. I see none here to frighten me."

At that moment, Miss Phoebe came riding up. Her cheeks were flushed and her eyes were abnormally bright. She was shortly followed by Captain O'Connell and Mrs. O'Connell. Without preamble, she addressed her sister. "Annabelle, I wish to go home now. I have developed the headache."

"Oh! Of course, Phoebe, we shall do so at once," said Miss Stallcroft. She stammered their excuses to the company, then she and her sister turned aside with their grooms.

Megan glanced swiftly at her sister-in-law, but Mrs. O'Connell briefly shook her head. Megan interpreted that to mean that Sophronia would tell her later what had occurred. She had naturally noticed that Sophronia had lingered behind with her brother and Miss Phoebe, and had wondered what had kept them from coming up to the rest of the party for so long. Obviously something of moment had happened. Her brother Colin was looking as black as a thundercloud as he stared after the Misses Stallcroft.

"I should accompany them at least to my own door," said Miss Bancroft. "For we all came together."

"Allow me to count myself your escort," said Lord Dorsey promptly.

"And I!" exclaimed Mr. Peasbody. "You will not have it all your own way, Dorsey."

"You will not go alone," said Lord Haven gaily. "I am ready to cut you both out for the pleasure of Miss Bancroft's company."

Miss Bancroft protested with pretty confusion the vying for her favors, but she was pleased nevertheless. Before too many minutes had passed, the riders had separated into two parties. The Stallcroft girls and Miss Bancroft carried off with them the majority of the gentlemen, including Captain O'Connell, while Megan and Mrs. O'Connell were escorted by Sir Lawrence and Mr. Newton.

Prince Kirov took his leave, citing an engagement that he could not shirk. He rode off with his silent companion. Sir Lawrence glanced after the prince. He smiled lazily, sliding his intelligent gaze at Megan. "That is a rare gentleman," he remarked.

Megan was embarrassed to feel heat rise into her face. Sir Lawrence had caught her staring after the prince. "Yes, he is," she said quietly.

Before turning off into her own street, Mrs. O'Connell held out her hand to each of the remaining gentlemen. When she parted from Megan, she said in a hurried aside, "I shall send a note round to you later!" Mr. Newton gallantly constituted himself her protector and turned off with Mrs. O'Connell to see her to her door. Sir Lawrence saw Megan home and used his time well by soliciting her for a dance at a ball later that evening.

Chapter Sixteen

Megan heard from Mrs. O'Connell as promised. Her hurried note notified Megan that she was off that moment to Lady Stallcroft's residence, for things had taken such a turn with Colin and Phoebe Stallcroft that she wasn't quite certain how it would end. It seemed that Colin had declared himself to Phoebe and she had flatly refused him! However, Captain O'Connell had not accepted this rebuff and had vowed to seek an audience with both Lord and Lady Stallcroft that same day to apologize for his previous outrageous behavior and to beg their consideration of his suit.

Megan had heard nothing more from Mrs. O'Connell before she and Mrs. Tyler set out for the ball that evening. She thought that her sister-in-law would probably be among the guests, and contained her impatient curiosity with the hope that sometime during the evening she might be able to learn from Sophronia what had happened. The burgeoning romance between her brother Colin and Phoebe Stallcroft was becoming dear to her heart.

Lady O'Connell came in a separate carriage escorted by her son, Mister O'Connell. "It is no use saying that we four might ride together, Lionel," said her ladyship, when her son pointed out that it must look odd for Megan to arrive on her own with no one but Mrs. Tyler to accompany her. "I absolutely refuse to feel crowded in my own carriage."

Lady Bishop's ball was an extravaganza to which all of the *ton* had been invited. Long before the hostess was able to leave her station in greeting her guests, she was gratified by hearing the function described as a terrible squeeze. The crowds, bejeweled and magnificently attired in silks and satins, milled around the dance floor. An orchestra played con-

stantly for the dancers and the din of conversation and laughter
was such that none could hear their neighbors without raising
their voices. The refreshment room was next to the orchestra
and it was nearly as loud. It was quieter in the card room, located at the far end of the ballroom, where several tables had
been set up for the pleasure of those whose tastes ran to games
of chance.

Megan's hand was solicited for nearly every dance, Sir
Lawrence having the honor of bearing her off first. He was tall
and personable and Megan enjoyed his company very much.

It was not long before she had the strangest feeling of being
under observation and she turned her head. She discovered
that Prince Kirov's unfathomable gaze was fixed upon her,
and Megan gave the slightest nod. The prince scowled, but
Megan was not displeased. She had told him that she had acquired admirers. It would do Prince Kirov good to realize that
she had spoken nothing less than the truth.

Megan knew virtually everyone in attendance, since she had
been on the town long enough to have been introduced into all
the polite circles. She moved among the company with the
ease of familiarity, her eyes sparkling as she exchanged witti-
cisms and laughter.

Sometime in the progress of the evening, when the ballroom
had become stiflingly warm, a gentleman volunteered to go
after an ice for her, and Megan remained in her seat. She
watched Mrs. Tyler finish a country dance with Mr. Bretton, a
solid-looking gentleman of middle years. Her companion was
returned with heightened color and a bright look in her eyes.
"Are you enjoying yourself, Gwyneth?" asked Megan, leaning
over.

"Oh, very much! I do not believe that we have ever been to
a better party," said Mrs. Tyler, fanning herself. Her gaze followed Mr. Bretton's retreating form for a moment, before she
suddenly turned to Megan. "My dear! Did you chance to see
the meeting between Lionel and Sophronia?"

Megan chuckled. "Indeed I did, and I was never more entertained. I do not believe that Lionel even recognized her for
several seconds. Then I saw him go straight up to her and say
something that I could see put her into an absolute flame."

"He demanded that Sophronia leave with him at once and she refused!" said Mrs. Tyler.

"So that was why Lionel turned on his heel and stamped off. His expression was thunderous, too. It set a few tongues wagging, I'll wager," said Megan.

"Of that there can be no doubt. I was asked who Lionel was by Lady Mansfield's sister, a dear creature but a sad gossip, I'm afraid, and when I told her, she positively radiated interest," said Mrs. Tyler. She shook her head. "I really fear that Lionel's arrival, and the way he has already behaved just tonight, will set in motion a rare scandal."

"Yes, I shouldn't wonder at it in the least. It can't be helped, however. Lionel *will* try to bully his way," said Megan. "We will be questioned, naturally, by all sorts of people. For my part, I shan't say anything that will add fuel to the fire."

"No, indeed! Silence is certainly the best course," agreed Mrs. Tyler.

Megan's gallant returned with the cold refreshment and sat down beside her to dally in a light flirtation. This pleasant interlude was interrupted by Lord Haven, who claimed Miss O'Connell's hand for the next set. When the other gallant had gone off, Lord Haven confided, "I was hoping that you would prefer going into the card room with me, Miss O'Connell. There is a famous game going forward. I left Nick Peasbody and Newton in dire straits and I am anxious to see how they fare."

Megan laughed. "Of course! How shabby it would be of me to keep you in suspense of their fate by tying you to the dance floor."

"I knew you would understand," said Lord Haven with boyish naïveté. He bowed to Mrs. Tyler and escorted Megan toward the card room.

When Megan and Lord Haven entered the card room, it was to a hushed atmosphere. All eyes appeared to be fixed on the players at the table in the middle of the floor. Mr. Montebatten Swail, Mr. Peasbody, Mr. Newton, and two other gentlemen were engaged in a serious struggle, as could be seen from the mound of guineas, notes, and scribbled IOUs in the middle of the table.

Only the whisper of the cards against the green baize broke the silence as each man discarded and more cards were dealt. At last the hand was played out, and a collective breath was loosed around the room. There were a few chuckles as Mr. Peasbody shook his head and snorted in disgust. Mr. Swail smiled and gathered in the pile of clinking coins and notes.

"Well, Swail, your luck is in at last," said one of the losing gentlemen, rising.

"I think it must be," agreed Mr. Swail suavely. He looked up just then and caught sight of Megan standing beside Lord Haven, who was commiserating with his friends. "Ah, Miss O'Connell! Do you play cards?"

It was an era when knowing the rudiments of card playing was almost a prerequisite in polite society. Megan had several times enjoyed making up one of a foursome. "On occasion, sir. But I am no real hand at it, I fear."

"You must allow others to judge that, Miss O'Connell. Pray sit down with me for a friendly turn. I give you my word that I shall not fleece you," said Mr. Swail.

"Take my revenge for me, Miss O'Connell!" said Mr. Newton laughingly. Several of the other gentlemen joined in urging the lady to acquit the losers. Before she quite knew how it came about, Megan found herself sitting opposite Mr. Swail. She knew herself to be fairly competent with the pasteboards and so it did not cross her mind that what she had lent herself to could be in any way dangerous.

Within minutes, however, Megan realized that she was in a fight for her life. Mr. Swail was a gamester through and through. He did not play except to win and there was no such thing as mercy either in the astute placing of his cards or in his heart. Megan looked across at the urbane, smiling gentleman, seeing for the first time the cold, calculating light in his eyes. She recalled Sir Lawrence's offhand warning to Miss Bancroft about Mr. Swail during the ride in the park, and with a sinking feeling felt herself to be lost. She was not a gambler and to see her vowels in the hands of a gentleman who was minute by minute proving himself to be quite without character was sobering.

Finally, she refused to stake another vowel. "I am sorry, Mr. Swail. But I have nothing more," said Megan quietly.

Mr. Swail laughed. He was the only person present who was in the least amused. What had begun in good fun had taken an ugly turn, and there was not a gentleman present who did not know it. "Come, Miss O'Connell! Have you nothing left?"

She shook her head. "I fear not, Mr. Swail."

He suddenly reached out and pushed all of his winnings into the middle of the table. "All or nothing, Miss O'Connell! Does that not persuade you?"

Megan did not allow her expression to betray how uncertain she felt. That would have been fatal. One did not reveal weakness on the hunting field or at the card table.

She unclasped the bracelet from around her slim wrist and tossed it onto the table. "A lady's token, sir. Surely as such it must match the challenge?" It was a grand gesture and unexpected. She calmly looked across at her opponent.

"By Jove, yes! I for one shall back that bet, Miss O'Connell," said Lord Haven, leaning forward to put down a small pile of guineas. Someone laughed and another gentleman declared himself quite as ready to back Miss O'Connell's hand and thrust forward with his own offerings.

Mr. Swail smiled. There was even a flicker of amusement in his gray eyes. "Very well. We shall see if your luck is in, Miss O'Connell." Deliberately he dealt the remaining cards and swept up his own.

Megan looked at her cards, careful not to allow by even the flicker of an eyelid any betrayal to her opponent. Without a word passing between her and Mr. Swail, the hand was played out. By a narrow margin, Megan rose the winner, amid the laughter and congratulations of her cavaliers.

"Allow me to gather your winnings for you, Miss O'Connell," said Mr. Newton, bowing over her hand.

"Thank you, Mr. Newton, I would be grateful," said Megan.

"Your bracelet, Miss O'Connell," said Mr. Swail with a saturnine smile.

Megan accepted it from his hand with thanks. She clasped it about her wrist again, silently vowing never again to be caught in such harrowing circumstances. It was one thing to play cards and quite another to plunge over her head.

"Perhaps you will honor the loser with a turn about the dance floor, Miss O'Connell?" asked Mr. Swail suavely.

Megan hesitated; then she heard the striking up of a country dance. It was treading dangerously to encourage the gentleman after making such a spectacle of herself. But she would not run frightened of shadows. She smiled and laid her fingers on the gentleman's arm. "I would be delighted, Mr. Swail."

However, before the couple had reached the floor they were intercepted. Captain O'Connell smiled at Mr. Swail with a somewhat steely look in his eyes. "I beg pardon, Monty, but I've come to steal my sister away for a few moments. You do not mind, I hope?"

"Of course not. Why should I?" Mr. Swail smiled and bowed, gracefully relinquishing Megan. But not before he had turned over her hand and pressed a kiss into her palm.

Without further ado, Captain O'Connell steered his sister away. "I don't know what maggot has got into your brain tonight, Megan. I'm just glad that I am at hand to keep you from compounding your mistake!" he said in a low, terse voice.

"Colin, whatever do you think you are doing?" asked Megan, shaking off her brother's hand. "I was simply going to go down a country dance with Mr. Swail."

"Yes, after playing cards with him! Monty Swail, of all people! I was never more shocked than when I came out of the refreshment room and someone told me! The whole room is buzzing, Megan," said Captain O'Connell.

"Oh, is it? How gratifying, to be sure," said Megan with a small chuckle. She could envision Prince Kirov's expression at learning of her slightly scandalous escapade. It was worth every nerve-racking moment if it served to incite his protective nature.

"That fellow is not someone you should even acknowledge. He's a rotter of the worst sort," said Captain O'Connell. He was still scowling after the retreating gentleman. If he had ever thought about the Honorable Montebatten Swail, it was to regard that gentleman with a sort of friendly indifference. How-

ever, that was at an end now that the gentleman had made his
sister the object of every whisperer in the place.

"I am well aware of that, now," said Megan. "That is precisely why I agreed to dance with him."

Captain O'Connell swung his head around and stared hard
at her. "Have you gone mad?" he demanded.

Megan smiled up at him. "Not at all. I am quite aware of
what I am doing. It is a little game all my own."

"Little game? Megan, you could find yourself ostracized for
associating with such scoundrels," said Captain O'Connell.
"Pray enlighten me. What exactly are you attempting to accomplish by running such a ridiculous risk?"

"Never mind, Colin," said Megan, chuckling. "My affairs
are not your concern."

Captain O'Connell was angered by her amusement. "What
do you mean by that? I am your brother, Megan! Of course I
am concerned for you."

Megan raised her brows slightly. There was a sudden coolness in both her expression and her voice. "Colin, you astonish
me. Why, we have neither of us ever interfered in the other's
life, nor have we ever put ourselves out for one another. I can
perceive no reason why you must needs change that unspoken
rule now."

Megan swept away, leaving her brother prey to angry
thoughts and the unpleasant suspicion that he was reaping
much of the disinterest he had sown in his past relationship
with his sister. The irony of it was that he had always cared
about Megan, if only in a loosely affectionate way. If he could
help her without putting himself to any trouble, such as staving
off one of their brother Lionel's tirades, then he was willing to
do so. But he had never put her interests before his own and
now saw what was coming of it. Megan was unwilling to listen to his advice because he had never proven himself worthy
of either her respect or trust.

"Damnation!" he muttered under his breath.

Captain O'Connell frowned as he watched his sister's
progress. Megan was laughing and flirting in what he considered to be a manner just short of shameful. She had a coterie

of gentlemen surrounding her again, but at least that bounder was not one of them at the moment.

It was odd, he thought. Why had he never realized before just how beautiful his sister was? Megan had an alluring quality that he had never noticed until he had come across her quite by accident here in London. He had been surprised to see her because he had quite understood that she was situated in St. Petersburg indefinitely.

Perhaps that short sojourn in Russia was what had made the difference, Captain O'Connell reflected. Why, Megan had positively blossomed into a woman of the world in only a few months. She was confident, beautiful, and apparently irresistible to the London *ton*. Something must have happened while Megan was residing with Princess Kirov. Something so completely overwhelming that overnight she had become this alarming diamond of the first water.

Captain O'Connell had been idly watching the activity around his sister when his gaze abruptly sharpened. He watched the immensely tall Russian forge a path through the other gentlemen. He observed the faintest hint of hesitation in his sister's manner, the tinge of color that rose in her face, as Prince Kirov bowed over her hand, soliciting her for the waltz.

Captain O'Connell's lips thinned. He thought that he had discovered a piece of the puzzle and it was not a pleasant possibility. Megan would naturally deny anything of the sort. But he would have the truth, one way or another. And then, if what he suspected was true, he would cheerfully murder the Russian.

Prince Kirov whirled Megan expertly around the floor. Her skirt billowed out behind her. He looked down at her with a gleam of amusement in his eyes. "You need not have flirted so desperately with that gamester, mademoiselle. I know that you are too sensible to be caught up in that one's sweetened flatteries."

Megan met his gaze. "Of course I am," she agreed. "Just as I am far too sensible to be caught up in a certain Russian prince's flattering phrases."

"Touché, mademoiselle. You are very quick," said Prince Kirov appreciatively. "Who was the swain who rescued you?"

"Why, do you not know him?" asked Megan, surprised.

"There is something familiar about him. But no, I do not
know him," said Prince Kirov, casting a glance in the direction
he had last seen the tall young gentleman in military togs. He
was startled to meet a smoldering stare from the unknown
man. Instantly, he instinctively recognized a force of character
that challenged his own dominant personality. "Who is he,
Megan?" he said abruptly.

At his tone, Megan looked up at him quickly. "Why, I believe that you are jealous! Surely you are not jealous, Mikhail!"

"Of course not! I merely do not wish you to be importuned
by every jumped-up soldier in town on leave," said Prince
Kirov with dignity.

Megan started to laugh. "You do not understand, Mikhail.
That is my brother, Colin. He would take exception to your
unflattering description of him, I assure you!"

Prince Kirov's stern features relaxed. He recalled that his
trustworthy companion had told him that Miss O'Connell had
a brother in the Lifeguards. It would behoove him to get on a
friendly footing with this fierce-looking brother, he thought.
"Of course that is your brother. Did I not say that he looked familiar? He favors you in coloring."

"Do you think so? Most people think that he and my sister
Celeste are closer in appearance, for they are twins. I am the
youngest and not thought to resemble anyone," said Megan.

"Ah, a swan among less graceful birds," said Prince Kirov
softly.

Megan shook her head, smiling. "Did I not say I was wise to
the flatterer, your highness?"

"I do not offer empty words, Megan," began Prince Kirov.

Megan threw him an amused glance. "No, merely ones of
sweetened froth."

His arm tightened about her waist. He stared down at her, a
somewhat grim line forming about his mobile mouth. "You do
not believe me, mademoiselle?"

"Oh, Misha. I only know that you believe all that you say to
me," sighed Megan.

His anger vanished. "Trust me, Megan," he urged. "That is
all that I ask."

"Then you ask for my life," said Megan quietly.

Prince Kirov was taken aback. He realized that what she said was true. But she had not carried her conclusions far enough. "And I offer you mine in return," he said with equal quiet.

Megan's eyes rose, a startled question in their smoky depths.

The waltz was concluding, but neither noticed straightaway. Prince Kirov slowed their steps until they came to a stand. He loosed her, only to raise her gloved fingers to his lips. "Megan, I—"

They were interrupted. Captain O'Connell took his sister's elbow. "Megan! I am glad that I have found you. I hope that you have not yet been solicited for dinner, for I am counting on escorting you in myself."

"I don't know. That is, I—" Megan looked from her brother to the prince.

Prince Kirov stepped back. He smiled. "It is never the appropriate time, it seems. Mademoiselle, pray introduce me."

"Oh! Of course! Your highness, this is my brother, Captain Colin O'Connell of the Lifeguards. Colin, Prince Mikhail Sergei Alexsander Kirov. The prince was my host during my stay in St. Petersburg," said Megan.

Captain O'Connell smiled. He was himself a tall man, but the Russian topped him by an inch or two. He disliked it. "Prince Kirov, it is a distinct pleasure. St. Petersburg must be a wondrous place. My sister returned to us a different woman."

Prince Kirov sensed the latent hostility underlying the other man's words. He smiled also, but the wolf in him gleamed from his eyes. "Ah, Captain O'Connell, you are too kind. We must talk sometime. I am certain that we shall have much to discuss."

"Agreed, your highness," said Captain O'Connell.

Megan looked from one to the other, puzzled. Both men were smiling and they spoke with perfect amiability. However, there was a tension between them that she did not quite understand. She laid her hand on her brother's muscular arm. "Colin—"

"Perhaps I should explain, Captain O'Connell, that my intentions toward your sister are honorable," said Prince Kirov abruptly, his gaze studying the other man's face. "I have always regarded Miss O'Connell with the highest degree of respect. She has never, nor shall she ever, take injury from my hands. I give you my word of honor on that."

Captain O'Connell regarded him unsmilingly. He made a slight bow. "It is understood, your highness." He held out his hand. "Will you accept my friendship, Prince Kirov?"

Prince Kirov smiled and shook hands. With greatest good humor, he said, "Of course. Why should there be enmity between us? We are to be brothers."

Startled, Captain O'Connell glanced quickly at his sister. She was blushing fiercely and there was a spark of anger in her eyes. He grinned. "Are you indeed! Megan had not informed me."

"She is overly cautious," said Prince Kirov, dropping his voice to a confidential level. He was watching Megan's face while he spoke. "I have protested my love for her, but she continues to hold me at arm's length. Perhaps I might enlist your influence on my behalf, Captain O'Connell?"

"Oh!" Megan was thoroughly embarrassed and incensed. "You are impossible, Misha! Do go away! Colin, take me in to dinner. I have heard quite enough nonsense."

Prince Kirov laughed, bowed, and strolled away. Captain O'Connell offered his arm to his sister, saying, "He'll have you, Megan."

"He is a bold, arrogant—" Words failed her and Megan shook her head.

"For my part, I was prepared to dislike him. But I have changed my mind," said Captain O'Connell. "You have my blessing, Megan." With that, he escorted his outraged sister into dinner.

Chapter Seventeen

It was not to be thought that Captain O'Connell could keep such a good joke to himself. He confided to two of his closest cronies, Lord Dorsey and Lord Haven, that he suspected that his sister was in a fair way to accepting a suit. "Prince Kirov announced himself to be as good as betrothed to her already," he said with a laugh.

Lord Haven repeated those carelessly uttered words to a friend or two, and it swiftly became general knowledge that Prince Kirov had staked his claim to Miss O'Connell. Other suitors protested that they had as much chance as the prince. A wager was made and accepted, the betting book at White's was called for, and the white heat of competition was born. Odds ran slightly in favor of Prince Kirov. It was argued that he possessed much in his favor, but there were a few others who were thought to stand an even chance.

Miss O'Connell appeared to be unconscious of the sharp interest that society was taking of her. She attended the routs, balls, soirees, and other functions without exhibiting a clear partiality for any one gentleman. Her seeming indifference only lent spice to the sporting atmosphere. It was all very entertaining.

There was another noteworthy source of amusement for the *ton* that Season. The ongoing feud between Mrs. O'Connell and her husband had generated both laughter and ridicule. It had quickly become apparent to everyone with eyes that Mr. O'Connell was jealous of his wife's admirers. There were several gentlemen, and, regrettably, ladies, too, who thought it amusing to further Mr. O'Connell's spleen. Mrs. O'Connell suddenly skyrocketed to a pinnacle of popularity. It was rare to either find her at home of an evening or without a flock of gallants crowding around her, eager to snatch her hand out from under her husband's disjointed nose.

Megan sympathized with her brother Lionel. He found himself placed in the awkward position of wooing his own wife. It was an affront to his dignity and his pride, but it served as well as a frontal assault against his former indifference and contempt for Sophronia. That was what Megan hoped (and knew that Sophronia had also pinned all of her hopes on) would attach Lionel's devotion in a way that he had never before experienced.

While Megan felt a small measure of pity for her brother, it did not lead her to accept his strictures upon her own life. There came a time when she was unable to avoid Mr. O'Connell's insistence for private speech. With as much cheerfulness as she could muster, Megan sustained the interview with her brother, during which he taxed her with her unconventional behavior in returning to England without leave and of causing their mother so much concern with her activities.

"Really, Lionel, you are making a great piece of work out of nothing," said Megan. "Mother is simply put out of countenance that she has a daughter who is enjoying the same sort of popularity that she is used to for herself."

"She has informed me that she has actually received offers for your hand from a smattering of gentlemen that she has described as mushrooms and tufts," said Mr. O'Connell bitingly.

"No, has she indeed?" exclaimed Megan, chuckling. "I knew that I had engendered admiration in several breasts, but I had no notion that it had blossomed into full-blown passion!"

"You choose to treat it all very lightly," said Mr. O'Connell. "Allow me to tell you that our mother and I take a far dimmer view of your progress, Megan. I have myself observed your free and easy manners and I am appalled! You have become an accomplished flirt of the worst sort, encouraging every male within your scope, as it were."

"Are you saying that I have crossed the mark, Lionel? For if you are, then perhaps you should direct some of your oration to Sophronia, for I have been much in her company of late! But I don't suppose that Sophronia has accepted your scoldings any better than do I!" said Megan tartly.

Mr. O'Connell stiffened. "We will leave Sophronia's name out of this, if you please! My object is to bring you to a sense of your failings. Heed me, Megan, for I warn you that the consequences shall be dire if you do not!"

"Lionel, you have no authority over me whatsoever. Pray do not think that you will browbeat or bully me into cowering under your thumb, for I shall not do it!" said Megan. "Now you must excuse me, for I must dress. Lady Mansfield has invited me and Mrs. Tyler to join her in her box at the theater."

"I suppose that Kirov fellow is to be one of the party?" inquired Mr. O'Connell sharply. "I've seen the way that he looks at you. Pah! As for his effrontery, it passes all bounds! He has made a laughingstock of you, Megan, whether you know it or not! Why, everyone is saying that he is going around declaring that he is as good as betrothed to you!"

Megan looked at her brother, her expression perfectly still. But her smoke-gray eyes flashed. "Prince Kirov is a gentleman and of royal blood. Pray recall that when you speak of him to me!"

Mr. O'Connell flushed at his sister's cold tone. As she swept toward the door, he called out furiously, "You are riding for a fall, Megan! Mark me if you don't! You will regret all of this one day!"

Chapter Eighteen

Not every gentleman regarded Prince Kirov with such rancor. At a ball a few nights later, Sir Frederick Hawkesworth, formerly assigned to St. Petersburg in a diplomatic capacity and newly arrived in London, recognized Prince Kirov. He had been brought to the ball by his friend, Mr. Bretton. Sir Frederick at once reminded himself to the prince.

Prince Kirov expressed himself delighted to see Sir Frederick again. In fact, the prince greeted him with such a pounding on the back that Sir Frederick was staggered. "You will join a small party that I am hosting tomorrow! We are attending a balloon ascension. I will introduce you to the company of the fairest lady in all of England. You must come, too, Mr. Bretton. I have naturally included Mrs. Tyler in the party and she will be glad to see such a good friend," said Prince Kirov.

Mr. Bretton reddened. "Thank you, your highness. I will be pleased to join you."

"Word has it that you are paying serious court to a lady, your highness," said Sir Frederick, quirking his brow.

Prince Kirov flashed a wide grin. "Ah, so you have already heard of Miss O'Connell! Excellent! Then you will understand when I issue a friendly warning to you, Sir Frederick."

Sir Frederick flung up his hand. "Unnecessary, your highness! I would not dream of trespassing upon your preserve. At least, not this time."

Prince Kirov nodded. There was a gleam in his ice-blue eyes. "You are wiser than some. Now come! I shall take you over to make your bows to Miss O'Connell and Mrs. Tyler. Then I shall make you known to some very unexceptional young ladies."

Sir Frederick burst out laughing. He went off in the company of Prince Kirov and Mr. Bretton.

Unaware of the three gentlemen bearing down on them, Megan and Mrs. O'Connell had their heads together. They were discussing the promising attachment between Captain O'Connell and Miss Phoebe Stallcroft.

"I am glad that all misunderstanding has been smoothed away. I was afraid for a while that Phoebe would never forgive Colin for that idiotic proposal. Offering for her in order to retrieve her tarnished reputation, indeed! Was there anything more calculated than that to put Phoebe into a flame?" said Mrs. O'Connell.

"No, indeed. But I believe that it did Colin good to be turned down. He is a bit more considerate of others lately," said Megan. "I never really thought to see Lady Stallcroft actually smile on Colin."

"Her ladyship has been all complacency since that disastrous day when Phoebe refused Colin and he swore to make all right with her parents," said Mrs. O'Connell. "He apologized very handsomely, too. Lord Stallcroft was quite won over."

"But not her ladyship?" suggested Megan. "You never have told me exactly what took place, you know."

"Oh, it was no great thing. Lord Stallcroft tentatively suggested to his spouse that to deny an upstanding and rather well-heeled young man from courting their daughter was not the wisest thing to do. I clinched the matter when I hinted that to continue to turn Colin away was generating speculations of the sort of intrigue that Lady Stallcroft most despises, which of course could ruin Phoebe's chances altogether," said Mrs. O'Connell with a laugh.

Megan regarded her sister-in-law with respect bordering on awe. "You didn't, Sophronia! But what did Lady Stallcroft say then?"

Mrs. O'Connell pointed with her fan to the dance floor, where Captain O'Connell and Miss Phoebe Stallcroft were going down a country dance. "As you have seen, her ladyship bestowed her approval on Colin's suit," she said with satisfaction.

"That is wonderful, indeed! If only your own interests were going as smoothly," said Megan. She put out a hand quickly when a shadow crossed her sister-in-law's face. "Forgive me! I did not mean to say that."

"It is quite all right. Of course you have noticed that Lionel and I continue to have our differences, and so has all of society," said Mrs. O'Connell with a sigh. She managed a credible smile. "But I have hopes of Lionel. Lately, there has been a look in his eyes that— Well, suffice it to say that he is adjusting his previous conceptions of me!"

"I should hope so!" said Megan warmly. She knew that her brother had been thrown into a passion of jealousy over his wife's new image. It remained to be seen whether that would be the spur that would heal the rift between Lionel and Sophronia.

"Here is Lionel now," said Mrs. O'Connell from behind her fan. "I have given him the next waltz. Wish me luck, Megan." She rose as Mr. O'Connell presented himself and offered his hand.

Megan watched them go, a handsome couple with troubles. She sighed, wishing that her own affairs were progressing better. She had known such success, had been the object of much admiration, and had also received a handful of offers. However, the one gentleman who could command her heart had yet to make a formal proposal. There had been hints in that direction, but it always seemed to be an inappropriate time for Prince Kirov to declare himself.

Lately, Prince Kirov appeared content simply to continue as her faithful admirer. It was rather daunting, she thought. But she kept recalling how he had said she was worthy of a magnificent courtship. Megan supposed that was what Mikhail was attempting to give her. How quickly she would dispense with it, if only he would ask her to marry him. She must have been mad to turn him away at all.

Sensing someone's presence, Megan looked up. She colored when she met Prince Kirov's eyes, thrown off balance by his sudden appearance just when she was thinking about him. Embarrassed, she unconsciously put her hand to her throat. "Prince Kirov! How delightful."

Prince Kirov made an elaborate bow. His eyes gleamed in comprehension of her flustered manner. "Miss O'Connell. I am astonished to discover you sitting alone rather than dancing."

The audacious observation steadied Megan. She flashed a brilliant smile. "Your pity is wasted, your highness, I assure you! I sit out only two sets tonight and that of my own choice."

Prince Kirov laughed. "I do not doubt it. Miss O'Connell, allow me to introduce an old friend to you, Sir Frederick Hawkesworth. He is late of the diplomatic services, having just returned to England. He is a guest of Mr. Bretton's, whom you know, of course."

"Of course. Sir Frederick, I am pleased to make your acquaintance," said Megan. She exchanged a few pleasantries with the gentleman. Then, at Mr. Bretton's inquiry, she said, "You will find Mrs. Tyler with Mrs. Hadcombe, Mr. Bretton."

Mr. Bretton bowed and took his leave, going in search of Mrs. Tyler. Prince Kirov also took his leave of Megan, saying, "I promised Sir Frederick that I would make him known to Miss Stallcroft and Miss Bancroft. But after I have performed this duty, I shall return to make your sitting out of this set less tedious."

"Thank you, your highness. That is truly noble of you," said Megan dryly with a shake of her head. But her fine eyes smiled at him.

Keeping his promise, Prince Kirov shortly made his way back to her. But he did not sit down. Instead he held out his hand. "Will you step out on the balcony with me, Miss O'Connell? I know that you do not like the heat of a ballroom."

"It is rather hot tonight," agreed Megan, rising and placing her fingers upon his elbow. She and Prince Kirov walked to one of the tall windows.

Prince Kirov unlatched it and pushed it open so that he could escort her out onto the marbled balcony. Megan stepped to the stone balustrade, cupping the cool stone under her hands. Her silk shawl slipped from her shoulders. Prince Kirov caught it and placed it gently back onto her shoulders. Megan had half-turned, her face tilted. They were very still, looking into one another's eyes, a tableau touched by moonlight.

"You are slowly driving me mad, Megan," he muttered. He took her into his arms and kissed her. He suddenly stepped back, dropping his arms from about her. "I had not intended to do that."

Megan laughed a little breathlessly. Her heart was pounding and she had to grasp the balustrade for balance. "You remain impulsive, Misha. But I do not dislike it."

Prince Kirov started forward, then stopped. "I think it is time to return to the ballroom, mademoiselle. I do not trust myself alone with you any longer."

Megan accepted his hand. She glanced up at his face as she passed by him through the door. His expression was inscrutable, but there was a warmth in his eyes that could not be hidden.

"I shall look forward to the balloon ascension tomorrow, your highness," she said quietly, dropping her gaze. "I have always wanted to see one."

Sir Lawrence stepped into view. "My dance, I believe," he said, glancing at the gentleman behind Megan.

Prince Kirov bowed and walked away. Megan did not see him for the rest of the evening. She heard later that the prince had left the gathering early.

Much later, after returning home and getting ready for bed, Megan heard a knock at her bedroom door. She opened it. Mrs. Tyler stood outside in the hall, wrapped in a robe and with a pretty lace cap covering her hair. "May I come in for a moment, Megan?"

"Of course, Gwyneth." She let Mrs. Tyler into the room and together they sat down on the settee that was in front of the fire. Megan studied her companion's somber expression. "What is it that makes you look so anxious, Gwyneth?"

She was astonished when Mrs. Tyler rather hesitantly informed her that she had received an offer from Mr. Jeremy Bretton that evening and she had accepted. "Oh, Gwyneth! I am so happy for you!" exclaimed Megan, hugging her.

"Are you really, Megan?" asked Mrs. Tyler anxiously. "I could not be certain, for I feel almost as though I am abandoning you. I was afraid that you might be upset."

"You goose, why should I be upset? Why, I have known for ages that you and Mr. Bretton were meant for one another," said Megan. "Why do you think that I have been so willing to accept Lady Mansfield's invitations of late? I wanted to be certain that you and Mr. Bretton were thrown together as often as possible!"

Mrs. Tyler blushed rosily. "Oh! How very scheming of you, Megan!"

"I was not the only one, for Lady Mansfield confided to me some time ago that you were the very one that she would choose for her nephew if she had been given the opportunity," said Megan, with a twinkling laugh.

Mrs. Tyler was completely overcome. She went quite pink with pleasure, and did not know where to look. "I—I believe that I shall retire to my room now, my dear," she stammered.

Megan let her go, promising to send word at once if Mr. Bretton should take it into his head to serenade his lady love. This sped Mrs. Tyler on her way in pretty confusion.

Megan gave a gurgling laugh. She sobered soon enough, however, with the thought that she would miss her good friend and mentor. It would be very different without Gwyneth to confide in and enter into all of her sentiments and aspirations.

The following afternoon Prince Kirov's party set out for the fairgrounds, where the balloon ascension was to be conducted. He rode beside the carriage conveying Megan and Mrs. Tyler. The prince's companion Fedor came on horseback behind. Captain O'Connell and Miss Phoebe Stallcroft were accompanied by that lively young lady's maid. Miss Phoebe announced that her sister was unexpectedly occupied that afternoon and sent her regrets. Mr. Bretton was riding his own hack. He was also the bearer of regrets, Sir Frederick having begged off due to an urgent engagement. Their defection was felt, but it did not dampen the high-spirited aspect of the rest of the party.

It was a simple matter to locate the balloon ascension. Crowds had flocked from miles around. The gaily colored silk balloon already towered overhead as it was filled with hot air heated by the burning of bundles of stubble. The heavy woven basket was tied to the ground by ropes and bobbed impatiently to be off. The balloon master was making grand claims on the advantages of flight and invited a few brave souls to enter the basket with him.

"What fun that would be!" exclaimed Megan, her head tilted back so that she could see the billowing sides of the balloon. "I have always wondered what it would be like to soar like a bird. One takes flight for only a second when jumping a horse. Or when riding an ice sled! Oh, I *should* like to try it!"

"I forbid you to even consider such a thing!" said Prince Kirov quickly.

"My sister was merely making an observation, your highness," said Captain O'Connell lazily. "Of course she has no such intention. However, if she did I am certain that I would not stand in her way."

"Would you not, indeed, Colin?" asked Megan, her eyes beginning to dance.

"Megan, what are you thinking of? Oh, no! Pray do not say it!" begged Mrs. Tyler.

"But what a wondrous adventure, Gwyneth. Can you not see?" said Megan with a laugh, alighting out of the carriage.

Mrs. Tyler resigned herself. "I must go with you, I suppose. It is my clear duty." She followed Megan down out of the carriage.

"Madame! Miss O'Connell! What are you doing?" asked Prince Kirov sharply.

"Why, Mikhail, we are going to go sailing into the sky," said Megan merrily.

Mr. Bretton at once came up beside Mrs. Tyler. He took her arm. "I shall go with you." Mrs. Tyler looked up at him with gratitude and nodded.

Prince Kirov strode after Megan and caught her arm. "Megan! You cannot do this! I forbid it!"

"So you already said. However, my brother surely has more cause to question my decisions than have you, your highness, and he has already granted me his approval," said Megan. She was smiling as she removed her elbow from his grasp. "Dear Misha," she whispered, "when will you learn that you cannot command me?"

Prince Kirov stared at her, completely bereft of speech. He was left standing while Megan walked away to talk to the balloon master, with Mrs. Tyler and Mr. Bretton in her wake. He muttered an angry phrase in Russian, which made Fedor glance up into his face.

The balloon master bowed to the brave ladies and their escort. In short order, the four were standing in the basket and the balloon master shouted for his assistants to untie the ground ropes.

The balloon lifted slowly, majestically, and the crowds shouted wildly. Within minutes the occupants of the basket were floating high above the green. The balloon's dark shadow passed over the upturned faces of those below.

Megan leaned over the side, laughing delightedly. The wind tugged at her bonnet. She waved to Prince Kirov and the others. "Isn't it marvelous, Gwyneth?"

A sudden gust of wind surged under the balloon. The basket jerked violently. Megan lost her hold. She felt herself falling over the edge and screamed. She reached out, grabbing for anything. The ground rope whipped around her wrist. Her shoulder was nearly jerked from its socket, but Megan caught hold of the flapping rope with both hands.

"Megan!" screamed Mrs. Tyler, rushing to the side. The equippage tipped dangerously and she grabbed the corner rope before she, too, was toppled over the side. Mr. Bretton caught her around the waist.

Megan looked up. Her face was perfectly white. She gently swayed with the air currents. She held onto the guide rope tightly with both hands. She dared not look down. She knew that she did not have the strength to pull herself hand over hand back into the basket.

Mr. Bretton took charge. "You, there! Move to the opposite side of the basket. Mrs. Tyler, pray do the same! We must keep the basket level, while I endeavor to pull Miss O'Connell up!"

The balloon master and Mrs. Tyler wordlessly did as they had been told. Mr. Bretton carefully braced himself in the dangerously swaying basket, aware that one move too quick or too wide could tip them all into disaster. However, he was a seafaring man and he adjusted quickly to the sway. He bent over the side of the basket to grasp the guide rope in his strong hands. "Hang on tight, Miss O'Connell! I shall pull you up," he shouted encouragingly.

Megan stared up at him, her eyes huge. Mutely, she nodded.

Hand over hand, inch by inch. Mr. Bretton pulled on the weighted rope. His hard muscles rippled smoothly under his coat. He breathed easily. The task was scarce different from drawing in an anchor or pulling in the heavy spray-drenched sheeting on a rig. But this time a young woman's life depended upon his strength. He did not dare to allow the rope to slip through his fingers even one jot, for fear that Miss O'Connell's precarious hold would be jarred loose and she would plunge to her death.

Sweat drenched him by the time his fingers closed at last over Miss O'Connell's wrist. With a final effort, he caught hold of her other arm and lifted her over the side of the basket. They both tumbled to the floor.

Megan instantly burst into tears. Mrs. Tyler dropped beside her, her arms closing tight around Megan's shoulders. "Oh, my dear! My very dear! I was so afraid for you!"

Megan returned the embrace fervently. "Oh, so was I, Gwyneth!"

Mr. Bretton got to his feet. Mrs. Tyler looked up at him, her eyes brimming. "Thank you, dear sir," she said in a choked voice.

"I am happy to have been of service, ma'am," said Mr. Bretton, managing a bow while holding onto a corner rope. He turned to the stupified balloon master, his eyes blazing. With a voice that cracked like a whip, he said, "Bring us down, you fool, and lightly! Or I swear that I will myself carve out your gizzard!"

The balloon master nodded several times, cringing from the gentleman's threatening stance. He began to let air out of the balloon. Soon the equippage began its descent. Within a very short time, though it seemed like an eternity to those inside the basket, the balloon settled toward the ground. The basket bounced, skidding across the green as it was pulled along by the balloon, before it came up against a hedge.

Mr. Bretton helped the ladies climb over the side to the ground. Almost immediately spectators surrounded the adventurers.

Prince Kirov pushed his way through the crowd. "Out of my way! Out of my way, I say!" Fedor kept hold of his master's coattails so that he was carried along. Captain O'Connell and Miss Phoebe Stallcroft crowded close behind, taking advantage of the Russian's path.

Prince Kirov took hold of Megan's shoulder. Urgently, he demanded, "You are unharmed? Speak to me, Megan!"

"Y-yes, I am quite all right," said Megan hoarsely. Her throat was still dry from fright. "I am only a little shaken."

"And so you should be! I could shake you myself for taking such a risk, Megan!" As soon as he had satisfied himself of her well-being, the prince's anxiety turned to wrath.

"We are in agreement in that!" exclaimed Captain O'Connell. "Of all the idiotic, stupid stunts! You might have been killed, Megan. Did it never occur to you?"

"Oh yes, at least once," said Megan. Her statement raised a laugh from the spectators.

"It was decidedly the most exciting thing that I ever witnessed," declared Miss Phoebe. Prince Kirov and Captain O'Connell turned as one to stare at her as though she was mad. Miss Phoebe ignored them and turned to Mr. Bretton. "And you, sir, pulled Miss O'Connell to safety. Why, you are a hero!"

"Instead of berating poor Megan, might I suggest that you gentlemen properly thank Mr. Bretton?" said Mrs. Tyler icily. She could feel how Megan was still quivering. It certainly was not the time for recriminations and scoldings.

Prince Kirov and Captain O'Connell were taken aback by Mrs. Tyler's anger. Flushing, Captain O'Connell offered his hand to Mr. Bretton. "Forgive me, sir. I know you will pardon my rude manners. I am somewhat distraught, as you will understand."

Mr. Bretton smiled as he shook hands. "There is no apology required, Captain. I understand perfectly."

Prince Kirov also expressed his fervent gratitude, before saying, "You have performed a service without price, Mr. Bretton. You will allow me to express my thanks with a token that is paltry by comparison." He snapped his fingers. At once, Fedor presented a wallet to his master.

Mr. Bretton's face darkened. "I will not accept payment, your highness," he said stiffly with restrained anger. "It would be an insult to the honor of a gentleman."

"Blimey, guv, take it! Honor be 'anged!" exclaimed a voice out of the crowd and the rest laughed and agreed.

"Enough!" roared Prince Kirov. He glanced around, his blue eyes hard. When the crowd had quieted, he again addressed Mr. Bretton. "You mistake, sir. I do not offer you money. Pah! What is money? No, my friend, I offer you something more valuable." He whipped a gold-edged card out of the wallet. "This is an invitation to a select private party at my residence. You will meet the world there, Mr. Bretton. I trust that I may rely on you to honor me with your presence."

Mr. Bretton glanced at the invitation in his hand. "Yes, of course." The flicker of a smile touched his face. "I shall be most happy to make one of your guests, your highness."

The crowd murmured in disappointment. " 'e should have gone for a reward," remarked someone. "Aye. Wot good is a party invite?"

"Good! Now, where is that idiot balloon master?" said Prince Kirov. "I have business to transact with him." He flexed his hands suggestively, while a certain cold gleam entered his eyes.

"Yes, by Jove!" exclaimed Captain O'Connell, turning around and looking for the man. "I should like a word or two with him, too. The man should be horsewhipped for his negligence."

"He's gone," said Miss Phoebe calmly. "He disappeared into the crowd a few minutes ago. I can't say that I blame him, either, for it can scarcely be considered his fault that the wind took such a turn."

Captain O'Connell scowled down at her. "What a birdwitted thing to say! The man is a fool and must be brought to book, as anyone with the least bit of sense would agree."

Miss Phoebe drew herself to her full height. Her eyes snapped wrathfully. "How dare you address me in such periods, sir!" While Captain O'Connell was still gaping at her, she turned her shoulder on him. She said to Megan and Mrs. Tyler, "Let us go over to my carriage. Mama's coachman has drawn up on the edge of this crowd. He is very trustworthy. I shall tell him particularly to go slowly so that you will not be jarred, Miss O'Connell. You are still so pale, poor thing! My maid always carries a smelling salt. I feel certain that you will benefit from it."

"That is indeed most considerate of you, Phoebe," began Mrs. Tyler.

"Miss O'Connell and Mrs. Tyler came with me. Naturally it is I who will see to their comfort," said Prince Kirov quickly. "I shall have my coachman come up at once. Fedor, see to it at once!" The dwarf flitted away.

"You were the one who brought Megan to this dastardly balloon ascension," said Captain O'Connell accusingly. "She will do better to return to town with me and Miss Stallcroft."

"Bah! Is it my fault that she is a headstrong hoyden? No, a thousand times! I forbade her to get into the balloon. It was you who urged her to take her life in her hands," exclaimed Prince Kirov, his expression darkening.

"Megan is my sister. I shall naturally uphold the stands she takes against impudent outsiders," said Captain O'Connell loftily.

"Impudent! I? I am Kirov! You dare to insult me to your peril, sir!" roared Prince Kirov.

Captain O'Connell looked at his fingernails and yawned. "I am at your service, your highness."

The gentlemen looked prepared to come to blows, a state that highly entertained the spectators. Megan could not bear any more. All she wanted to do was to go home and the two great idiots stood faced off to one another with mayhem on their minds. "How I should like a cup of hot strong tea," she said longingly.

"And you shall have it," said Mrs. Tyler firmly. She graciously bid Mr. Bretton good-bye, giving her hand to him briefly. Then she turned. "Miss Stallcroft, we shall be delighted to ride in your carriage."

Prince Kirov and Captain O'Connell turned as one, their enmity forgotten.

Miss Phoebe waved in a friendly way at her former escort. "Captain O'Connell, I enjoyed the afternoon very much. I am sorry that I cannot offer you a place in my carriage just now. However, I am persuaded that Prince Kirov shall not mind in the least in giving you a lift back into town."

"Here now!" exclaimed Captain O'Connell, starting forward. "Megan, you are going back to town with me."

"No, she is not, Colin," said Mrs. Tyler with finality. She bestowed a frosty nod on Prince Kirov and Captain O'Connell. Then she and Phoebe Stallcroft ranged themselves on either side of Megan and walked off with her.

Prince Kirov stared after the departing trio. "This is not to be borne."

"You're right, there," agreed Captain O'Connell. "We have been shabbily treated, indeed."

"That is the ladies for you, gentlemen," said Mr. Bretton, amused. "When they draw up ranks, it is odd's-time for us."

Prince Kirov shrugged. He slapped the other men on the shoulders, staggering them. "Ah, well! Such is life. There is my carriage. Let us go into the village to the inn. I thirst for ale. We will eat and drink together, my friends!"

Chapter Nineteen

Lady O'Connell sulked. Her ladyship's displeasure was centered upon Megan's social ascendancy. Her sense of self was offended. She could not bear that first her daughter-in-law, and now her own daughter, were garnering as much, if not more, attention than she was herself.

"It is utterly incomprehensible to me! I feel as though I have had the rug jerked out from under my feet. Not once does a day go by that someone does not say something to me about Sophronia or yourself, Megan!" lamented Lady O'Connell. "I am going distracted, for you must know that I am unused to these scores of completely negligible gentlemen beating at my door. I have actually been forced—*forced*—to deny certain ones entrance. It is too fatiguing by half!"

"It is a great deal too bad, indeed, Mother," said Mr. O'Connell with a censorious glance at his unrepentant sister. "You have no consideration at all, Megan. I do not mind telling you that I am surprised. You were not used to be so forward or disobliging at home."

"Perhaps you should move up your departure date, Lionel," suggested Megan cordially.

Her brother flushed and opened his mouth. But Lady O'Connell forestalled whatever he was about to say. "Megan! How can you, when you know that Lionel has been so hardily afflicted by Sophronia's shameful conduct!" exclaimed Lady O'Connell.

"Pray, Mother!" began Mr. O'Connell, throwing a glance of warning at his parent. Though the family, such as it was, was dining informally at home that evening, there were servants serving them at table. It was no wish of his to air his concerns before the entire household.

Lady O'Connell rushed on, unheeding of her son's ill-concealed discomfiture. "When I think of that minx getting up to all of her tricks, it is enough to give me palpitations! She denied Lionel's right to stay at the town house, if you please! And now she is sending him back to Ireland without even a blush of shame! My poor Lionel! Sometimes I think that I should not have written to you at all, so that you could have been spared all this humiliation and trouble."

Without a word, his expression stiff, Mr. O'Connell put down his napkin and left the table. The footman rushed to open the door of the dining room for him.

"Poor Lionel, indeed," murmured Megan.

Her brother's circumstances appeared to have come to a final and depressing conclusion. Megan was convinced of it the next day when her sister-in-law called at the town house. Megan quickly entered the drawing room. She was concerned, for she knew that Sophronia had refused to set foot in Lady O'Connell's residence for several months. Only something of grave proportions could have brought her sister-in-law there that morning. She shut the door. "Sophronia!"

Mrs. O'Connell turned. Her face was very pale. "Megan, I had to come!"

Megan met her outstretched hands and clasped them. "Oh, Sophronia, I am so very sorry! Naturally you are upset and—"

Mrs. O'Connell looked taken aback. "What?"

"Why, about sending Lionel back alone to Ireland. Isn't that why you came?" asked Megan, bewildered by the queer expression on her sister-in-law's face.

"No, no! Lionel and I have come to an agreement. I shall be going back to Ireland at the end of the Season for a trial period. That is why Lionel is leaving," said Mrs. O'Connell. She squeezed Megan's hands. "You thought that— My poor dear! You have not heard, then!"

"What, Sophronia?" Megan's heart began to beat faster. There was such a look of pity in her sister-in-law's gaze that she began to feel fright. "What have I not heard?"

"There has been a duel fought over you, Megan. One man was wounded. I do not yet know how badly. But Prince Kirov was one of the principals," said Mrs. O'Connell baldly.

Megan felt the blood drain from her face. "Then he might be hurt? Oh, dear God! I must go to him at once!" She started to turn toward the door.

Mrs. O'Connell caught her back. "No, Megan! That is just what you must not do! That is why I came to warn you. It would be fatal for you to show any knowledge of the affair at all. You would plunge all of us into terrible scandal. You must let me find out for you. Do you understand?"

"Yes, yes, of course! I shall do just as you say," said Megan, passing a hand over her eyes. "I will wait here for your message, Sophronia."

"Then I shall be off at once. One or two of my friends might know more, and as soon as I can, I shall send word," said Mrs. O'Connell. She suddenly reached out and embraced Megan. "He will be all right, my dear. I know it!"

"Pray do not fail me, Sophronia!" whispered Megan. "I do not think that I could stand it otherwise." She let Mrs. O'Connell go and watched that lady hurry out.

Megan informed Mrs. Tyler of what she had been told and Mrs. Tyler was equally horrified. "I shall stay at home today with you, Megan. After that terrible experience at the balloon ascension yesterday, you will not wish to keep such a vigil alone. No, do not protest! My mind is quite made up," said Mrs. Tyler firmly. "Oh, my dear! I am certain that Sophronia will let us know as soon as she is able."

However, it was not Mrs. O'Connell who informed Megan of the truth of the affair, but Prince Kirov himself. When the prince was ushered into the drawing room, Megan flew up out of her chair and ran to him with a glad cry. "Misha!"

Mrs. Tyler quietly picked up her embroidery and exited the room, leaving the two locked in embrace.

Megan stepped back suddenly, hurriedly inspecting him. "But you are not hurt? Oh, thank God! I have been beside myself with anxiety."

"I was never in danger, my dove. It was not I, but that foolish young poet, Milfred, who threw down the challenge. You recall, of course, that sonnet he wrote to your eyes," said Prince Kirov. "I was merely privileged to act as his second."

"Privileged?" gasped Megan. "Mikhail, that is the stupidest

word I have ever heard! What happened, pray? Was—was anyone killed?"

"No, of course not! My man Milfred was wounded, but it is only a scratch. As for his opponent, he came off unscathed," said Prince Kirov. He frowned thoughtfully. "It was rather a tame affair, as such things go. I had expected more, but there was more passion than courage when all was said and done."

"How can you speak about it so calmly?" demanded Megan.

"How else should I speak?" asked Prince Kirov, slightly puzzled.

"Oh, you are impossible! Mikhail, Sophronia told me that this duel was fought over me. Is that true?" asked Megan.

"It was over the color of your eyes," corrected Prince Kirov. Megan stared at him, completely bereft of speech. He saw that more explanation was needed. "Young Milfred's sonnet was ridiculed, you see. It was said that he had not got the color of your eyes down correctly. Milfred flew into a frenzy and tossed a glass of wine into the man's face. After that, there was no question, of course."

"Couldn't you have done something? Why did you not put a stop to it?" asked Megan.

"But how could I do so? It was a question of honor," said Prince Kirov reasonably.

"Oh, honor!" exclaimed Megan. "Someone could have been killed! Why did they not simply apply to me if they could not decide what color my eyes are? I certainly could have told them!"

"That is not the way of gentlemen," said Prince Kirov with dignity. "We do not involve ladies in our disputes."

Megan virtually snorted and flounced out of the room.

When news of the duel became public, Lady O'Connell was appalled. She could scarcely believe that her daughter had suddenly become so notorious. It was unthinkable that Megan was actually the cause of a duel.

Lady O'Connell could no longer take the comments and the inquiries that she had been receiving about her daughter. Even her closest friends and acquaintances were beginning to ripple with catty laughter and declare themselves deliciously scandalized by Miss O'Connell's wide progress.

One of Lady O'Connell's oldest and dearest friends took her aside once news of the duel had broken and gave her ladyship a piece of advice. "It is obvious, Agatha. You cannot control her. You must take drastic measures," said the dame.

"But what can I do?" Lady O'Connell almost wailed. "I have tried everything. I have talked to Megan until I am blue in the face. I have spoken to my cousin, Mrs. Tyler, who is her companion. Nothing has been of the least use!"

"If I were you, I would send a packet off to Lord O'Connell this very day," said the dame.

Lady O'Connell immediately rejected the suggestion. "His lordship would not be pleased to be bothered. Besides which, I do not think that he would bestir himself in the least."

"If you do not do something, and quickly, then your own reputation and name will be dragged under the same harsh scrutiny as Miss O'Connell's," said the dame. "You are her mother. Ultimately her manner must reflect upon you!"

When her free-spoken friend had left her, Lady O'Connell was left in a state of high anxiety. She did not know what to do. Her daughter had metamorphosed into some sort of society monster, becoming talked about and recognized and feted and pointed out to no little degree. If it was not so terrible, she would have been jealous of Megan's meteoric rise. As it was, however, Megan was hurtling toward destruction. Up to this point, Lady O'Connell had only been able to stand by and shudder.

Now her own social rank was said to be teetering on the brink of disaster. The specter, once raised, could not be forgotten. Lady O'Connell fretted far more about her own preservation in a few hours than she had done on her daughter's behalf in weeks.

Lady O'Connell finally did as her friend had suggested. She penned an urgent, if somewhat incoherent, letter to her spouse and sent it off immediately. She hoped that his lordship, if he chose to act at all, would be able to rein in their suddenly uncontrollable daughter.

Lord O'Connell arrived in London on a gray day late in

May. It was raining heavily when he was ushered into the town house. He was soaked between the carriage and the door and the butler immediately put out orders that a fire be made up in the master's bedroom. Lord O'Connell had never slept in the largest bedroom in the town house before, but it was still the master's bedroom and kept prepared for him always.

Lord O'Connell was ushered upstairs by the butler, followed by his lordship's valet. The first order of business was to make his lordship comfortable. Perhaps then the thunderous expression on his lordship's face would ease.

Lady O'Connell had the first intuition that her lord had arrived when she languidly made her way downstairs for luncheon and walked into the drawing room to find him sitting beside the fire, reading the London papers. "Oh!"

Lord O'Connell lowered the newspaper. His expression had scarcely changed from the time of his arrival. When he saw his wife, his frown deepened. He tossed aside the papers, demanding, "What is this farrago of nonsense, pray? You have got me to London on some hum, I daresay."

He had been reluctant to leave his horses. He had scarce interest in anything beyond his beloved racing stables and so he was not in any good humor. No amount of good brandy or a change into dry raiment could alter his disgruntlement.

"I told you all in my letter, my lord. Megan has become impossible," said Lady O'Connell. "She has made herself a byword, a scandal, a—a scapegrace!"

"Nonsense. Megan is a good, steady girl. I have never had the least trouble in managing her," said Lord O'Connell irritably. "She knows her place and her duty well enough."

"That is what I thought until this Season," said Lady O'Connell bitterly. "It is worse than with Sophronia. At least Sophronia did not do such outrageous things, nor encourage every jackanapes in town! You would not believe me even if I told you, my lord, of the—the *riffraff* that I have been forced to give the office. Then there was that horrible balloon ascension when Megan fell out of the basket. She was dangling from a rope, her skirts blowing every which way in the wind while a crowd of commoners stood gawking up at her! I was never more humiliated."

"What is there in all that to dash off a damned queer letter to me?" demanded Lord O'Connell. "You are her mother. It is your responsibility to properly chaperone your daughter. Get the girl married off. That will settle the dust quick enough."

Lady O'Connell burst into flame. Her ample bosom heaved in outraged injury. "My daughter, sir? Megan is *your* daughter, for I wash my hands of her!"

"You are hysterical," said Lord O'Connell with disgust. "If Megan is not toeing the line, it is because you have not kept a tight enough rein on her. As her mother, your example must influence her."

"I am certain that I never influenced her to try her luck at the faro table or the races!" exclaimed Lady O'Connell. "As for marrying her off, I have never been more certain in my life that I shall detest a son-in-law more, whomever he might be, for it is fact that he will have placed a bet at White's in favor of his odds in winning Megan's hand!"

"What!" Lord O'Connell stared at his wife, suddenly straightening in his chair. "What is that about bets being laid? What was that, madame?"

Lady O'Connell looked at her spouse with a degree of grim satisfaction. "Did you hear that, at least? Yes, my lord, our daughter is the subject of betting at White's. I have it on perfect authority that there are several gentlemen who have entered the lists and placed bets on their chances to win Megan's hand!"

"I do not believe it!" exclaimed Lord O'Connell, scowling. He had always delighted in horseracing and betting was a natural part of the racing atmosphere. He thought nothing odd in the fact that his daughter might place a few genteel bets of her own at the races. Even playing at faro was not outside what might be acceptable. He himself delighted in the odd chance. However, it was quite a different matter to be informed that his daughter was being touted like a two-year-old filly at the gates. His sense of rigid propriety was insulted.

"Go to White's yourself, my lord. I should like to be informed that my sources were inaccurate," said Lady O'Connell.

Lord O'Connell lunged to his feet. "I shall do so at once.

And if I find that it is true that *your* daughter is the focus of such ill-bred controversy, I shall have much to say to you, my dear lady!" he said wrathfully. He strode out of the drawing room, ignoring his wife's scandalized disclaimer.

Lord O'Connell repaired at once to White's. It had been many years since he had entered its portals, but the porter recognized him nevertheless and greeted him. Lord O'Connell ordered a brandy from a waiter and settled into a deep chair in the gaming room. He listened to the conversations around him in an idle fashion. Just when he began to relax, enjoying the excellent brandy, and suspect that Lady O'Connell's outrageous contention had been false, he overheard his daughter's name.

Lord O'Connell listened intently and with gathering wrath. The betting book was called for and a bet placed amid much laughter and raillery among the parties. Shortly thereafter, Lord O'Connell left White's in a towering rage. His scowling expression was so intimidating that the porter did not dare to wish his lordship good day.

Lord O'Connell returned to the town house. He sent word upstairs that he wished to speak to his wife and daughter. He was not happy to learn that neither lady was at home and were not due to return until several hours later. "Am I supposed to kick my heels here all day waiting for them?" he inquired wrathfully of the butler.

Digby retained his wooden expression. "No, my lord."

Lord O'Connell snorted. He waved the butler out and flung himself into an easy chair with the racing journals. After reading the racing news, Lord O'Connell decided to go to Tattersall's. Perhaps there might be a nag or two that would be worth bidding on. At least he would not be wasting all of his time in London.

Lord and Lady O'Connell both returned to the town house about the same time. They met politely in the drawing room to discuss their daughter. For once they found themselves in complete agreement. A halt had to be made to Megan's wild progress.

When Megan returned late that afternoon, she was informed by the butler that his lordship was in residence and had requested that she wait on him when she came in.

Megan looked at the butler in mild surprise. "My father here in London? It scarcely seems possible. Why has he come, Digby?"

"I cannot say, miss," said the butler. He hesitated, then said, "His lordship seemed strangely exercised over something, miss. His lordship and Lady O'Connell have been closeted together for the last hour in the drawing room."

Megan raised her brows slightly. "Odd, indeed. Very well, I shall come down again as soon as I have put off my pelisse and bonnet. Is Mrs. Tyler about?"

"She returned some minutes earlier, miss. I believe she is still abovestairs," said Digby.

Megan thanked the butler and hurried upstairs. She could not imagine what her father was doing in London. It had to be a matter of great urgency to tear Lord O'Connell from his stables. Perhaps Mrs. Tyler would know.

Mrs. Tyler could not enlighten her, however. "I am as much in the dark as you are, my dear," said Mrs. Tyler, perturbed. "When I returned, I was informed of Lord O'Connell's sudden appearance, of course. But I have heard nothing about what has brought him here. I hope that there has not been an accident or something of that sort."

"To Lionel, you mean, on his trip home? That wouldn't worry my father in the least," said Megan practically. "No, it more than likely has something to do with the horses, which means that his lordship will be in a true state."

"Shall I go down with you?" asked Mrs. Tyler.

"I cannot conceive any reason why you should," said Megan. When Megan entered the drawing room, she was surprised that both of her parents turned at once to look at her. She did not recall ever having gained their instant attention upon entering a room before. She paused, trying to assess their expressions before she went forward to greet her father. "My lord, it is good to see you," she said.

Lord O'Connell frowned at her. "I daresay! It is on your account that I am come to London. I shall tell you now that I am extremely displeased, Megan."

Megan stared at her father, taken aback. "I do not understand." She looked to her mother for enlightenment.

Lady O'Connell was not behind in explanation. "I wrote your father, Megan. I felt driven to do it. I have told him everything! Simply everything! He agrees with me that we cannot have this any longer. Our very reputation is at stake."

"What are you talking about?" asked Megan, though she was beginning to have an inkling. But such a thought was sheer nonsense and only to be regarded with astonishment.

"Your rake's progress, miss! Yes, you may stare, but so it is!" exclaimed Lord O'Connell. He thrust forward his jaw. There was outrage in his stance. "There are bets laid against your name at White's, Megan. You have become the object of vulgar speculation and scandal. I will not have it, do you hear? I will not have it!"

"Pray calm yourself, my lord. Shouting will certainly not accomplish our purpose," snapped Lady O'Connell. She turned to her daughter. "Megan, your father and I have agreed. Your outrageous behavior must be curtailed. You will return to Ireland at once. I shall set it about that you have gone on a repairing lease because you were going the pace too fast. That at least will be believed! Then perhaps this terrible gossip will die away."

Lord O'Connell nodded. "You will be forgotten soon enough. Then we may be comfortable again."

Megan looked from one parent to the other. She was dumbfounded. Then a rising anger began to darken her eyes. "Excuse me, sir, but *I* shall not be comfortable! How dare you say that you will pack me off just when I have at last embarked upon the Season that has been promised to me for two years past? I positively refuse to be buried again without hope of any sort of future. Not once have either of you paid much attention to me. And now, because I have earned a sort of harmless notoriety, you have bestirred yourselves to decide what is to be done to best insure *your* comfort!"

"Do not dare to speak to me in that tone, daughter!" roared Lord O'Connell.

"Why should I not?" inquired Megan. Her eyes flashed. "Perhaps if I had done so anytime these years past you might have realized that I am your daughter and that I do have an existence outside of my ability to sit a horse!"

"What has happened to you, Megan? You used to be so biddable, so unselfish. Now look at you! You defy us without a hint of remorse!" exclaimed Lady O'Connell, staring at her as though she was looking at something horrifying.

"I have grown up, Mother. I turned twenty last month. Do you not recall? I am not a girl any longer," said Megan. A twisted smile touched her lips. "I am nearly on the shelf and you are determined to put me there. Well, I have decided that I am not going without a struggle." She took a breath. "I am sorry, Father, but I shall not return to Ireland. I intend to remain in London for the remainder of the Season."

"Nonsense! You cannot remain. We have decided it, your father and I," said Lady O'Connell.

Lord O'Connell raised his hand. "One moment, my lady." He looked at Megan. "Have you indeed turned twenty?"

Megan almost laughed. "Yes, I have. A fortnight past."

"I had no notion. And you have never had a Season." Lord O'Connell turned to look an accusation at his wife. "That was your duty, ma'am, surely? Providing a Season for our daughter?"

Lady O'Connell avoided his lordship's eyes. "There never seemed to be a convenient time. And Celeste never required a Season, after all! I quite thought that Megan might—"

"What, Mother? Form a runaway connection as did Celeste? Though I love my sister, I never thought what she and Patrick did was quite right," said Megan.

"No, indeed!" exclaimed Lord O'Connell. "I never approved of the manner in which Celeste left our roof. It was a scandal. You have the right of it, Megan. Runaway matches are not good *ton*. I am glad that you have the sense to see it."

He lowered his glowering gaze onto his wife. "Madame, I demand an explanation. You have shamefully neglected Megan's interests. This is a reflection upon me as well. No one likes to admit that he is left with a spinster daughter on his hands!"

Lady O'Connell was thrown into self-defense. "Megan cannot say that I have not done well by her! Why, I sent her off to St. Petersburg with the certainty that Princess Kirov would give her entrée into the most unexceptional company. Yes, and footed the bill for a new wardrobe besides! For her *and* Mrs. Tyler! Is it my fault that she did not take?"

"On the contrary, Mother, I did take! I was immensely popular. I learned a great deal while under Princess Kirov's aegis, which I have put to good use this Season," said Megan. "Perhaps you do not care for the responsibility of chaperonage. Nor the way that I am talked about. But I do have any number of possible suitors from which to choose a husband. And I have strong hopes of being able to do that very thing before the Season is out."

"Do you, indeed!" said Lord O'Connell, looking at his daughter. He saw the confidence in her proud stance. Respect stirred slightly somewhere deep within him. He suddenly smiled. "Then we must not stand in your way, Megan. By all means you shall finish out the Season."

"But, my lord! That is not what you said twenty minutes ago!" exclaimed Lady O'Connell in dismay.

"It is what I say now, however. Megan is to be given her chance at contracting a decent match, my lady," said Lord O'Connell.

"But what about the scandal? What about the duel and the betting? Yes, and what about my own commitments! You cannot expect me to shepherd her everywhere," exclaimed Lady O'Connell. "I am utterly distracted as it is! Why, I have not once enjoyed an evening all Season. Someone is always mentioning Megan's name or inquiring about her latest exploit. It is quite unnatural."

"Obviously, then, you require help," said Lord O'Connell. "What of Mrs. Tyler?"

Lady O'Connell stared. "My cousin? Why, she is Megan's companion!"

"Precisely. I see no reason why Mrs. Tyler cannot accompany Megan into company. She is perfectly respectable," said Lord O'Connell.

"Gwyneth enjoyed as much popularity in St. Petersburg as did I," said Megan quietly. "And she is quite willing to accompany me whenever I go out. She has done so except when my mother has deemed the party to be too rarefied."

"The problem is solved, my lady," said Lord O'Connell.

"You will allow Mrs. Tyler the liberty to choose her own entertainments and thus she will be available at all times to help you chaperone Megan."

"Oh, very well!" snapped Lady O'Connell. "But I do not agree with raising my cousin's expectations too high. Inevitably the moment will come when she is horridly snubbed by some extraordinarily proud personage."

"I assure you, Mother, Gwyneth's skin is thick against all such insult," said Megan dryly, reflecting that it was her mother who had most often pointed out to Mrs. Tyler their differences in social standing.

"There is also Sophronia," said Lord O'Connell. "I assume that she will be willing enough to bear-lead Megan on occasion?"

"Oh, Sophronia! She is almost as bad as Megan for flouting convention," said Lady O'Connell. When she saw her spouse's lowering frown, she hastily amended her statement. "What I mean is, she is known as a wonderful hostess. Simply everyone may be found at her little soirees. She has greatly changed, my lord."

"I hope that the change is for the better," said Lord O'Connell. "Very well, then. We go forward with the Season. Megan, I request that you give more thought to your reputation and mine! That is all I ask of you at this point."

"I am quite willing to agree, sir," said Megan with a smile. She was almost dizzy with the realization that she had gained everything that she had wanted. Instead of exile to Ireland, she would triumphantly finish out the Season.

Megan had very little doubt upon whom she would bestow her hand. The wild courtship would be over and she would become betrothed to Prince Mikhail Kirov. The thought left behind a tingling feeling of pleasure and anticipation.

Lord O'Connell's next words fell like a bucket of cold water splashed over her head. "There is one stipulation that I shall make, however. You are not to encourage that Kirov fellow," he said. "I have heard enough in the short time that I have been in town to form the opinion that he is completely contemptuous of convention. I am thus able to see quite clearly that your present wildness stems from your sojourn under Princess Kirov's roof. I do not wish that influence to continue. I therefore forbid you to entertain his advances any longer, Megan. Do you not agree, my lady?"

"Oh, indeed! I was never more shocked than at the transformation of my dear sweet daughter upon her return from St. Petersburg," said Lady O'Connell quickly. She was anxious to establish once and for all that she was not in any way to blame for Megan's recent behavior. "I shall bar the house from Prince Kirov on the instant."

"But—but that is ridiculous! Prince Kirov is one of my most ardent admirers," stammered Megan. She dared not reveal just how dear she held him to be. "He is certainly far and away much more eligible than many of the others!"

"Eligibility is what one makes it. I already have the jawbone of an ass for a son-in-law. I do not intend to risk acquiring a heedless hedonist," said Lord O'Connell. "I approve of your decision, my lady. By all means, instruct the staff that Kirov is no longer welcome."

Megan instinctively began to protest. "But, sir!" At her father's darkening expression, however, she swallowed back the tumble of hasty words that was choking her. He was looking at her with a particularly obdurate glint in his eyes. Now was certainly not the best time to persuade Lord O'Connell of his massive mistake.

Instead Megan requested permission to be excused. It was granted to her and she left the drawing room. Once outside the closed doors, she picked up her skirts and flew upstairs. She had to tell Mrs. Tyler at once of the awful thing that had just happened.

Chapter Twenty

The injunction against Prince Kirov was swiftly carried out and he learned of it in very short order. Prince Kirov frequently called at the O'Connell town house. He was astonished the next day when he was denied the door. "What did you say?" he asked with liveliest astonishment.

The porter who barred the door to him repeated his orders. "Begging your pardon, your highness, but there it is," he added with some sympathy.

Prince Kirov shoved his shoulder into the door, sending the porter flying. The man skidded across the marble tiles and brought up against the opposite wall. Prince Kirov did not notice. His eyes extremely hard and cold, he strode down the hallway. "Where is Lady O'Connell? I wish to have a word with her!" he snapped.

Digby appeared, along with two footmen. "Your highness!" With a comprehensive glance at the porter, the butler drew himself up. "I am sorry, your highness, but you shall have to leave."

"You mistake. I do not leave until I have seen Lady O'Connell," said Prince Kirov conversationally. He smiled, but it was a wolfish expression. "And do not think to set your accomplices on me, Digby, for I should very much regret breaking their heads." He flexed his large hands suggestively, still smiling that disturbing smile.

The butler inclined his head. He was not a coward and nor were the footmen. However, the gentleman standing before them was in truth virtually a giant, and a very angry one at that. Digby considered himself to be a prudent man. He would allow his master to deal with the prince. He motioned to the footmen to step aside, to their patent relief. "Very well, your highness. Allow me to show you into the library, where you will find Lord O'Connell. He will receive you."

Prince Kirov laughed, but his ice-blue eyes glittered. "You may rest assured of that!"

The short interlude had been loud enough to bring Lord O'Connell to the door. "What is going forward, Digby?" he demanded. With growing astonishment, he realized himself to have come under the narrowed scrutiny of a very tall, very large gentleman. His lordship's bushy brows met over his hard eyes, for he was not used to be regarded in such a way. His voice chilly, he inquired, "Yes? Do you have business here, sir?"

"I am Kirov," announced Prince Kirov. "I desired to speak to her ladyship. However, I address my query to you, my lord, since I discover you to be in residence."

"Kirov!" Lord O'Connell glanced accusingly at his servants. For the first time he took note of the porter, who was still holding his head. His gaze raked back to the prince. "You have had the audacity to force your way into my house! Outrageous!"

Prince Kirov bowed. "I am a man of decision, my lord. We shall discuss the matter."

"There is nothing to discuss, your highness! I have decided that your suit for my daughter is not welcome to me. That is all," said Lord O'Connell hastily.

Prince Kirov raised his brows. "Indeed! May I inquire Miss O'Connell's preference in the matter?"

Lord O'Connell began to redden. He was fully aware of the servants' lively curiosity. "That is quite beside the point! However, if you must have it, my daughter shall naturally obey my wishes. She will not receive you. I bid you good day, Prince Kirov!" He started to turn away.

"You have the right to deny me entrance, my lord. However, you do not command me otherwise. I shall continue to make Miss O'Connell the object of my honorable attentions," said Prince Kirov silkily. "None shall say me nay, my lord."

Lord O'Connell glared at the arrogant prince. The effrontery of the man was unbelievable. His lordship was more than ever convinced that his decision had been the right one. He would not have any connection between his family and one so lost to propriety and a sense of consequence. "I do not bandy words with you, Prince Kirov. Now I demand that you leave this place instantly!"

"I do not think that you understand whom you are addressing, my lord." Prince Kirov smiled again. There was such a savage expression in his eyes that Lord O'Connell took an unconscious step backward. "Ah, perhaps you discern a little, my lord. We shall speak again, I promise you."

Prince Kirov bowed. Then he spun around on his boot heel and strode down the hall to the front door. He opened it, paused to glance back with a flash of glittering anger, and exited. The door was pulled shut with resounding force.

Lord O'Connell discovered that he had been holding his breath. It greatly annoyed him. He glared around at the butler and other servants. "What the devil are you staring at?" He stepped back into the library and slammed the door.

The tale went through the household with amazing speed. Within minutes every servant in the house was in possession of the facts of the astonishing confrontation. Simpkins heard it belowstairs and though the dresser preserved a dignified front, she at once went up to apprise Mrs. Tyler of the news. "I'll not be saying that the story has not been somewhat exaggerated, ma'am. However, I thought you would wish to know," ended the dresser.

"Yes, of course," said Mrs. Tyler, her brows drawn together. Arousing herself out of her reflections, she smiled at the dresser and dismissed her. Then she went to the sitting room to pen a short note addressed to Prince Kirov. She called for a footman and requested that it be delivered at once.

This interesting communication was given to Prince Kirov before he set out for an evening with friends. The prince frowned over its contents, then folded it away. It did not surprise him that Mrs. Tyler stood his friend; nor that that good lady had chosen to set down some carefully chosen words of advice. What did surprise him was the explanation for Lord O'Connell's incomprehensible bias against him.

Prince Kirov could only shake his head over the rigid rules of etiquette that formed Lord O'Connell's personality and character. He, for one, saw nothing at all improper in Megan's success. And to place the blame for any perceived wildness in Megan at his door was ludicrous in the extreme, he thought. Megan was certainly much more the product of her upbringing than of any influence that her short sojourn in St. Petersburg might have brought to bear!

Prince Kirov left his residence still exercised by his reflections. He shortly came to realize that the English milord's mind was virtually alien to his experience. Much as he was reluctant to admit it even to himself, Prince Kirov needed help to crack the shell of this particular nut.

Sir Frederick happened to be at the party. Prince Kirov at once realized that here was just the gentleman who might be depended upon to give him the insight that he desired. He sought him out, saying, "I have a diplomatic problem, Sir Frederick. I hope that you will be able to help me."

Sir Frederick was instantly curious. "I should be most happy to lay my experience open to you, your highness."

Prince Kirov gestured to a card table in an alcove and the two gentlemen repaired to it. They were trailed by Fedor, who took up a wary stance a few feet away, out of earshot but near enough to his master to obey his summons.

Once seated, the prince seemed at a momentary loss. He sat frowning into space before turning to Sir Frederick. "You may know that I am a suitor for Miss O'Connell's hand."

Sir Frederick nodded. A flicker of amusement touched his face. "I believe all the world knows that you have aspirations in that direction."

Prince Kirov smiled, a sudden wolfish expression. "I have not made a secret of it. It is good that Miss O'Connell's admirers know this."

"What is the problem, then, your highness? Does not Miss O'Connell favor your suit?" asked Sir Frederick boldly.

Prince Kirov stiffened. His eyes flashed. "Miss O'Connell has indeed honored me with her favor, Sir Frederick. That is not where the trouble lies. It is with Lord and Lady O'Connell. I had hoped that you might shed some light on the workings of the English mind, for I am at a loss to understand the action that they have taken against me. Do I not love their daughter?

Am I not an eligible parti? Am I not wealthier than most men? Is not my birth superior to their own?"

Sir Frederick eyed the Russian with fascination. "What precisely have Lord and Lady O'Connell done, your highness?"

"They have denied me the house and I am told by Mrs. Tyler that Miss O'Connell has been ordered not to think of me any longer as a principal suitor," said Prince Kirov heavily.

There was a moment of incredulous silence. "You astonish me, your highness," said Sir Frederick with perfect truth. "I cannot perceive how your suit could be so repugnant to them if Miss O'Connell herself is amenable." He shot a swift look at the Russian. "Unless, of course, Miss O'Connell is not as willing as you believe?"

"I have told you! Miss O'Connell is in love with me. She would accept my suit in a trice if it were not for this ridiculous ban against me," said Prince Kirov. He audibly ground his teeth. "I do not deal in dishonor, Sir Frederick. You know enough about me to know that is true. I say that Miss O'Connell is in love with me and that the desire of my heart is to make her my wife. You may believe that it is so."

"Yes, I know well your sense of honor, Prince Kirov," said Sir Frederick.

Prince Kirov felt a release of tension inside him that surprised him. He had not realized how much he wanted Sir Frederick to believe him. "Then you will help me." It was not a question but a statement.

Sir Frederick laughed. "Yes; at least, I shall try. What do you wish me to do? Do you want me to act as your intermediary with Lord and Lady O'Connell? The position of marriage broker is a bit outside my realm of experience, but I suspect that it is not much different than other types of negotiations."

Prince Kirov thought over Sir Frederick's offer. It was an attractive one, but he realized that it held no guarantee of success. He preferred to rely upon his own resources. "Perhaps. We shall see. At the moment, I request only that you explain to me how I might bring myself back into Lord and Lady O'Connell's good graces."

"My good man! You ask the moon. I cannot very well read their minds," said Sir Frederick, taken aback.

Prince Kirov flashed a grin. "Ah, but you can! You are English. You know how your countrymen must reason, just as I know how a Russian must reason. You have been in diplomatic circles and must know a score of tricks, besides. You shall tell me what I must do." He settled back in his chair and confidently savored his wine while Sir Frederick stared across the parquet table at him.

"The devil. You are right," said Sir Frederick finally, ruefully. "I, better than anyone, should be able to aid you. Very well. Let me think for a moment."

Prince Kirov gestured graciously. "Of course, Sir Frederick. I am a patient man."

Sir Frederick cracked a disbelieving laugh at that, but he merely shook his head at the prince's look of inquiry. "I'll not muddy the waters with my opinion of that, your highness."

"I am Kirov. What more is there to say?" asked Prince Kirov.

Sir Frederick did not reply to what he felt certain was a rhetorical question. Instead he bent his mind to the prince's problem. After several frowning minutes, he glanced again at the prince. "Are you certain that Miss O'Connell's affections are engaged?"

"You have my word of honor that it is so," said Prince Kirov quietly.

Sir Frederick was impressed that the prince did not respond with his usual arrogance but instead with dignity. "Very well, then. I shall help you to her hand. My advice to you is to make your suit indispensable to Lord and Lady O'Connell."

Prince Kirov stared at his companion. His well-marked brows lowered. "I do not understand. How am I to do this?"

"Think, your highness! You have told me yourself all of your excellent points. But none of these are vitally important in and of themselves to the O'Connell's. In one form or another, a score of other gentlemen can fit those same requirements," said Sir Frederick.

"There is no one better than I!" declared Prince Kirov. At his ringing tone, his silent and ever-present companion started toward the table. The dwarf's hand had slipped to the knife only partially hidden beneath his coat front.

"Perhaps, but not in the eyes of your prospective in-laws," retorted Sir Frederick. "And you had best call off Fedor, for I do not go unarmed myself."

"You are right," said Prince Kirov. He waved the dwarf back. "Though I suspect that Fedor might give a very good account of himself. Now, Sir Frederick, I place myself in your hands. How do you suggest that I accomplish my purpose?"

Sir Frederick frowned thoughtfully. "From all accounts, and judging from my own observations, Lady O'Connell is a rather vain, self-indulgent woman. She is undoubtedly motivated by self-interest."

"That much is true. Her ladyship is not moved by an appeal to her softer nature," said Prince Kirov. "In fact, I do not believe that she has one. This very afternoon I sought out Lady O'Connell, knowing that she takes tea with Mrs. Hadcombe, and walked her to her carriage. When I declared myself in love with Miss O'Connell and requested her clemency, Lady O'Connell refused. She called for her servants to give me the go-by!"

There was such outrage in the prince's expression and voice that Sir Frederick could hardly stop himself from laughing. That would not have done at all and so with all the command of his years as a diplomat, Sir Frederick replied gravely, "An unpleasant experience indeed, your highness. But let us turn our thoughts to what we know of Lady O'Connell's character. What will turn her about? What is it that she prizes? What is so important to her that she will give you permission to extend suit to her daughter in exchange for it?"

"Pah! You make it sound like a horse trade," said Prince Kirov, grimacing.

"And so it is," said Sir Frederick, lounging at his ease with his hands thrust into his coat pockets. "That is negotiation in its most primitive form, your highness. Ferret out what your opponent wants to acquire and hold it for ransom until he gives up what you want."

There were a few moments of silence while Prince Kirov frowned over what Sir Frederick had told him. "I think I see my way becoming clear," he said slowly.

Sir Frederick sat up, immediately curious. "Do you, indeed! What do you intend to do?"

Prince Kirov laughed. "I shall tell you one day, perhaps. But now I must go speak with Mrs. O'Connell. I hope to enlist her to my cause." He rose to his feet and Sir Frederick also stood up. Prince Kirov held out his hand to the other man. "You have been a friend to me, Sir Frederick. One day I trust that I shall be of similar valuable service to you."

Sir Frederick clasped the prince's hand warmly. "Dash it, Kirov, I have always liked you. Good luck to you, man."

Prince Kirov bowed and moved away. The dwarf followed him, casting an unsmiling glance back at Sir Frederick. Sir Frederick waved at him in a friendly way. Fedor's impassive face creased in the slightest of smiles.

Sir Frederick watched the prince bear down in a leisurely fashion on Mrs. O'Connell. The lady looked up at Prince Kirov, listening to something he was saying. She nodded, then excused herself to her friends and went off on the prince's arm. Their heads were bent together while they conversed. Sir Frederick lifted his wineglass in a silent toast.

Chapter Twenty-one

L ady O'Connell was surprised to receive a note from her daughter-in-law. She was even more surprised by its content, which begged her to call on Mrs. O'Connell that same morning. The note hinted at a reconciliation. "Well! This is something indeed," exclaimed Lady O'Connell, vastly pleased.

Her ladyship ordered out her carriage and during the entire ride she entertained herself with a pleasant scene. Her repentant daughter-in-law would apologize for all of the slights and cuts that she had directed toward Lady O'Connell that Season, at which time she would magnanimously forgive Sophronia and advise her to return to Ireland. Naturally Sophronia would instantly take her advice, close the house, and retreat back into her dutiful role as the colorless wife of her ladyship's eldest son. Then Lady O'Connell would ascend once more into the social heavens.

Buoyed by this imagination, Lady O'Connell was at her most gracious when she was ushered into her daughter-in-law's drawing room. Mrs. O'Connell received her cordially, if somewhat ironically. However, Lady O'Connell was too caught up in visions of her own spinning to notice. She pulled off her gloves, signaling that she meant to make a lengthy visit.

"I was quite happy to receive your communication this morning, Sophronia," said Lady O'Connell. With a smile, she added, "I am certain that we shall have a very comfortable little coze. We used to be rather good friends, after all."

Mrs. O'Connell blinked, but she returned the smile. "Were we, my lady? No doubt you are right. Will you take tea and perhaps a biscuit?"

Lady O'Connell gave a nod. Obviously her daughter-in-law was anxious to establish a polite atmosphere. She was nothing loathe, for it would make the coming victory all the sweeter. How wonderful it would be to send Lionel's wife back to him. "Have you heard anything from Lionel?" she asked brightly.

Mrs. O'Connell cast an amused glance at her mother-in-law. "As a matter of fact, I have. He has written to me several times since he left London. I am considering a visit home to Ireland shortly, for he tells me that we have several things to discuss between us."

Lady O'Connell felt herself to be approaching the pinnacle of her pleasant daydream. "How nice, to be sure," she said, lifting her teacup to her lips.

The door of the drawing room opened and the butler entered. Mrs. O'Connell responded to his apology for the interruption and his request for a private word by turning to her guest with a smile. "I do hope you will not mind, my lady? It will take but a moment."

Lady O'Connell was displeased, but she nodded. "That is quite all right, Sophronia. I shall await your return."

Mrs. O'Connell left the drawing room and the butler closed the door behind her. It was not more than two minutes by the clock on the mantel before the door opened again. Lady O'Connell was just setting aside her teacup and she looked up. Her face creased in a satisfied smile. "Well! That was indeed quick, Sophronia."

"Lady O'Connell, there is someone here whom I think that you should see," said Mrs. O'Connell. She moved out of the doorway to make room for a gentleman to enter. Then she exited and began to close the door.

Recognizing the gentleman, Lady O'Connell surged to her feet. "Sophronia! This is an outrage!"

Mrs. O'Connell merely smiled and finished closing the door.

Since Prince Kirov stood between her and the door, Lady O'Connell felt that she had no easy way of escaping an uncomfortable scene. Vowing vengeance upon her daughter-in-law, Lady O'Connell turned to the waiting prince.

"Prince Kirov"—she acknowledged in freezing accents—"obviously you have managed to get around Mrs. O'Connell. She has always wanted for sense! However, I warn you that I am an altogether different matter. I will not be so easy to get around. If you have come to try to persuade me to accept your suit for Megan, then—"

"My dear Lady O'Connell, I promise you that I shall not utter one word on that matter," said Prince Kirov with a smile. He gestured at the settee. "Pray be seated, my lady. I merely request your indulgence for a few moments, for I have asked for this interview to solicit your advice."

Lady O'Connell was thrown off guard. "Oh!" Eyeing him with uncertainty and a large degree of suspicion, she said, "Well, if you truly do not wish to talk about Megan, then I suppose that I may listen to whatever you might have to say." She sank back down on the settee.

"May I?" inquired Prince Kirov. Without waiting for her acquiescence, he seated himself on the settee. A leather case had been tucked under his arm and he set it down onto his knees. "This is what I wish to solicit your opinion about, my lady. I shall have it unlocked directly."

Lady O'Connell had not noticed the case until that moment. Instantly she recognized it for a jewel case. Her curiosity ignited, she watched while the prince took a small key out of his waistcoat pocket and fitted it into the brass locks.

He grunted in satisfaction when he had turned the key in both locks. Prince Kirov opened the top of the case. "This, my lady, is something that no one else has yet been privileged to view," he said solemnly. "It is a gift for a very special occasion." He turned the case around for her inspection. On a bed of pale blue velvet was nestled a magnificent set of jewels.

Lady O'Connell looked at the gold necklace, the matching bracelets, the earrings, the tiara. The sunlight winked a shower of sparks from the dazzling array of diamonds and rubies. Her ladyship's eyes glistened. "My dear Prince Kirov! Such an extraordinarily fine gift. It is quite priceless. No woman would be able to resist."

"Indeed, my lady? But you do not speak of yourself, of course. You are not moved by such a paltry offering, I know," said Prince Kirov, turning the case around to look at the set for himself. He pointed at a star-shaped brooch. "That alone costs more than most men see in all of their lives. What a pity that I cannot bestow this set upon you, my lady."

Lady O'Connell raised her eyes and asked sharply, "Bestow it upon me? That is what you said, was it not?"

Prince Kirov heaved a sigh and shook his head. "Indeed, yes, my lady. It is an old custom in my family to give a lavish gift of jewels to one's mother-in-law. When I had hopes of making a successful bid for Miss O'Connell's hand, I at once commissioned that this set be created with your ladyship in mind. It arrived from St. Petersburg the very day that I learned that I was no longer to aspire to Miss O'Connell's hand."

Lady O'Connell made inarticulate sounds that might have been thought unladylike. Prince Kirov politely ignored them. "My suit has not prospered and so I must regretfully look elsewhere for a bride. I have only shown this set to you today so that you may give me an unbiased opinion. Do you think that Lady Bancroft will be flattered by diamonds and rubies, my lady?"

"Lady Bancroft?" repeated Lady O'Connell stupidly. She was still reeling at the thought of actually losing the opportunity of owning such a magnificent set of jewelry. Possessing that set would make her the envy of all her friends. She would be the envy of everyone she knew. She would be the envy of the entire world.

As Prince Kirov turned the case back so that he could look at the contents more fully, it was all Lady O'Connell could do not to snatch it out of his hands.

"Yes, my lady. Do you think that this set would compliment Lady Bancroft's style? Her ladyship's daughter is a handsome young lady and good-natured. I have thought that an alliance with—"

"An alliance with the Bancroft chit? And this lovely set to be given to Alicia Bancroft, to be worn by her!" exclaimed Lady O'Connell, her fingers curling.

"That is what I had in mind, yes," said Prince Kirov gravely.

"Never! Never will I countenance it!" declared Lady O'Connell. "You cannot marry the Bancroft chit, your highness!"

"Forgive me, my lady. But I must remind you that my intentions are no longer of your concern," said Prince Kirov gently. "I merely desired your opinion about whether this set would compliment Lady Bancroft and—"

Lady O'Connell struggled to find adequate words to express the emotions that she was feeling. Finally she managed a credibly restrained, polite reply. "My dear prince, Alicia Bancroft would look atrocious in diamonds and rubies. My advice to you is to forget the matter altogether."

"But what is to be done? I have gone to great trouble and time to have this set commissioned. It would be wasteful to discard it," said Prince Kirov. He shrugged. "I suppose that I shall send it back to St. Petersburg. I have several minor cousins who would no doubt be overjoyed to take the set into their possession. Of course, they do not often frequent the sort of society where such jewels are meant to be displayed. Such a pity that these will not be worn where they can be best appreciated."

Lady O'Connell appeared to be laboring under grave stress. In truth, she was nearly strangled by the thought of such largesse handed over to some obscure Russian woman. It would be absolutely criminal.

"There is no need of that, Prince Kirov. I assure you that I would be delighted to take the set off of your hands," she said hastily.

Prince Kirov stared at Lady O'Connell. Then he smiled. He shook his head. "You are generous, my lady. But I shall not be so insensitive of your feelings. I know that possessing and wearing this set would only remind you of a painful episode which is better forgotten. No, I could not trespass on your good nature so far."

"Trespass!" Lady O'Connell attempted a laugh. "My dear prince, you misunderstand me entirely! Why, I would think no such thing. No, indeed! Why would I think such ill about my own dear son-in-law! I assure you, I would regard you in just such a light!"

"My lady, are you saying that you approve once more of my pressing my suit with Miss O'Connell?" asked Prince Kirov.

Lady O'Connell looked at him fleetingly, then down at the case. "Prince Kirov, I was too hasty in my judgment of your suit. I have since revised my opinion of you. I shall most assuredly welcome you as a suitor for my daughter's hand."

Prince Kirov closed the case and rose to his feet. He tucked the case under his arm and with the other hand gallantly lifted Lady O'Connell's hand. He raised it to his lips. "Thank you, my lady. You make me happier than you can conceive," he said.

"Yes, I am so glad," said Lady O'Connell, never taking her eyes from the case. "Er, the custom which you referred to, your highness. I suppose that one is made recipient of the gift immediately?"

"Oh, do you mean this?" Prince Kirov tapped the case. Cheerfully, he said, "The jewels represent an occasion for great celebration and therefore are given with much pomp and ceremony to the new mother-in-law at the wedding reception. If my suit prospers with Miss O'Connell, I will present this set with much trumpeting. There will not be a single guest who will not know that you have come into possession of these jewels."

"How nice," murmured Lady O'Connell. She was torn between her ardent desire to have the jewel set in her possession at once and the pleasing vision of parading her triumph before all of her friends and acquaintances.

"Lady O'Connell, I must take my leave. Before I go, however, I should like to make clear my intention of persuading Miss O'Connell to dispense with a long engagement. I hope that this will meet with your approval," said Prince Kirov.

"Your highness, the sooner you wed my daughter, the better I shall feel," said Lady O'Connell frankly, her eyes straying again to the case.

Prince Kirov smiled lazily. He bowed once more. "Thank you, my lady. I shall leave you now. Pray inform Miss O'Connell that I shall call on her tomorrow."

"We shall be attending the Smythe soiree and later go on to the theater. Perhaps we shall see you there?" said Lady O'Connell.

Prince Kirov's brows rose, but he politely replied. "Perhaps, my lady. Good-bye."

As soon as the prince had left, Lady O'Connell made a beeline for the bellpull. She tugged on it vigorously.

The door opened. Mrs. O'Connell quietly entered. She wore

a smile, but there was a combatant light in her eyes. "Well, my lady? Are you so eager to rake me down in my own house?"

Lady O'Connell rushed at her daughter-in-law and enveloped her in a hug. "My dear Sophronia! Rake you down, indeed. How silly of you, my dear! No, no, I am very happy with you. I have quite made my peace with Prince Kirov. Now where is dearest Megan? So silly of me not to inquire of her last night what she meant to do today, but you are familiar with her habits, are you not? Sophronia, I must speak to her at once."

Mrs. O'Connell shook her head, having difficulty believing her reception. "Why, I suppose that she is out shopping. Or perhaps she has gone to call on Miss Stallcroft, which she is often in the habit of doing. They have become quite good friends. I really cannot tell you."

"That is not at all convenient. But it cannot be helped, can it?" Lady O'Connell grabbed up her gloves and began to pull them on. "My dear Sophronia, I must leave you now. I have something of great import to attend to and I know that you will excuse me. Pray give my love to Megan if she stops by to see you. I shall see her tonight, of course. Advise her to wear her most stunning gown. Now I really must run." She snatched up her reticule, pecked her daughter-in-law on the cheek, and exited smartly.

Mrs. O'Connell stammered a wondering good-bye even as her mother-in-law flew out of the drawing room. She went to the door of the drawing room. In a matter of seconds, Lady O'Connell's carriage was brought up to the front steps and her ladyship had well and truly left.

"What in the world did that man say to her?" asked Mrs. O'Connell aloud. She was not destined to know the answer and her lively curiosity was left unsatisfied.

Lady O'Connell could scarcely attend to her own obligations that day. She could not get that magnificent set of rubies and diamonds out of her mind. Her thoughts dwelt lovingly upon them as she imagined pinning the brooch to her gown, putting the tiara in her hair, wrapping the shimmering necklace about her throat . . .

When Megan returned from a long day with friends, she

was met with the intelligence that she was to wear her newest gown to the soiree. "But whatever for, Simpkins? It was meant for the grand ball next week, as her ladyship well knows," said Megan.

When the dresser merely shook her head, Megan turned to Mrs. Tyler. "Gwyneth, what notion has my mother taken into her head? Why does she wish me to wear this particular gown?"

"I haven't a clue, Megan," said Mrs. Tyler, frowning slightly. "But I will tell you this. I spoke with her ladyship very briefly not an hour past. I have never seen her in such high alt, nor so anxious that you accompany her to a function."

Megan stared. She could think of only one explanation for her mother's odd solicitude. "Depend upon it, then," she said decisively. "She has discovered some eligible gentleman that I have not already met or whom I have not already turned down. Ever since my father decided that I should remain for the Season, she has become eager to see me betrothed and off of her hands. I think that it is only Prince Kirov who is still denied the house!"

"Yes, it has had me in quite a pucker," said Mrs. Tyler worriedly. "I have felt very guilty to be thinking of myself so much. Perhaps I should not have accepted Jeremy's proposal so soon."

Megan hugged her. "You are not to start thinking like that, Gwyneth. I should be made very unhappy if I thought I was the cause of delaying your happiness. I have told you, wed dear Mr. Bretton at once. My muddled affairs shall not be any less tangled regardless of your presence."

"I suppose that it is true," said Mrs. Tyler hesitantly.

"I know that it is! Now pray do not give it another thought. You must finish planning your trousseau. The wedding is only a few weeks away," said Megan.

A soft flush mounted in Mrs. Tyler's face and a glad light sprang into her eyes. "Oh, my! So it is. And I am not nearly ready. Megan, I do not know how it is, but I seem to have become the most shatterbrained creature alive. I keep forgetting the oddest things!"

"That is what comes of daydreaming constantly about your handsome betrothed," said Megan.

Mrs. Tyler flushed bright with embarrassment. "Really, Megan! As though I am some giddy young girl!" She got up from the chair and smoothed her skirt with a distracted air. "I shall go along to my own room now and let Simpkins help you finish getting dressed for the evening."

"Will you be going with us to the soiree and the theater?" asked Megan.

Mrs. Tyler shook her head. She started to smile again. "Not this evening, my dear. I have had a note from Jeremy, you see, and—"

"And he will be dining with you here again," finished Megan. "How perfectly lovely for you, Gwyneth. But how scandalous, too! Perhaps I should stay at home and play chaperone."

"I'll not listen to any more of your teasing," said Mrs. Tyler as she went to the door.

Megan laughed as her companion exited. "Well, Simpkins, that is a truly happy romance. I am very glad of it."

"Yes, miss. One naturally wishes Mrs. Tyler all the best," said the dresser. "Now, miss, if you please! We do not wish to keep her ladyship waiting."

"Oh, very well! I suppose that I must comply with her ladyship's wishes. I wonder whom she hopes to snare for me?" said Megan, sitting down at the dressing table.

"I could not say, miss," said the dresser, taking up a hairbrush.

Megan was ready to accompany Lady O'Connell a quarter hour before they were to leave. Her mother was in an affable mood, which continued until halfway through the soiree. Lady O'Connell scanned the company every few minutes, obviously in hope of catching sight of a certain personage. When they left the soiree and went to the theater with their party, Lady O'Connell spent most of the performance looking out of her box at her fellow theatergoers rather than turning her attention to the stage.

Megan knew that whomever it was that Lady O'Connell had been hoping to see all evening had never materialized when her ladyship complained on the drive home that she had had a perfectly horrid time. "I am sorry for it, Mother. Perhaps you will feel more the thing tomorrow," she said soothingly.

"There is only one thing that will make me feel better," declared Lady O'Connell, stepping out of the carriage with the help of one of her footmen. "And that is to see you properly betrothed!"

Megan sighed and followed her mother up the steps into the town house. She, too, had had a rather insipid evening. Indeed, the entire week had dragged past. Wherever she went, she was constantly hoping to catch a glimpse of Prince Kirov's tall handsome figure, perhaps even to be allowed to exchange a few words with him. But only a few scant times had the opportunity risen and such polite stilted phrases had passed between them that Megan was left hollow afterward.

Upon wishing her mother good night, Megan went upstairs to her bedroom. She allowed Simpkins to undress her and ready her for bed. However, when she was laid down and the candle was blown out, she did not go to sleep. Her unhappy state preoccupied her thoughts to the exclusion of all else. For the thousandth time, Megan wondered if there was any way to restore a relationship with Prince Kirov. But the melancholy truth was that, short of throwing herself into his arms, in complete defiance of her parents, she could do nothing.

And perhaps Prince Kirov no longer wished to further his suit for her hand, besides, she thought despondently. It would not be surprising if that was so, for what proud gentleman would swallow such blatant rejection as had been handed out by the O'Connells? Certainly not one so proud as Prince Kirov. Unless his heart was truly engaged, whispered her practical mind. Megan found no solace in that thought.

Chapter Twenty-two

Megan's depression did not lessen over the next few days. She still attended routs and balls, but the previous pleasure that she had taken in them had disappeared. More than once, a friend or acquaintance inquired solicitously whether she was feeling unwell. Megan denied it, claiming that she was merely feeling the effects of the unseasonal heat. This was accepted without question, for it was an exceptionally warm spring.

It was difficult for Megan to attend the wedding of her friend to Mr. Bretton, but not for the world would she have wanted dear Gwyneth to guess how miserable she felt at watching such a happy ending and know that she would not experience one of her own. So she smiled and laughed and in general gave all the appearance of being absolutely delighted by the entire affair.

The pain in her heart was certainly not soothed when announcements appeared in the *Gazette* of the betrothals of Miss Stallcroft to Sir Frederick Hawkesworth; of Miss Phoebe Stallcroft to Captain Colin O'Connell; and of Miss Bancroft to Lord Henry Dorsey. It seemed as though all about her everyone was deliriously happy and was embarking on matrimony. Megan began to toy with the notion of taking the veil or of exiling herself to some tiny cottage hidden away in the hinterlands. Or perhaps she would just go home to Ireland.

Megan finally realized that these depressing thoughts were coming into her head with more frequency than they should, and were being dwelled upon. She had always loathed self-pity and it was a shock to discover that she could actually be subject to it. She gave a hiccup of laughter. "What a stupidly morose female I have become!" And she went off to put on her riding habit, for generally a good hard ride would clear the cobwebs from her mind.

It was during one of these rides, solitary except for the groom who always followed her, that Megan made up her mind to forget might-have-beens. She had told her father that she was confident of achieving a respectable match that Season. Very well! She would do so. There were several gentlemen who were still expressing interest in her. She would choose from among them the most eligible and acceptable one and settle comfortably into a new position.

It was not to be thought that her decision lifted the pall of gray that seemed to have been cast over her, but Megan refused to allow that consideration to alter her determination. She had known that Prince Kirov was unattainable. She had always known that. The prince's gold signet ring was still in her possession. Megan supposed that one day she would show it to her daughters as the keepsake from a long-ago romance. How perfectly insipid it would all be!

When Megan entered the town house, she was met with the intelligence that a visitor awaited her pleasure. Megan frowned as she gave her whip to the footman and peeled off her gloves. "Who is it, pray?"

"That I could not say, miss, me not being on duty when the gentleman arrived," said the footman apologetically. He gave a cough. "I apprehend that the gentleman is something of a friend of the family, miss. Her ladyship is with him now in the sitting room."

At that moment, Lady O'Connell emerged from the sitting room. "I thought that I heard your voice, my dear," she said. "Come in! There is someone here that I feel sure you will be delighted to see."

"But I am in all my dirt, Mother," began Megan, gesturing down at her riding habit.

"It does not signify in the least. Do come along, Megan!"

Mystified, Megan walked past her mother into the sitting room. She stopped, her eyes becoming at once fixed upon the large gentleman standing at the window. The door was closed quietly behind her, leaving her alone with the visitor.

The gentleman turned. His expression was somber.

"Prince Kirov!" Megan advanced a few faltering steps to grasp the gilded back of a chair. Her thoughts were thrown into a whirl. What did it mean that her mother had so smilingly granted her this interview with Prince Kirov? Her heart thumped with a wild, impossible hope.

"Megan." Prince Kirov walked over to her and raised her hand to his lips, bowing gracefully. He straightened and looked down at her with a faint smile. His ice-blue eyes were curiously softened. "You are always beautiful."

Megan colored fierily. She did not understand how it was that the same compliment if uttered by any other man could never bring her to the blush. She laid her palms against her hot cheeks. "Oh! You should not say such things. You know that you should not."

"I tell you what is in my heart, Megan," said Prince Kirov quietly.

Megan could scarcely bear it. She had not seen him for a fortnight and now, when she had all but given up hope of ever seeing him again except in social settings where they must meet as strangers, he appeared. And with wonderful, painful words that pierced her very being. "Why have you come? Why has my mother allowed me to see you?"

"Her ladyship did not tell you?" asked Prince Kirov, not greatly astonished.

Megan shook her head. "She has said nothing to me." For the first time she noticed that he was dressed for travel. His greatcoat was buttoned back and underneath it he was attired in a serviceable coat, buckskins, and boots. Driving gloves were stuffed in his pocket. She raised her eyes to his face, her expression stricken. "Are you leaving London?"

"Yes, I am leaving for Dover as soon as I have taken my leave of you," said Prince Kirov.

Megan felt suddenly stifled with despair. He had come to say good-bye, then. That was why her mother had allowed her to see him alone. "I—I hope that you have a pleasant journey, your highness." She could scarcely look up at him, afraid that he would see the tears that threatened her. She was crying out silent denial inside. Surely he was not leaving forever. Surely he was not! "Shall you be gone from London long?"

"For a short time only. I am going to Calais to oversee for myself the safe transport of a Kabardian trotter," said Prince Kirov gravely.

"A Kabardian trotter?" Megan looked up at him quickly, searchingly. She shook her head, confused. "I do not understand."

"I have lately been in Paris. I have purchased the mare from a cousin who is presently sojourning there. He never travels without some of his own horses. He was persuaded to part with the mare and has sent her to Calais so that I can take possession," said Prince Kirov. He cleared his throat. "I have been in close correspondence with your father. I am giving the Kabardian trotter to Lord O'Connell as a bride-price."

Megan's eyes widened. "As a what?" she asked faintly.

"I have also assured Lady O'Connell that a very costly set of jewelry which I commissioned many months ago will be given into her possession at our wedding reception," said Prince Kirov. He cleared his throat again. "Megan, I have bought you from your parents."

"You have bought me?" repeated Megan, stunned. She stared up at him with a dawning comprehension.

Prince Kirov nodded, watching her expression closely. "But I shall withdraw from all of these negotiations if you do not wish the match. I—I do not force you to come to me, Megan." There was an uncharacteristically vulnerable look in the prince's eyes.

"You would break your pledged word of honor?" asked Megan slowly.

Prince Kirov's somber expression deepened. "My honor is everything to me. But my love for you is a stronger bond than even that, Megan. Say the word, and this very instant I shall inform Lord and Lady O'Connell that I withdraw from all that I have promised."

There was a short silence. Megan drew a design with her finger on the smooth chair back. "Why have you not kissed me, your highness?"

Prince Kirov drew in a deep, haggard breath. He felt his self-control waver for just an instant, but he steeled himself. He shook his head. "I do not sway you with unfair tactics this time, Megan. I am Kirov, a gentleman and a prince. I have my scruples."

Megan threw a glance up at him from under her lashes. "Your reputation says otherwise," she said demurely. "And your scruples have not stood in your way before."

His face paled and his eyes became bleak. "You think to torment me, mademoiselle. Truly I deserve such treatment, for before I have thought only of myself and my own desires."

Megan stepped very close to him. She reached up and took hold of his lapels. "I would cheerfully shake you if I could, but you are too large," she said, "Misha, I have loved you since before I ever left St. Petersburg. I denied you because I did not trust my own heart, nor yours. That is why I was so furious when you took advantage of me. And now! Misha, never did I think that I should have to beg you to kiss me!"

With a sound very like a growl, Prince Kirov swept his arms about her. Ruthlessly he kissed her, lifting her feet quite off of the floor. Megan returned his attentions with fervor, winding her arms around his neck.

It was Prince Kirov who first broke the embrace. Breathing heavily, he stared down into his future bride's radiant face. "We shall be married at once by special license and you will accompany me to Calais," he declared.

"Then we'll go to Paris for our honeymoon," said Megan, nodding.

"Yes, and then we shall go to Paris," said Prince Kirov, his eyes brightening. He had immediately perceived the benefits of leaving all family and social entanglements behind and having Megan to himself.

Happy with the thought, he kissed her again, and again, until Megan uttered a faint protest. Holding on to his lapel, she said breathlessly, "Misha! If you do not allow me to breathe, I shall quite faint away."

Prince Kirov laughed. "You are safe in my arms, my dove. I will not let you fall. Megan! I do not wish to be parted from you for even a moment more. You must go with me now, and we will be wed. Then we shall set out at once for Paris."

Megan saw nothing to object to in this whirlwind plan, but

there were threads left untied. "But what about my father's horse? And the presentation to my mother of the jewels?"

"Your father may take possession of the horse for himself. As for the jewels, we shall hold our first public reception in Paris and present them to Lady O'Connell there," said Prince Kirov decisively.

"You are Kirov," said Megan, laughing up at him. "Of course it shall be just as you say."

"Yes, I am Kirov," declared Prince Kirov. "I sweep all before me."

ONYX

ROMANCE FROM THE
PAST AND PRESENT

☐ **DEVOTED by Alice Borchardt.** Elin, a daughter of the Forest People, was mistress of the forbidden powers granted by the old gods. Owen, the warrior-bishop, was his people's last hope against the invading Viking horde, and against the powerful ruler who would betray them. They came together in a love that burned through all barriers in a struggle to save France. "Love and treachery ... a marvelous, irresistible novel."—Anne Rice

(403967—$6.99)

☐ **LILY A Love Story by Cindy Bonner.** Lily Delony has no reason to doubt the rules of virtue and righteousness she has been brought up with until she meets the man who turns her world—and her small town—upside down. The odds are against her forsaking her family for an unknown future with an outlaw who shoots first and thinks later. (404394—$4.99)

☐ **DUCHESS OF MILAN by Michael Ennis.** Once upon a time, in fifteenth-century Italy, two women faced each other with a ruthlessness and brilliance no man has ever matched. Enter their world of passion and evil in Italy's most dazzling and dangerous age! "Two young women who had the power to change history ... Be prepared ... you won't want to put this one down."—Jean M. Auel

(404289—$5.99)

*Prices slightly higher in Canada

Buy them at your local bookstore or use this convenient coupon for ordering.

PENGUIN USA
P.O. Box 999 — Dept. #17109
Bergenfield, New Jersey 07621

Please send me the books I have checked above.
I am enclosing $_____ (please add $2.00 to cover postage and handling). Send check or money order (no cash or C.O.D.'s) or charge by Mastercard or VISA (with a $15.00 minimum). Prices and numbers are subject to change without notice.

Card #_____ Exp. Date _____
Signature_____
Name_____
Address_____
City _____ State _____ Zip Code _____

For faster service when ordering by credit card call **1-800-253-6476**

Allow a minimum of 4-6 weeks for delivery. This offer is subject to change without notice.